Trace did not move as the warrior passed the crevice where he sat. The Blackfoot was no more than twenty feet below him now, and Trace could plainly see the young brave's face, his forehead and cheeks painted black with white stripes like lightning flashes at his temples. He was armed with bow, axe, and lance. *Good,* Trace thought, *he passed right by.* But it was not to be. In no more than a few seconds, the Indian reappeared at the opening in the rock.

Startled to see Trace calmly sitting there above him, the warrior hesitated, his eyes wide and wild. He raised his lance over his head, ready to attack—fearful that the man before him might suddenly turn into a hawk and fly—but still he did not release his weapon.

Seeing his hesitation, Trace did not move. His rifle lay on the rock beside him, the barrel pointed at the warrior, his hand resting on the trigger guard. When the warrior appeared to make up his mind to act, Trace spoke. "I am not your enemy. Why do you attack me?"

Taken aback, the Blackfoot continued to stand ready to strike. After a moment's pause, he asked, "Are you the Mountain Hawk?"

"I am a man, trying to live in peace," Trace answered.

"You are the Mountain Hawk." This time it was not a question. "The man who kills you takes your medicine. . . ."

# The Mountain Hawk

Charles G. West

A SIGNET BOOK

SIGNET
Published by New American Library, a division of
Penguin Putnam Inc., 375 Hudson Street,
New York, New York 10014, U.S.A.
Penguin Books Ltd, 27 Wrights Lane,
London W8 5TZ, England
Penguin Books Australia Ltd,
Ringwood, Victoria, Australia
Penguin Books Canada Ltd, 10 Alcorn Avenue,
Toronto, Ontario, Canada M4V 3B2
Penguin Books (N.Z.) Ltd, 182–190 Wairau Road,
Auckland 10, New Zealand

Penguin Books Ltd, Registered Offices:
Harmondsworth, Middlesex, England

First published by Signet, an imprint of New American Library,
a division of Penguin Putnam Inc.

First Printing, January 2001
10   9   8   7   6   5   4   3   2   1

PUBLISHER'S NOTE
This is a work of fiction. Names, characters, places, and incidents either are the
product of the author's imagination or are used fictitiously, and any resemblance
to actual persons, living or dead, business establishments, events, or locales is
entirely coincidental.

BOOKS ARE AVAILABLE AT QUANTITY DISCOUNTS WHEN USED TO PROMOTE PRODUCTS
OR SERVICES. FOR INFORMATION PLEASE WRITE TO PREMIUM MARKETING DIVISION,
PENGUIN PUTNAM INC., 375 HUDSON STREET, NEW YORK, NEW YORK 10014.

If you purchased this book without a cover you should be aware that this book is
stolen property. It was reported as "unsold and destroyed" to the publisher and
neither the author nor the publisher has received any payment for this "stripped
book."

*For Ronda*

# CHAPTER 1

*How can this evil spirit be allowed to remain in these mountains?* This was the question that bothered Two Horses. This country belonged to the Blackfeet, and no outsider had any right to be here—no matter if he was man or spirit. When Broken Wing's crumpled body was found at the base of a cliff, Two Horses made up his mind. He would avenge his friend's death.

No man in Little Bull's camp was as powerful as Two Horses. He had killed eight enemies before reaching the age of twenty summers. Now he was at the age of twenty-five, and no warrior had counted as many coups as he. And no man among them hated the white man more than he. Two warriors had been killed already this summer by the white devil who had come to nest on the upper slopes; the most recent death had been that of his best friend. Two Horses clenched his fist in anger when he recalled the battered body of Broken Wing.

Knowing that he would be facing the most powerful enemy of his life, Two Horses began careful preparations for his quest. He fasted for three days, then rode into the hills to meditate and seek spiritual guidance. Satisfied that his medicine was strong, he then nourished his body to regain his strength. Next, he sought the advice of those who were respected in the village. Medicine Horse, one of the elders, talked at length about the white man the Blackfeet had given the name of Mountain Hawk. It had been his belief, when the stranger was sighted by members of a hunting party in early summer, that he was no more than a mortal white man—a trapper perhaps—who chose to live in the high country. Now he was not so sure. Little Bull himself had been with a later hunting party when he spotted the stranger, and it was Little Bull who had discovered the spiritual powers of the white man. "It is a brave quest you have chosen for yourself," Medicine Horse said. "But you must be wary of his guile. If you kill this Mountain Hawk, you will take his power—and that would be a great thing." Before they parted, Medicine Horse advised Two Horses to seek Little Bull's counsel, since he was one who had witnessed Mountain Hawk's transformation.

Little Bull was not surprised when told of the plan of Two Horses to avenge his friend's death. Broken Wing and Two Horses had been the closest of friends since they were small boys. Like Medicine Horse, Little Bull advised Two Horses to exercise great caution in stalking the lone white man. "Shoot him if you can before he sees you. If you cannot, if you have to fight him hand to hand, you must hold on to him very tightly so he can't turn into a hawk and escape."

Two Horses listened carefully to his chief's counsel. What he said was good advice—the safest thing to do would be to kill Mountain Hawk with a rifle ball from a distance. But there would be much greater honor in killing this white man with hand weapons. And Two Horses was confident that no man was a match for his own physical strength. Nevertheless, he thanked Little Bull for his words of advice. After all, the chief was one of only a few men who had witnessed the medicine of the Mountain Hawk. Although no one had seen the actual transformation as it was taking place, there was no reason to doubt it had happened. The white man was sighted on a rocky cliff above them. They immediately set out to capture him, but when they climbed up to the cliff, there was no sign that anyone had been there. Standing on the brow of the cliff, Little Bull looked up to see a hawk circling high above. Though they looked carefully around them, they could not discover any way the man could have escaped. This was sign enough for Little Bull to assume that the man they had seen was, in fact, a spirit who had turned into a hawk when he saw them approaching.

The sun was barely peeking through the tall pines that ringed the slopes to the east when Two Horses rode out of the village. His face was painted with his favored designs of jagged lightning bolts, as was his war pony. Medicine Horse stood before his lodge and nodded solemnly to the young warrior as he rode by. Two Horses, confident in his mission, returned the greeting with a single nod of his head, gently kicked his pony into a canter, and headed toward the mountains.

Trace McCall sat quietly watching the progress of the lone warrior making his way cautiously up through the boulders and random patches of bear grass. He was a powerfully built young brave, scaling the steep slope with apparent ease after leaving his pony in a grassy meadow below. As Trace watched, the warrior paused and listened, then seemed to be testing the wind, like a coyote sniffing, searching for prey. The warrior started climbing again, through the stunted pines that had been formed into twisted shapes by the strong winds that swept the higher ridges. *Blackfoot,* he thought, *the third one this month, coming to make a name for himself.*

Trace had a notion what had started it all, but he still found it puzzling that it had developed into such a big deal to the Blackfoot tribe. Some folks, Buck Ransom for one, would say Trace was crazy to make his summer camp in the middle of Blackfoot country. Trace did not discount the danger there, but he had confidence in his ability to hang on to his scalp. To further ensure his safety, he made his camps

high up in the mountains, coming down only occasionally to hunt.

He was sure that he had been seen on one of his
trips to the lower elevations, alerting the Blackfeet
to his presence in their land. While following an elk
down through a mountain meadow, he happened
upon a small hunting party working their way up
to the higher elevations. He was not aware of their
presence until he walked out onto a rocky ledge, trying to spot the elk. He and the Indians saw each
other at the same time, too late to hide, so they stood
gazing at each other for several long moments before the Blackfeet sprang into action and rushed to
give chase. Trace was forced to give up his elk and
disappear into the rocky cliffs above. Even though
his presence in their country was now known, he
was still reluctant to leave these mountain heights
that filled his soul with awe and reverence for the
hand that made them. At this point in his young life,
Trace desperately needed the pure solitude that the
mountains offered. And he intended to stay until the
coming winter dictated a move to warmer climes.

What he could not know was that he had been
spotted at a distance several times by the sharp-eyed
Blackfoot hunters. Yet when they tried to track him
they could find no trail. It was as if he had taken
wings and flown away. Being a highly superstitious
people, they soon created a legend about the man
who dwelled high up in the mountains.

Trace had no notion that he was known to the

Blackfoot tribe as the Mountain Hawk. What he *was* aware of, however, was that there seemed to be some big medicine to be gained by the warrior who was successful in finding him and bringing back his scalp—a thought that brought his focus back to the warrior now picking his way slowly across an open area of loose shale and gravel. Trace hoped the warrior would not discover the narrow slash in the rocks where he sat watching. He had no desire to take another young warrior's life. The first two had given him no choice. If the Blackfoot did find him, perhaps he could talk some sense into this one.

Trace did not move as the warrior passed the crevice where he sat. He was no more than twenty feet below him now, and Trace could plainly see the young brave's face, his forehead and cheeks painted black with white stripes like lightning flashes at his temples. He was armed with bow, axe, and lance. *Good*, Trace thought, *he passed right by*. But it was not to be. In no more than a few seconds, the Indian reappeared at the opening in the rock.

Startled to see Trace calmly sitting there above him, the warrior hesitated, his eyes wide and wild. He raised his lance over his head, ready to attack—fearful that the man before him might suddenly turn into a hawk and fly off—but still he did not release it.

Seeing his hesitation, Trace did not move. His rifle lay on the rock beside him, the barrel pointed at the warrior, his hand resting on the trigger guard. When the warrior appeared to make up his mind to act,

Trace spoke. "I am not your enemy. Why do you attack me?"

Taken aback, the Blackfoot stood ready to strike. After a moment's pause, he asked, "Are you the Mountain Hawk?"

"I am a man, trying to live in peace," Trace answered.

"You are the Mountain Hawk." This time it was not a question. "The man who kills you takes your medicine."

Their gazes locked, and they stared at each other for a long moment. Trace was about to try once more to reason with the warrior when the Blackfoot suddenly cast the lance. Trace's reaction was lightning-fast, but his aim was thrown off. The Hawken barked, sending a lead ball whistling past the charging warrior's head. In an instant, the Blackfoot was upon him, and it was all Trace could do to avoid the war axe as it crashed down, bouncing off the boulder behind his head and dropping into a crevice in the rocks. Unfazed, the Brave unsheathed a hunting knife. The battle was joined as each man strained to overpower the other. It took all of Trace's strength to hold Two Horses' knife hand, but gradually he forced the warrior's arm back until he was able to shove him backward toward the narrow ledge. As the Blackfoot regained his balance and braced to charge again, Trace was able to draw his own knife and set himself to meet the assault.

Once again they clashed, slamming their bodies

together like two mountain rams, struggling to wrench a hand free for a fatal thrust. Face-to-face, each man looked deep into the other's eyes, measuring the courage there. And Two Horses, reading the stony gaze of the mountain man, suddenly experienced his first misgivings that he might have underestimated the power of his enemy. In a desperate lunge, he managed to free himself and step back, swinging wildly in an attempt to slash Trace's ribs. Trace easily stepped to the side, at the same time coming up under Two Horses' arm with his long Green River knife. The Blackfoot grunted as the blade of Trace's knife sank deep under his breastplate. A look of shock and startled disbelief glazed Two Horses' eyes as he tried to back away from the knife. Trace stepped with him, forcing the knife in as deep as it would go.

Suddenly the strength left Two Horses' knees and he began to sag. Still, he courageously tried to strike out again with his knife. Trace easily blocked the thrust, trapping Two Horses' wrist in his powerful grip, and held the Blackfoot until the remaining strength drained from him. Then, supporting the Indian's body with the knife in his gut, he backed him to the ledge and with one sudden shove hurled his body down the mountainside. Tumbling over and over down the steep slope, Two Horses came to rest some fifty yards below, against a stunted pine.

"A damn waste," Trace said. He stood there for several minutes longer, looking at the corpse lodged below him on the scrub pine. This one had gotten too close. Trace's camp and his horses were only a quarter of a mile below, on the other side of the mountain. Perhaps it was time to move on anyway, for the cold weather would soon be here. He admired the beauty of this place, but it was difficult to decide if he would come back in the spring, since the Blackfeet had made him a legend. He had no desire to be a Blackfoot legend.

There were no further encounters with ambitious Blackfoot warriors over the next few weeks, but it was because the Indians who came in search of the Mountain Hawk did not venture near his camp. However, they still searched for him—he sighted at least one every day or two—so Trace finally decided to leave his camp high up in the ridges and head down past the Absarokas, to the Wind River Range, maybe go on down to Fort Laramie if the notion struck him. He had some plews to trade, and he could use some powder and lead for his Hawken rifle. Then, too, his supply of coffee beans had long since been depleted. Having spent four years of his life living with a band of Crow Indians, he got along just fine without flour, baking soda, sugar, and other staples that most trappers craved. But he did miss his coffee. If it was necessary, however, Trace could be content living without most civilized conveniences. With his bow and knife—along with a flint and steel—he could not only survive but prosper, using only what nature provided.

After three days of following an old hunting trail, he put the Absarokas behind him and struck the Wind River, constantly alert for signs of Indian hunting parties. This time of year there was generally a great deal of activity among the tribes. It was the end of summer, and the Sioux and Cheyenne were at war with almost every tribe in the area. A white man was smart to stay out of the way of all of them— even the Crows, whom Trace had lived with. He wasn't quite sure what his reception might be if he paid a visit to his old village, since he had chosen to leave the Crows and throw in with the likes of trappers Buck Ransom and Frank Brown. He often thought of his boyhood friend Black Wing and his father, Buffalo Shield. The years Trace spent with them were not unhappy years, and he hoped that he was still considered a friend in Red Blanket's village.

Following the river, he made his way in a leisurely fashion toward South Pass, stopping to hunt when he felt the need, resting the horses frequently. He crossed a wide coulee that was now dry and was about to climb the other side when his eye caught a movement on the horizon. Trace immediately pulled his Indian pony up short and strained to identify the travelers. Because of the distance between them, however, it was difficult to determine if it was a hunting party or a war party—but whichever, it was not a large group.

Turning the paint, he rode down toward the river,

using the side of the coulee as cover until he reached the trees that lined the river. Then he continued on a course that would intercept the party. When he was close enough to get a better look at what manner of travelers he had discovered, he couldn't believe his eyes. It was not an Indian party at all. It was a wagon, pulled by a team of six mules, flanked by two riders. "What in hell are they doing up this way?" he muttered. *Pilgrims*, he thought, *and as lost as a pilgrim can get.*

It made little sense to Trace for a wagon even to be trying to cross this country. They were almost to the confluence of the Wind River and the Big Horn. If they were looking for South Pass and the trail to California, they had sure as hell missed it. And if they continued in the direction they were heading, they would end up staring at a mountain they couldn't get over.

Trace prodded the paint to a faster gait so he could intercept the wagon as it entered a treeless ravine that led from the flat down to the river bottom. After about a fifteen-minute ride, he came to the head of the ravine, where he could watch the pilgrims from above as they followed the ravine down to the river. There was no need to expose himself until he got a closer look at who it was he was about to meet. So he sat on his horse and patiently waited for the wagon to approach.

When the party finally entered the ravine and ambled slowly by below him, wagon wheels creaking in protest to the rough floor of the gully and pots and pans clanging noisily as the wagon lurched to and fro, Trace shook his head in amazement. There were two men on the seat, father and son, it appeared, with a woman and a little girl in the back. *Typical*, he thought. What was not typical, however, were the two riders that had flanked the wagon until it descended into the draw. As Trace watched, they fell behind, apparently conferring about something. It was the look of the two that troubled Trace. Even at that distance, he could sense something strange about them. Trace dismounted and carefully made his way to the edge of the ravine, where he crawled up behind a screen of brush. Unseen by the travelers, he could plainly hear the conversation between one of the men and the woman behind him in the wagon.

"Paul, there's no trail here," the wife complained, "I don't think they know where we're going."

Her husband didn't answer right away. He had constantly reassured his wife and son that the two men who had so graciously offered to guide them to Fort Bridger knew the country. But now he began to have doubts himself. Until that morning, they had followed a well-traveled trail with evidence that countless wagons had passed that way before. But when they broke camp that morning, their guides had led them in a more northerly direction, away from the beaten track—a shortcut, they assured him, that would save them a full day's travel. They were late for their rendezvous with the main party as it was, so a day's time saved would be welcome. But now he began to share his wife's suspicions, especially when he looked at the mountains before them, standing like giant, impenetrable palisades. There was no sign that anyone had ever traveled this way before, and the rough terrain threatened to tear his wagon apart. Their guides had promised that the trail would become smoother a few miles ahead, but he feared he might bust a wheel before they reached better ground. The wagon was in sore need of repair as it was, and he had been anxious to reach Fort Bridger to get the work done.

Finally he answered his wife's troubled comment. "I don't know, Martha. Mr. Plum told me this shortcut would save us at least a day, but it don't look to me like this trail leads anywhere. We'll stop at the river to water the mules—I'll talk to 'em about it then." He lowered his voice and threw an aside to his son. "William, why don't you ease back in the wagon, and make sure those rifles are loaded and handy? This thing is beginning to smell a little like trouble. We'd do well to be prepared for some funny business." He glanced back to see his wife's troubled expression, and said, "Now, there ain't nothing to worry about. It just pays to be cautious, that's all."

A dozen feet above them, Trace heard every word of the conversation clearly. Now he knew why he had sensed something wrong about the two guides following along behind the wagon. The one word that had alerted him was the name Plum. For now he recognized the two baleful-looking blackhearts with the family—not by sight, because he had never come face-to-face with either of them before, but by a reputation earned by a long history of double-dealing. Plum and Crown—the two renegades were said to be raiding with a band of Blackfeet, and Trace could only wonder what business they had with this family of emigrants. *Well, we'll soon find out,* he thought as he moved slowly away from the edge of the ravine and returned to his horses.

Jack Plum, vicious as a wolf, was also as wary as a fox. He did not miss young William's quick move into the bed of the wagon. "Best watch yourself, Crown," he warned softly. "That young pup might be up to somethin' back there. Might be they's gittin' a little suspicious."

Crown grunted contemptuously, then replied, "Won't do 'em much good if they are, will it?" He failed to see much threat from the boy and his father. His mind was already thinking beyond the murders they were about to commit. "Remember, Plum, I fancy the girl for myself."

"I said you could have her," Plum shot back. While he might amuse himself with the child's mother for a while before he killed her, Plum was more interested in the load of supplies Paul Murdock had in his wagon. Plum's taste in women ran toward younger girls, but only Crown was sick enough to lust after children.

Paul Murdock guided his team of mules through a stand of trees near the river and hopped down from the wagon seat, his rifle in his hand. William followed close behind his father, also carrying his rifle. Riding up to the wagon, Plum and Crown exchanged cautious glances, both noticing that father and son were armed. Their caution irritated Plum, as he had planned a simple slaughter, with Murdock and his son unsuspecting victims. Now he had to try to put them at ease again.

"It's been a little rough," Plum said, trying his best to convey a cheerful tone, "but it'll be like riding the streets of St. Louis after we cross the river." He swung a leg over and dismounted. Being as obvious as he could, he walked over and propped his rifle against the wagon, then moved back beside his horse. "We'll be eating supper at Fort Bridger tomorrow. That'd be all right, wouldn't it, missy?" He gave Murdock's daughter a playful wink. The little girl responded with a slight smile of embarrassment.

"Mr. Plum," Paul Murdock said, his face a mask of serious concern, "I'm not so certain that we're on the right trail. You say we have to cross the river here? Seems to me Fort Bridger oughta be yonder way." He pointed toward the southwest.

Plum strained to maintain his cheerful facade. *You dumb-ass farmer, it's the right trail, all right, and it's gonna lead you straight to hell.* But to Murdock, he said, "Oh, yes, sir. It's the right trail, all right. You're right, Bridger is yonder way. When we cross the river, we'll pick up a trail on the other side of them hills ahead that cuts right back toward Bridger. Be there tomorrow for supper. Ain't that right, Crown?"

Crown's response was a slight curling of one side of his mouth, forming a sinister grin. Unnoticed by Murdock or his son, Crown had casually moved over near the back of the wagon to a position that placed him off of young William's right shoulder. His eyes shifted constantly from Plum to William and back, with an occasional glance at Murdock's twelve-year-old daughter.

Murdock was not convinced. He caught his wife's worried eye and knew that she was trying to signal her lack of confidence in Plum's word. More than ever, he began to suspect that he had led his family into danger, and he was not sure if he could extricate them peacefully. The one thing he was convinced of, however, was that he would not follow these two wild mountain men any farther into the wilderness. "Well, Mr. Plum," he began, "we're much obliged to you and Mr. Crown for guiding us this far. But my wife and I have decided to turn around and go back."

Noticing that Crown had eased himself around almost behind William's back, Plum smiled and said, "Well, now, that don't make no sense a'tall." His hand came casually to rest on the butt of one of two pistols stuck in his belt.

"It damn sure makes sense to me." The voice came from behind Crown, causing him to jump. All heads turned as one to discover Trace McCall, standing easy, his Hawken rifle cradled across his arms with the casual confidence of a mountain lion.

"Where the hell did you come from?" Crown demanded.

Trace ignored him. "Where are you bound for, mister?" he addressed Paul Murdock.

This stranger was as wild-looking as Plum and Crown, but Murdock sensed an absence of the treachery that Plum and Crown reeked of. "Fort Bridger," he immediately volunteered.

William, realizing that Crown had gotten behind his back before the stranger startled them all, turned now toward Plum's sinister partner, his rifle in hand. Father and son stood shoulder to shoulder, facing the two renegade mountain men. Plum, though angry as hell, was smart enough to know the odds had just shifted Murdock's way. He held his tongue while he and Trace eyed each other like two rogue wolves. Plum didn't like what he saw in the tall young hunter dressed in animal skins. He carried a bow as well as a rifle and gave the distinct impression that he knew how to use them.

Talking to Paul Murdock, his eyes never leaving Plum, Trace asked, "Are these two your guides?"

"We run up on them after leaving Fort Laramie. They said they were going to Fort Bridger, so they offered to travel with us and show us the way." Murdock looked nervously at Plum while he talked. It never occurred to him to question this stranger's authority to interrogate him.

"Bridger, huh?" Trace cast an accusing eye in Plum's direction. "Well, mister, the company you keep is your business, but if Fort Bridger is where you're headin', you picked a sorry pair of guides. You're about a half a day too far north now, and if you keep going in this direction, you ain't ever gonna see Fort Bridger."

Plum felt the bile rise in his throat, but he fought to keep his anger from showing on his face. Forcing a smile, he said, "Mister, you've took a mighty harsh tone here. Me and Crown here was just doin' our best to help these people. We're lookin' for a shortcut a feller told us about."

It was all too obvious to Trace what these two scoundrels were about. He had little patience for men who preyed on the greenhorns who ventured west in search of a new life. "Is that a fact?" Trace replied, looking Plum straight in the eye. "Well, mister, you're either a liar or just plain stupid. A blind man oughta be able to lead a party over South Pass to Fort Bridger." Anger flashed in Plum's eyes, and his hand tightened on the butt of his pistol. Trace did not move, but he warned in a soft and deadly voice, "I've already figured you for a liar. Now if you want to prove you're stupid, too, go ahead and pull that pistol."

Plum's body went rigid, his hand still gripping

the handle of his pistol. One glance at Crown told him that his partner was not comfortable with the odds facing the two of them. Both Murdock and his son had raised their rifles and stood ready to fire. Plum could feel the flames of frustration and anger consuming his insides, and he knew he had lost his opportunity to capture this wagonload of plunder. Knowing he was beaten but reluctant to admit it, he continued to stand there, glaring defiantly at the tall mountain man, who returned his glare with cool, clear eyes that knew no fear. At that moment it crossed Plum's mind that this formidable figure standing firmly before him might be the one that the foolish Blackfeet called the Mountain Hawk. The thought made Plum even more irate, but he knew he would be flirting with death if he made a move. Finally he surrendered.

"Well, mister—whoever the hell you are—them's pretty harsh words to use on two honest fellers trying to do a good turn for these folks." He motioned with his head for Crown to back away, then spoke to Murdock. "Mr. Murdock, I'm sorry to see you side with a total stranger when me and Crown has gone outta our way to give you folks a hand." He removed his hand from his pistol, held both hands up in front of him, palms out, and slowly backed toward his horse. "But we'll take our leave now with no hard feelin's—nobody's got hurt. We'll just be on our way."

Plum and Crown climbed into the saddle, both

men keeping a cautious eye on the three facing them, and slowly backed their horses away from the wagon. When they were some twenty yards away, they turned and galloped off toward the north.

Paul Murdock exhaled noisily and put his rifle down. "Mister," he said, extending his hand, "I'm sure glad you came along when you did. I'm Paul Murdock. This is my wife, Martha. Over there's my son, William, and that skinny little towhead is Beth."

Trace accepted Paul's hand and shook it. "Trace McCall," he replied and nodded to Martha Murdock. "Ma'am." Turning back to her husband, he said, "I wouldn't advise you to camp here. There's still plenty of daylight left, so you've got plenty of time to find another spot." Murdock didn't reply at once. Instead, he stood with his hands on his hips, looking back the way he had come and then out toward the southwest, where he imagined Fort Bridger to be. Trace could see that the man couldn't decide which way to start out, so he said, "Go back the way you came and pick a camping spot near the river somewhere. I'll be along directly—I want to make sure those two polecats don't decide to double back." He walked back through the trees along the riverbank to retrieve his horses.

When he returned, he paused again at the wagon. Looking down at Paul Murdock, he answered the worried man's unspoken question. "You can't drive that wagon straight through the mountains—there's no way over them. You'll have to go back and pick up the trail to South Pass." Reading the concern in Murdock's eyes, he added, "I'll take you to Fort Bridger when I catch up with you."

Murdock was visibly relieved, even more so when Trace tied his packhorse behind the wagon.

"Yes, sir, Mr. McCall," Murdock said cheerfully as Trace gave the paint a gentle kick with his heels. "How will you know where we camped?" he called out.

"I'll find you," Trace called back.

There had been more than a few tales told about Jack Plum and his sadistic partner, Crown. Trace figured that if half of them were true, it was enough to make a man watch his back. To be safe, he wanted to see for himself that the two renegades were not circling around to bushwhack Murdock's family. If Trace could have had firsthand knowledge that the grisly stories he had heard about Plum's raids with the Blackfeet were true, he might have considered executing the pair when he'd had the chance. But since he didn't cotton to the role of executioner, he would content himself with the knowledge that Plum and Crown were no longer in the area.

He had ridden no farther than three miles when their trail led off to the west and down to the river again. Trace circled into the trees and made his way carefully along the bank until he sighted the two of them standing near the water's edge. They appeared to be arguing.

"Dammit, I say we oughta go back and kill that

son of a bitch," Plum fumed. The more he had thought about being driven off by Trace, the more livid he'd become.

Crown, who had long ago become a devout practitioner of the art of back-shooting, was not as eager to tangle with the tall mountain man who had suddenly materialized behind them at the wagon. Crown preferred longer odds in his own favor, and this stranger looked to be extremely dangerous. To be sure, Crown would have loved to get a clear shot between the man's shoulder blades. But somehow he got the feeling that it would be difficult to catch Trace with his back turned.

"Well?" Plum demanded when Crown made no response to his ranting. "Are we gonna let him have that wagon to hisself?"

"I reckon it's better'n havin' to shoot it out agin three of 'em," Crown calmly replied. If Plum was hoping to appeal to Crown's pride, he was wasting his time. Crown had no more pride than a coyote.

"Damn you, Crown. You ain't worth the powder it'd take to blow you to hell. I'm goin' back to settle with that bastard."

Crown stared at Plum with eyes as devoid of expression as a corpse's. He didn't like Plum—he didn't particularly like anyone—but Plum was in tight with the Blackfoot chief, and so it was to Crown's benefit to partner with him. *One of these days I might be lookin' down a rifle barrel at your shoulder blades*, he thought. "All right, Plum," he said, "we'll go back and take a look."

Leading his horse back through the willows that lined the bank of the river, Plum heard the distinct call of a sage thrasher in the trees to his right. It registered in his brain, but he gave it no importance. Less than a minute passed before he heard an answering call, but this time it seemed to come from a position to his left. He stopped dead still. Looking back, he saw that Crown had also stopped in his tracks, listening. They had ridden on too many Blackfoot war parties to ignore such obvious signals.

"See anything?" Plum whispered.

"Not a damn thing," Crown replied. "I think they're on two sides of us."

"Damn!" Plum spat as he took a few steps toward a large cottonwood. Using it as cover, he strained to see through the trees around them. "Maybe it ain't nothin' but birds," he said, moments before an arrow smacked into the tree trunk beside his head. "Let's git outta here!" he yelled and leaped upon his horse.

Crown was already in the saddle, hightailing it back toward the river. Plum galloped right on Crown's heels. Into the shallow water they plunged, kicking their mounts violently. When they reached the far side, they didn't hesitate for an instant but escaped into the hills. Back by the river, Trace walked over to the cottonwood and pulled his arrow out of the trunk, satisfied that he had seen the last of Plum and Crown.

*        *        *

"Evening, Mr. Murdock." The voice came from out of the dark, directly behind Paul Murdock, causing him to jump, his coffee sloshing over the sides of his cup.

Gathering his wits as quickly as possible, Paul swallowed hard trying to get his heart out of his throat. "Glory be, man, you scared the life outta me!"

"I'm sorry, I didn't mean to," Trace said. He honestly had no intention of startling the man, he just naturally moved quietly.

"It's all right, it's all right," Paul hurriedly repeated, genuinely relieved to see the tall mountain man again.

A short time later, Trace sat by the fire and watched Martha Murdock as she prepared the dough for pan biscuits. It had been a long time since Trace had been able to watch a white woman as she worked at a cookfire, and he was fascinated by the efficient manner in which she went about making supper. It was simple fare, to be sure—biscuits, beans, and gravy made from the antelope meat Trace had provided—but to him it seemed a banquet. Making it especially satisfying for Trace was the coffee, made from roasted beans ground in a wooden coffee grinder, instead of green beans pounded between two stones, the way Trace usually made coffee.

"Here you are, Mr. McCall," Martha sang out cheerfully as she handed Trace a plate. "I'm going to let you get started while we wait for the biscuits."

Trace nodded and mumbled his thanks, suddenly embarrassed to be the focus of the Murdock family's attention. Paul Murdock, especially, realized that this rangy, sandy-headed mountain man had undoubtedly saved them from losing all their earthly possessions and possibly their lives. As a result of the family's appreciation, Trace found one or all of them constantly eyeballing his every move.

Taking a big bite of the antelope shoulder, he started to chew, then hesitated with his mouth full of meat when he suddenly remembered his manners. When Paul and William were served and had sat down beside the fire, Trace finished chewing and swallowed. "Can't remember when last I've had biscuits," he offered as conversation, eyeing the pan of them baking in the coals at the edge of the fire.

Martha stood behind him, watching the men eat. "Well, they won't be anything like my biscuits baked in a good oven," she replied, "but I don't reckon they'll kill you."

Paul Murdock grinned at their guest, openly proud of his wife's cooking. He reached over and gave his daughter a playful pinch on the cheek. "This'un's gonna be as good a cook as her mama. Ain't you, darlin'?" he said, laughing as Beth pulled away from him.

*This man's got himself a fine family*, Trace thought, letting his mind fantasize about the possibility that he might someday have a family of his own.

As if reading his thoughts, Martha asked, "Do you have a family, Mr. McCall?"

"Ah, no, ma'am," Trace replied, but his thoughts went immediately to a slip of a girl in Promise Valley. Jamie Thrash might be baking biscuits for her pa right now. He remembered the last conversation he'd had with her before he loaded his supplies on his packhorse and rode out of the valley in the early summer. Jamie had broadly hinted that he was going to have to settle down one day and end his love affair with the mountains. And she made it plain without actually spelling it out that she cared enough for him to wait until he got the mountains out of his system. It made him uncomfortable every time he thought about it. He admitted to having special feelings for Jamie, but it wasn't the same as the way he had felt about a little Snake maiden who was somewhere with her people in the high country. Sometimes he wished he did care for Jamie enough to marry her, but the fact was, he didn't.

He quickly put these worrisome thoughts out of his mind. "Where'd you folks come from?" he asked, changing the subject.

"Illinois," Paul answered. "Springfield."

Needing no further encouragement, he began an accounting of their journey up to that time, and where they planned to settle in the West. "We didn't have anything holding us in Illinois. I was working six days a week in a sawmill for four dollars a week and trying to raise enough to feed my family on a little thirty-two-acre farm my father left me. When I heard that these two fellows in Springfield—brothers they were—Jacob and George Donner, were organizing a wagon train for California, why, me and the missus didn't have to study on it very long. We were as ready to go as a body can be. Sold my farm to my brother, and we joined up with the Donners."

"These brothers," Trace asked, "they had been to California before?"

"I don't know—I reckon—they sent us a guidebook on how to get there." Paul turned to his son. "William, fetch me the book, son. I wanna show it to Mr. McCall." While William hopped up into the wagon to get the book, Paul continued. "The book tells you how to get out to Fort Bridger, where this fellow Hastings is gonna lead us to California." He paused to take the book from William, and he passed it over to Trace.

*Emigrant's Guide to Oregon and California, by Lansford W. Hastings,* Trace read across the front cover of the book before flipping through the pages. He nodded soberly as he glanced at the passages, stopping briefly to study the crude maps, trying to appear interested while marveling to himself that anyone would start out to cross the continent with nothing for a guide but a book. He glanced up at Murdock and said, "It's getting on a mite late in the summer to be starting out to cross the mountains. That is, if you wanna get over 'em before it snows."

Paul nodded but rushed to add, "That's the reason I'm in a hurry to get to Fort Bridger. I've got to catch up to the rest of the party."

"How'd you get behind?"

"Hard luck," Paul replied. "We've had our share of trouble ever since we left Grand Island on the Platte. We had a devil of a time crossing all the swollen branches of that river. I broke a wheel on a rock under the water—patched it up as best I could, but it didn't hold, and we had to drop out of line. I got the wheel fixed near Julesburg and we started out again, only this time, we didn't make it to Fort Laramie before we bent an axle. They left a message for us at Laramie to catch up as fast as we could because it was already getting late in the summer."

Murdock paused to light his pipe. "Hard luck," he repeated. "We were on our way to Fort Bridger when we met up with Plum and Crown." He glanced at Trace as if to apologize for his decision. "I knew the first time I laid eyes on those two that I was taking a chance going with them. But July's gone already, and I was supposed to get to Bridger by the first of August. Well . . . you know the rest."

Trace handed the book back to William. The boy accepted it with the same reverence he would have accorded a Bible, getting up immediately to put it away in the wagon. Trace watched William scramble up into the back of the wagon while he considered whether or not to offer any advice of his own. He had always been reluctant to tell anyone else what they should do, but there were some things he felt sure Mr. Hastings's guidebook might not tell, like that there are sometimes early snowfalls in the Wasatch and the Sierra Nevadas, not to mention a hell of a lot of desert in between. After thinking about it for a minute, he decided to speak his mind. "Mr. Murdock, I ain't trying to tell you what to do, but if it was me, I 'd have to say it's too late to start out now—especially in a wagon needing repairs."

Paul Murdock didn't reply for a long while. It was obvious that he had already spent a lot of time worrying over that very thought. But he was seriously lagging behind the rest of his party and anxious to get to California; it was just too difficult to give up now. After thinking about it a little longer, he said, "I hear what you're telling me, Mr. McCall, but I feel like if I can just catch up to Mr. Donner and the rest of 'em, I'll be all right. There'll be more'n ninety of us in the party, and I'm sure we can take care of each other. If I don't catch 'em before they leave Fort Bridger, then I guess I'll just have to decide then what's best to do."

Trace nodded thoughtfully. "Well, I'll get you to Fort Bridger as fast as I can."

# CHAPTER 2

It was the fourteenth of August when the log palisades of Fort Bridger were sighted, as Trace led the Murdock family across the broad, grassy river bottom. Jim Bridger had built his fort on Black's Fork of the Green River, and Trace had to admire his choice of sites. There was grass for the animals, and tree-lined channels of cool, clear water provided by the melting snows of the Uinta mountains. Little wonder Bridger called it one of the most beautiful spots on the face of the earth, and his paradise—although Trace himself was partial to the Bitterroot country. It was a disappointing sight to Paul Murdock, however, because there was no wagon train camped near the fort—only small groups of traders, mostly Indians from the Snake village, camped among the cottonwoods by the river.

Fort Bridger consisted of an eight-foot-high stockade with four log cabins inside. One of these housed Bridger's forge and workshop, and this is where Murdock pulled his wagon to a halt. Trace stepped down from the saddle as the familiar round figure of Louis Vasquez stepped out from another cabin that housed the store and trading post.

"Trace McCall," Louis called out, a wide smile on his face. "I figured surely you'd gone under."

"Howdy, Louis," Trace said with a grin. "I figured those Snake warriors you're so cozy with would have burned this place down by now." After they shook hands, Trace introduced the Murdock family. "Louis, this here is Paul Murdock, Mrs. Murdock, William, and Elizabeth. They were hoping to catch up with a party heading for California."

Vasquez frowned. "The Donner party? They left here ten or eleven days ago."

"Damn," Murdock complained. He turned to look at his wife. "Just more hard luck." Then he looked back at Trace, a spark of hope in his eye. "Maybe we could still catch up."

"I wouldn't advise it, Paul. There's some mighty rough country between here and California, and you'd best be on the other side of the mountains before October. I doubt you could make it by then."

Vasquez nodded his head in agreement. "Trace is right, Mr. Murdock. It ain't a good idea to drive a wagon off by yourself this late in the summer. Besides, the Donner party was planning to take a different trail to California, one I ain't familiar with. That feller Hastings was set up here for a spell. I understand he was supposed to lead the Donners over his new shortcut, but he left with another train before they got here. Left me a note to give 'em, said he'd mark the trail for them to follow."

"They left without a guide?" Murdock asked.

"They did," Vasquez confirmed. "Stayed here three days, deciding which way to go—finally decided to take Hastings's cutoff."

Trace helped a dejected Murdock family set up camp inside the stockade. They left the wagon to be repaired and turned the mules out in the corral next to the fort. Jim Bridger was away from the fort, but his wife, a heavyset, round-faced woman, came out with Vasquez's wife to make them welcome.

Resigned to the fact that he had missed his chance to get to California this season, Paul was now faced with a decision. Should he head back East, perhaps to winter at Laramie or Grand Island, or should he stay where he was and wait for a train to come through next spring? With some persuasion from Vasquez, and Trace's promise to act as a guide come springtime—or have his friend Buck Ransom take them through, Murdock decided to stay.

Trace was eager now to return to the mountains, but he offered to stay long enough to help Paul lay in a supply of meat for the winter ahead. After three days of hunting, Trace left the Murdocks in the hands of Jim Bridger's Indian wife, who took Martha under her wing and showed her the basics of drying meat to be stored away.

"My thanks, Trace, for seeing us through," Paul

said as Trace stepped up into the saddle and took hold of the lead rope on his packhorse.

"Glad I could be some help. I'm sorry you got delayed on your trip, but I think you'll be all right here till spring." He turned the paint's head to the north. "Take care of that family of yours."

"I will," Paul promised. "I just hope all the good land in California ain't gone by the time I get there."

Trace laughed. "I reckon there's land aplenty for everybody." He nudged the paint with his heels and was off.

"Hey, Trace," Vasquez yelled from the doorway of the store, "hang on to your topknot!"

"I aim to," Trace called back.

More than a month had passed since Trace left Paul Murdock and his family at Fort Bridger. In that time, Trace had not laid eyes on another white man, having trapped and hunted the mountain country up through the Yellowstone, over to Pierre's Hole, the Bitterroots, and back to the Wind River—managing to stay clear of the Blackfeet and the Shoshones. He was just following the wind, wandering, nursing off the clear mountain air, taking in nature's bountiful offerings.

On a cloudy morning in early October, Trace found himself near the Three Forks of the Missouri River. It had been cold in the mountains for several weeks now, each day promising that winter was not far away. Trace had even given thought to the possibility of going to Promise Valley to winter with his old friend and partner Buck Ransom. He had to smile when he thought about Buck. For one who so often scoffed at the notion of living inside a log house, Buck had looked mighty comfortable in his cabin by the river when Trace last saw him. *How many months ago was that?* Trace wondered. He had lost count. Folks in the little valley would be getting set to face another winter about now. As he rocked along comfortably with the easy rhythm of the paint's walk, Trace tried to picture Buck in his tiny shack on the river. Sometimes Trace wondered if the day would come when he settled down in one place. This invariably led to thoughts of planting corn, raising young'uns, and leaving the mountains. He shook his head to rid it of such thoughts.

North of the forks where the Missouri began, he had started looking for a place to camp for the night when he was brought up short by the sound of an axe. Not expecting to find anyone on this section of the river, he naturally followed the direction of the sound to find its source. Climbing a low rise that hid the river from view, he discovered a long gentle slope on the other side that led down to the water. At the end of the slope, where the trees lined the riverbanks, Trace spotted three men building a cabin.

Knowing it was never wise to show your hand until you were sure of the game, Trace stood motionless at the top of the rise and watched as the men notched logs and dragged them into place. After a few minutes, he decided there was nothing amiss about the three white men—they appeared to be trappers—so he nudged his horse and rode on down.

In order not to alarm them, Trace called out a hello when he was halfway down the slope. In spite of his greeting, the three were startled by his sudden appearance and scrambled to pick up their rifles. Trace continued down toward them, walking his horse slowly. When he was close enough to be identified as a white man, one of the men, a heavyset man with a bushy gray beard, cautioned his two partners to keep their eyes peeled. "Come on in, mister," he called out to Trace.

Boss Pritchard stood watching their surprise visitor approach. He still held his rifle in front of his chest, ready to fire if necessary, his feet spread wide to support his ample bulk, his eye steady and unblinking. Not many white men roamed around these parts alone, and this one looked about as wild as any Indian he had ever seen. Pritchard had heard some talk about a renegade who was running with a band of Blackfeet. A man like that might not be concerned about traveling alone.

"What do you make of him, Shorty?" Boss said, his voice low.

Shorty Whitehead squinted his eyes as if trying to make them see farther. "Can't say. Looks like he's by hisself, though."

"I wouldn't be too sure," Boss replied. "Could be that feller that raids with them Blackfeet. Jake, you'd best take a look back there at the horses. Make sure there ain't no damn Injuns sneakin' around back there while this feller makes talk with us." Jake Watson made no reply but slowly backed away from the half-finished cabin.

Boss Pritchard had been trapping the Rocky Mountains for fifteen years. He, Shorty, and Jake had been free trappers, working with the Rocky Mountain Fur Company when Jim Bridger was running things. When beaver were still shining, the three of them used to winter with large numbers of company men in log forts where they could hold their own against a sizable Indian war party. But in the last several years, most of the trappers had given up or were dead, so now there were just the three of them. That changed things a great deal. Most important, it made it necessary not to winter in the same place every year.

Trace was not surprised that the three men were greeting him with rifles in hand. A man couldn't be sure what manner of renegade might be riding into his camp.

"Hell, I know him," Shorty suddenly announced. "Ain't he that young feller that rode with Buck Ransom and Frank Brown?" Not waiting for an answer, he said, "Shore he is. We seen him at the rendezvous on the Green River, when ol' Joe LaPorte got killed." Shorty lowered his rifle. "Don't recall his name."

That served to revive his memory. "McCall," he said, and his face lit up as he remembered, "Trace

McCall, as I recollect. You recognize him now, don't you, Boss? He's changed some, but it's him, all right." Boss grinned and nodded, and Shorty called out to Trace, "Come on in and set by the fire, Trace." He walked over, propped his rifle against the cabin wall, and waited for their visitor to dismount and lead his horses up to their camp.

"It's Trace McCall, ain't it?" Shorty asked.

"That's a fact," Trace answered, smiling, but surprised that the man knew his name.

"Where's ol' Buck?" Boss asked when Trace came up to the fire to warm his hands. "He ain't gone under, has he? I heared about Frank Brown, but last I heared about Buck, he was leadin' a bunch of pilgrims out to Oregon Territory."

"Yeah," Trace replied, "Frank's gone under, but Buck's all right. Just been treed, that's all—took a piece of ground for himself in a little place they named Promise Valley. I guess he kinda got attached to the folks he was leading and just decided to settle down with 'em."

"Well, I'll be . . ." Shorty said. "I never woulda thought Buck would go civilized." He shook his head sadly, almost as if he had been told that Buck had died.

"I think he feels like he's getting too old to roam these mountains," Trace said. "I've got some fresh deer meat on my packhorse I'd be pleased to share with you."

"That shines," Boss quickly replied. "We got

plenty of coffee. We might as well cook us up some supper. We're about ready to quit workin' on the cabin for the day, anyway."

The rest of the evening was spent telling tales and recalling past rendezvous when beaver was prime and free trappers ruled the Rockies. Boss's eyes fairly sparkled in the firelight when he talked about the past. But now times were hard for the few free trappers who desperately clung to the old ways. For men like Boss Pritchard—and Trace McCall—there was never any thought about going back to the settlements to live. That was the reason the three partners were working hard to finish their cabin and get a roof on it before the severe weather hit. As soon as the cabin was ready, they would spend most of their time hunting for their winter supply of meat and laying in a stack of firewood. It would be a long, hard winter, but to them it was preferable to wintering in a settlement back East.

Trace bade them farewell early the next morning with the customary exchange of cautionary advice to watch their scalps. With a fresh breeze blowing off the river, he set out for Blackfoot country.

# CHAPTER 3

Buck Ransom sat on his horse and peered at the gathering of tipis on the creekbank. Clustered among the trees, the lodges were hard to identify from the ridge where he sat, so he prodded his horse and circled around to the south, keeping the ridge between himself and the Indian camp. Working up along the creek from the south, he moved up closer until he reached a point where he could get a clear view of the lodges.

He was on his way back to Promise Valley after a trip to visit his old friend Jim Bridger at Jim's fort at Black's Fork of the Green River. He had not encountered any Indians until now, and he wasn't in any particular hurry to return to his cabin in Promise, so he decided to have a look at this camp. It might be that he could spend a little time visiting, if they were a friendly band.

"Snakes," he murmured. "Ol' Broken Arm's bunch." He recognized the markings on the lodges, having spent some time with them at the last rendezvous held on the Green. Friendly enough, he figured, at least enough to sit down and have a squaw rustle up some supper for him. He rode out of the trees and approached the camp in the open, so the Snake warriors could clearly see him.

Recognizing the old trapper, Broken Arm himself walked out to welcome him. "Ransom," he called, "what brings you to this part of the country?"

Buck dismounted and clasped the old chief's arm in a gesture of friendship. "On my way back to the Blue Mountain country," Buck answered. "Been visitin' a friend of your'n, Jim Bridger." Buck knew it never hurt to drop Bridger's name—he was a big friend of the Snakes.

Broken Arm smiled and nodded his head. "Ah, Bridger. How is he? I have not seen him for many moons now."

"Why, he's passable, I reckon. He speaks often of his friend Broken Arm," Buck lied.

"Come, we will sit by the fire and smoke. My daughter will get some food for us." He led the way toward his tipi. Buck followed, leading his horse, exchanging polite greetings with some of the small crowd that had gathered.

Buck and Broken Arm sat beside the fire, smoking a pipe and talking. While they discussed the availability of game and the recent wars between the various tribes, Broken Arm's daughter came from inside the tipi and placed a pot of meat on the fire to boil. Her eyes averted, she did not acknowledge Buck's nod of recognition as she hurriedly prepared their supper. Buck remembered the girl—Blue Water was her name—and a right handsome maiden she was. As he recalled, she was the little Snake maiden who had seemed to be quite taken with his young friend Trace McCall—and had, in fact, figured in the trouble with Joe LaPorte.

Buck watched her as she moved quietly about the fire, tending the boiling meat, still keeping her eyes down when Buck looked directly at her. But out of the corner of his eye, he caught her staring at him when she thought her father wasn't watching. *She's shore findin' somethin' curious about me*, he thought. *Maybe she remembers I was with Trace at that rendezvous.*

He started to say something about the rendezvous on the Green River, but just then a small boy—maybe five or six years old—appeared out of nowhere and stood by Blue Water's side. Buck couldn't help but notice the striking resemblance between the girl and her son. But his features were also reminiscent of someone else, someone white, and without being told, Buck knew he was looking at Trace McCall's son.

"Leave us now," Broken Arm said, motioning for the child to leave.

Buck wanted confirmation. "That's a fine-lookin' boy there. Who is he?"

Broken Arm shrugged as if it was of no significance. "He is my daughter's son."

"Where's his father?"

"It is not polite to speak of the dead," Broken Arm answered, reluctant to discuss it, but after a moment he said, "His father was Eagle Claw. He was killed in the war with the Gros Ventres."

This was not the answer Buck had expected. He would have bet money that the boy was half white, and he was the spitting image of Trace McCall when Buck and Frank Brown had first found Trace. *Well, it ain't the first time I've been wrong.*

Old Broken Arm insisted that Buck should stay the night in his tipi, and Buck was more than happy to accept. They sat before the fire and talked of the old days when beaver was plentiful and when the trappers of the Rocky Mountain Fur Company worked the streams and rivers on both sides of the Rockies.

When Broken Arm finally announced that it was time to sleep, Buck, stiff from sitting so long, got up and stretched his back. "I reckon I'll take my horse down to the creek to give him a drink of water," he said and left the firelit circle, disappearing into the darkness. When he returned, Broken Arm's family was preparing to retire for the night. Blue Water, two older women Buck assumed were sisters of Broken Arm's late wife, and the boy all laid out sleeping robes around the perimeter of the tipi. A buffalo mat was spread out for Buck opposite the women, and he laid his bedroll on top of it. Blue Water ignored him, turning her back and apparently falling quickly asleep. When Buck looked over he encountered the wide-open eyes of the boy, staring at him. He winked and the boy smiled, then turned over and went to sleep.

Early the next morning, Buck awoke and looked around the tipi. Everyone else was still asleep, so he roused himself as quietly as he could and tip-toed outside. He walked down by the creek to relieve himself and to sprinkle a few drops of water on his face to chase the sleep from his eyes before returning to get his possibles packed to leave.

"You are Trace's friend?"

"Damn!" Buck uttered involuntarily. The woman's voice had come from the willows directly beside the path to the creek, startling him so much that he jumped. *Damn Injuns*, he thought, embarrassed to have been unaware of Blue Water's presence before she spoke. When his heart settled down again, he answered her. "Yessum, I'm Trace's friend. I was wonderin' if you was ever gonna recognize me." Then, seeing her puzzled expression, he repeated his words in her tongue.

She nodded excitedly. "Is he well?"

"As far as I know, he is," Buck answered. "I haven't seen him in many moons now. He lives alone in the mountains." Buck had some curiosities of his own to satisfy, so he questioned her. "I don't mean to offend you by talking about the dead, but Broken Arm said your husband was killed. Is that true?" She nodded, then dropped her eyes to look at the ground. He reached out and gently raised her chin, looking into her eyes. "That boy, he's Trace McCall's son, right?"

She nodded slowly. "I was carrying Trace's child when I was wed to Eagle Claw. He was a good man, and accepted the child as his own. Now the boy has no father, but my own father has taken him under his wing."

Buck had figured it right all along, and he didn't have to think too hard to realize why Blue Water had given no sign of recognition in Broken Arm's presence. Old Broken Arm may have been friendly toward a few white men—Buck himself and Jim Bridger in particular—but he wasn't too fond of white men in general. He didn't trust most of them, and Buck could understand that the old chief would have been pretty upset to learn that his daughter had borne a white man's child.

"You must not tell my father that we spoke of this," Blue Water cautioned.

"I know," Buck replied.

"Does Trace ever talk of me?" she asked, her dark eyes searching his.

"Oh, yessum, he does," Buck quickly responded. "He was quite taken with you—talks about you a lot." Then, realizing he had slipped back into English again, he answered her question with a simple "Yes." Buck had no knowledge of whether or not Trace ever thought about the pretty Indian girl.

He never talked about her, but Trace never let on to anyone what he was thinking, anyway.

His simple answer seemed to please her, for a soft smile appeared upon her face. "Tell him that his son is strong and smart and will be a fine young warrior some day." She gave Buck's arm a little squeeze, then turned and was gone.

*So ol' Trace McCall's a daddy. Ain't that somethin'?* Then Buck wondered if he should tell him or not. It might be best if Trace didn't know about the boy. On the other hand, Trace had a right to know. *Maybe I'll tell him—if I ever see him again. I'll think about it and decide later.*

When Buck returned to Broken Arm's tipi, Blue Water and the two older women were busy preparing food for him. Blue Water, as she had done the night before, did not look directly at him as she busied herself with her chores, then retreated to the tipi until he left. Buck said his good-byes, took his leave of Broken Arm's camp, and set out for Promise Valley.

Trace McCall knelt in the tall grass on the hillside, watching the seemingly endless herd of buffalo as it spilled out of the shallow draw and spread across the open prairie. Like a dark, rolling carpet, they covered the uneven ground as they bobbed and bumped along, all following one lead bull. Trace was in no hurry to make his kill. He would wait until the lead bull turned the herd toward the stream below him. Then he would work his way down the slope to a point where he would be close enough to use his bow. There had been a great deal of Indian sign in the Yellowstone country lately, too much to risk using his rifle. He suspected that a Sioux hunting party was waiting to ambush this same herd, probably no more than half a day's ride ahead of him. He had seen their scouts the day before as they followed the herd to make sure the massive beasts had not altered their pattern. Trace knew the Sioux would be near the river where the bluffs were steep, waiting to drive the confused animals over a cliff. It was late in the season, and the tribe wanted a large kill so they could store enough meat and skins for the coming winter. Trace's needs were on a much smaller scale. He required only one good-sized cow to replenish his meat supply and fashion a new robe for protection against the winter cold.

He tested the wind again to make sure it had not shifted. Satisfied, he pulled the wolf pelt over his shoulders and, crouching as he ran, moved quickly down along the slope. Buffalo have keen eyesight and miss very little around them. But Trace knew they were accustomed to seeing wolves following their flanks, and as long as the herd was bunched together, the buffalo would not be bothered by a single wolf.

Just as he figured, the herd turned and headed for the stream. As the lead animals thundered past the foot of the hill, Trace positioned himself on a knoll that afforded him an almost point-blank shot from above. His arrows ready, he set himself ready for the shot, waiting for the right animal. He soon spotted a cow the right size, but he waited, his bowstring drawn, the ground trembling beneath him as the sea of buffalo rumbled by him. She had a calf following her—good-sized, yet probably a spring calf and not old enough to fend for itself—so he spared the little one's mama. There were buffalo as far as the eye could see. He could afford to be selective. No need to make the little fellow an orphan.

He didn't have to wait more than a few seconds. He released his arrow, and it found its mark behind the lunging beast's front leg. She dropped like a stone. He waited for a few seconds while the river of animals veered away from the fallen cow. Then he placed another arrow in the wounded animal's side. She did not attempt to get to her feet but lay still, her heavy breathing and glazed eyes the only indication that she was not dead. In a few minutes the dark, rolling sea flowed past the foot of the hill and swept over the next rise, leaving Trace alone with his kill. She was done for, but still dangerous, so he moved to end her misery quickly and with caution—one toss of that massive head could throw a horse ten feet in the air.

After retrieving his horses, Trace worked quickly to skin the buffalo and take the cuts of meat he wanted. He did not want to linger in this open country any longer than necessary. As he butchered the cow and packed the meat on his horse, he was reminded of Buck Ransom and the time many years before when his old friend had shown him how to butcher his first buffalo. It seemed like a lifetime ago.

Thoughts of Buck naturally led to thoughts of Jordan Thrash and his daughter, Jamie. Trace paused for a moment while he formed a picture of the young girl in his mind. He knew that Jamie would have married him if he had asked, and on occasion he had allowed the notion to wander across his mind. Although he admitted to having strong feelings for the girl, he could not honestly say he loved her enough to tie up her life. When it came right down to the gristle of the matter, the call of the mountains was too strong to allow him to think about settling down with a wife. It left his mind in quite a quandary because he could not really say he had a strong desire to see her again. He was aware of her feelings for him, but he found it difficult to think of her in the same way.

Then he thought about the feeling of desperation that swept over him when he had first seen the cultivated land around Jordan Thrash's cabin in the little valley they had named Promise. The sight of groomed earth almost always caused him to feel a sickness in his stomach and renewed his craving for the mountains. He paused once more and took a long look around him to make sure he was still alone on the prairie before permitting his thoughts to wander again to the folks in Promise Valley.

A dozen families, most of them from the wagon train, had settled in Promise Valley. To Trace's surprise, even Buck had staked out a piece of the valley for himself next to Jordan's. Reverend Longstreet, who had captained the wagon train, cut out a piece across the river from Jordan. Farther up the valley, Travis and Nettie Bowen had settled, and next to them an old trapper named Slim Wooten had decided to try his hand at farming. Trace smiled when he thought of Slim—ol' Slim had spent too many years roaming the mountains to be content tied down in one place. Reverend Longstreet was determined, with help from the Good Lord, to build a town in Promise. *Maybe so*, Trace thought, *but there's a helluva lot of Injuns thereabouts that might not be looking for neighbors.*

Still, if folks were determined enough, they could stick, no matter how serious the threat of Indian trouble might be. Promise was settled mostly by hardworking, God-fearing folks who might not be experienced fighters. But they had good leadership in Reverend Longstreet and experienced Indian fighters in Buck Ransom and Slim Wooten.

Trace pictured the valley in his mind with thirty or forty more families settled there. It was not an image he particularly liked. Then the face of Jamie

Thrash formed in his mind and he dwelled upon it for a moment. Jamie's face gradually changed, taking on a darker, more rounded image. Her light-brown hair turned to midnight-black, parted in the center with braids down to her shoulders—and he realized he was thinking of a young Indian girl of the Yahuskin people, known to the trappers as Snakes.

Blue Water was her name, and he had to admit she might be another reason he felt hesitant about settling down in Promise Valley. Theirs had been a brief encounter, but one that would bind them together for as long as he had memory. Old Broken Arm, her father, had taken her away during the night, fearing a union between his daughter and a white man—but not before the two young lovers had come to know each other's passion.

Trace often thought about Blue Water and that night of magic on the banks of the Green River. Sometimes when seated before his lonely campfire at night, he could recall the soft, smoky scent of her dark hair and the warmth of her young body. As he thought about that time, years ago, he unconsciously fingered the otter-skin bow case and quiver she had made for him. There was no doubt in his mind that he would be married now if Blue Water had not disappeared in the night. He was young, and she had taken him to a place he had only dreamed about before. Sometimes the knowledge of that made him sad, for he had always thought that she could have come to him if she'd really wanted to. Then his thoughts flashed back to Jamie, and he once again contemplated the prospect of settling down in one place. He didn't spend more than a moment's thought on it before concluding that he was not ready to leave the mountains—and wouldn't be for a hell of a long time.

# CHAPTER 4

Jamie Thrash stared critically at her image in the small looking glass, one of the few things she had saved that had belonged to her mother. Holding the mirror's mother-of-pearl handle in her right hand, she moved the glass up and back, to each side, turning her face at first one angle and then another. She was not entirely satisfied with the reflection she saw, although she knew she was far from homely. Her father, and even Buck Ransom, constantly told her she was pretty. Still, it would have pleased her had she not inherited her mother's button nose. She unconsciously placed her left hand on the tip of her nose, grasping it gently with her thumb and forefinger and pulling on it as if to make it longer. When she saw how ridiculous she looked in the mirror, she made a face and stuck out her tongue. "That's for you, Trace McCall," she said, then immediately wondered why she had said that.

*Trace McCall*. It had been several days since she had brought that name to mind. When she and her father had first reached Promise Valley, not a day passed that she didn't think about Trace, wondering where he was and what he was doing—and when he might come back. She had gotten better about pushing thoughts of the tall, sandy-haired young man out of her mind, telling herself that it was foolish to pine for someone who was carrying on a love affair with a bunch of mountains. She felt her face flush in a fit of momentary anger. *To hell with him! I'm not waiting around for him to come to his senses. He can marry one of his damn mountains.* Now she glared at the image in the mirror as if daring it to contradict her. But she knew inside that she would probably wait around for Trace to marry her until she was too old to care—and that made her mad, too.

Replacing the mirror on the small chest by the window, she chided herself for indulging in self-pity and turned back to the stew she was making for supper. Slim Wooten had brought her a shoulder of deer that morning, as he often did, and as warm as it had been in the valley, she didn't want the meat to sit too long before she cooked it. It was handy having Buck Ransom and Slim Wooten close by. Buck had built a small cabin just north of them—little more than a shed actually, with one room. Her father had helped him build it, and Buck, in turn, had helped her father build their two-room cabin. By comparison even to Buck's humble dwelling, Slim had fashioned little more than a lean-to for himself. He was a few years older than Buck, and while both of the old trappers still talked about the mountains, Jamie suspected their wild days were long past.

*It's a pretty little valley,* she thought as she gazed out the window at her father struggling to break some new ground beyond his garden patch. There was still a lot of the summer left, and he wanted to see if he could get in a crop of fall beans before it got too late to plant. Jordan Thrash was a hard-working man, and he had done well by them, even if he wasn't much of a hunter. Buck and Slim supplied them with all the meat they needed, anyway, and Jordan repaid them with vegetables from the garden.

Promise Valley—Reverend Longstreet had named it that because of the prosperity it promised for all those souls who had survived the long trek from the East. He saw a great future for the modest community, built on both sides of the river. He was already talking about building a church next summer. Jamie would be satisfied just to acquire some chickens and maybe a cow. Longstreet had promised that they would soon come, along with a general store, and a blacksmith shop. *Maybe enough to entice Trace McCall to settle down,* she thought. *Dammit, there I go again.*

She picked up the bucket from the corner of the table and started toward the largest of two springs that fed into the river just below the cabin. The Tyler brothers had promised to come and help her father dig a well out back next week. She was looking forward to having a well, even though for a few days while the well was being dug, it would mean having Bradley Tyler looking moon-eyed at her. Bradley, a rail-thin, hawk-nosed bachelor, had made the trip out here with his twin brother, Bentley, and his family. Mrs. Tyler had hinted on several occasions that her brother-in-law was looking for a wife, a thought that usually made Jamie's skin crawl. Bradley Tyler was forty years old if he was a day. Jamie smiled as she thought about a comment Buck Ransom had made when he didn't know he was being overheard. He had joked to her father that it probably took both of those bony little Tyler twins to satisfy a woman as big as Bentley's wife, Rosemary.

She knelt down beside the spring and watched as the water bubbling out of the small opening in the ground slowly filled the wooden bucket. Their little valley was alive with color, which Jamie paused to appreciate. Much of the bottomland was already cultivated, but there was enough yet untouched to cast a green carpet that was sprinkled with thousands of bright summer flowers, spreading up the hillsides to the darker green of the fir trees.

She stood up and breathed in deep gulps of the gentle breeze flowing down through the valley. From where she stood, she could see Reverend Longstreet's log house across the river. Looking north, she could just see the front corner of the Bowens' place. It *was* a lovely little valley. Turning her gaze back toward the south, she looked at the undisturbed portion of the valley. Reverend Longstreet said that it wouldn't be long before folks would be coming to claim that land. Giving in to the temptation to stick a toe in the river, she put her bucket down and walked down to the water's edge.

Pulling her skirt up to her knees to keep it out of the mud, she started to step down from the low bank when she glanced down into the painted face of an Indian warrior, naked except for a breechclout. Stunned, Jamie stopped in her tracks, still holding her skirt, suspended in time for what seemed like minutes, his savage eyes locked on hers. Then, as if her nervous system was suddenly switched back on, she found her voice. Screaming, she turned and ran for the cabin. The warrior immediately sprang after her. On both sides of her, half-naked savages leaped out of the bushes and from behind trees, filling the air with terrifying war whoops and cutting off her escape. Turning away from the cabin, she tried to run toward the garden, but was overtaken in seconds. A hand grabbed her hair and almost yanked her off her feet. In the next instant she was snatched off the ground by powerful arms that held her helpless. She continued to scream until a hand was clamped roughly over her mouth, almost suffocating her. She tried to bite the hand and received a hard slap across her face in response. Still she struggled, but soon she was exhausted, and she knew there was nothing she could do to save herself. Her eyes wide with fright, she looked toward the lower end of the garden and saw her father running toward the cabin. Halfway through the garden, he suddenly stopped, seeing the overwhelming number of warriors swarming around his cabin. Jamie could see the terror in his eyes when he looked at her, helpless in the grasp of a naked brave. He looked back at a group of warriors destroying the inside of his cabin, then again at his daughter. "Run, Pa," Jamie cried softly, knowing he was too far away to hear her. He turned and fled for his life, leaving his daughter and his burning cabin behind him.

Buck Ransom pushed his hat back on his head and scratched his scalp thoughtfully as he listened to Jordan Thrash's recounting of the attack. Jordan was beside himself with grief, and though Buck was sympathetic with the slight man's anguish, there was little he could offer to give the man hope.

"They just grabbed her up and carried her off," Jordan wailed, tears welling in his eyes as he recalled the events of that terrible day a week before. "I did the best I could, Buck, but there was too many of 'em. I couldn't do nothin' to help my Jamie."

Buck nodded his understanding. "Don't reckon there was much you could do." It appeared to Buck that Jordan was looking for forgiveness for letting his daughter be carried away by an Indian raiding party. He wasn't in a position to judge, having been away from the valley when the Indians struck. Some folks would condemn a man for not giving his life in an attempt to save his own flesh and blood. Others would say it didn't make any sense to sacrifice yourself if there was no hope of success. Buck knew that Jordan Thrash was a hardworking man, and tough. But he was sweat and toil tough. He was not a fighter. Buck formed a mental picture of the Indian raid and how terrifying it must have been for poor Jamie. He wondered where Jordan had hidden while the abduction took place. *Every man's got to live with himself,* he thought, then quickly turned his attention away from the woeful little man.

"How many more got hit?" He asked the question of Reverend Longstreet.

"Just Jordan here, and the Tyler brothers' place upriver." In answer to the question on Buck's face, Longstreet answered, "Both men and Rosemary murdered. The little girl, Polly, ain't been found yet— we reckoned the Indians must have stole her."

Buck shook his head solemnly. "Dang. That shore is a shame. They was nice folks, too." He pictured little Polly—eight, maybe nine years old and bright as a new dollar. "What bunch was it? Anybody know?" He looked at Jordan, who shook his head sadly in reply.

"Slim Wooten said from the way Jordan described them, he thought they were Kutenai," Longstreet said.

Buck cocked his head and looked back at Jordan. "You got a look at 'em?"

"From a distance," Jordan answered weakly.

Buck fixed his gaze upon the mournful little man

for a long moment before turning back to Longstreet. "Where's Slim?" He didn't like the picture that was rapidly forming in his mind. Of all the little group of settlers in the valley, he figured Slim Wooten might have had the gumption to form a posse and go after the raiders.

"He went to find Trace McCall," Longstreet answered. "You were gone, and nobody else knows the mountains but you and Slim. He said he needed help to track them savages. You know, Slim ain't so young anymore."

This surprised Buck. Nobody had even seen Trace for almost a year. Buck himself had begun to wonder if his young friend might have gone under. It was a dangerous life Trace had chosen, living alone in the mountains, especially during these times when many Indian tribes were in a warring mood.

"How'd Slim know where to look for Trace?"

"Feller came through a couple of weeks back— said he camped one night with Trace above Three Forks, on the Missouri. So Slim set out that way, hoping to cut Trace's trail."

Buck scratched his chin while he considered what Longstreet said. "Three Forks, huh?" He speculated Trace McCall's probable whereabouts after passing through that territory. Knowing something of Trace's habits, he said with confidence, "Well, I guarantee you he ain't there now. He won't stay in one place for more'n a day or two until he holes up for the winter."

"I guess we should have formed a posse and gone after that raiding party, but we couldn't leave our own women and children unprotected," Longstreet said.

"Reckon not," Buck answered. He didn't say more about that suggestion, but he was thinking that if they *had* formed a posse from the farmers of Promise, they most likely would have gotten lost once they left the valley.

Just as he was reluctant to judge Jordan Thrash for not having the courage to stand and fight a Kutenai war party, Buck also could not question Slim Wooten's decision to go in search of Trace McCall, even though it meant losing a lot of time to a raiding party that already had a sizable head start. Slim knew the mountains as well as Buck did, but he was a couple of years older than Buck, and Buck was well aware of the toll that age takes on a man, especially in Indian territory. Although he would never admit it, he was painfully cognizant of the fact that his days of scouting were rapidly nearing an end— and it had happened so suddenly. He could still lead a party of immigrants up from Grand Island, up the Platte, over South Pass, and along the Oregon Trail. That trail was so familiar and well traveled by now, that he could follow it blindfolded. But to track a Kutenai war party through the mountains? Slim was right, you needed a younger pair of eyes for that. And there was no better man for the job than Trace

McCall, the man the Indians called Mountain Hawk. Finding him, however, would be the problem.

Suddenly aware that Longstreet and Thrash were gazing steadily at him, awaiting his advice, Buck reluctantly confessed. "Slim's right, he's too dang old to follow sign that's a week old—and so am I." He shifted his gaze to fix on Jordan Thrash. "I'm sorry to have to say it, but I don't hold much hope for finding them girls after all this time." When he saw the painful reaction to his statement in Jordan's eyes, he quickly added, "But if there's any man who can find 'em, it'd be Trace McCall." Glancing back at Longstreet, he said, "The thing I'd like an answer to right now is, where the hell is Slim Wooten? If Trace was on the Missouri, he should have found him by now."

"We can't just give up on it," Jordan wailed. "It's my daughter, Buck."

"No . . . and we ain't," Buck quickly responded. "I'll go look for Trace, myself. I know a lot of spots we used to camp when we was trappin'. Maybe I'll run into Slim, too. I'll start out first thing in the morning."

Slim Wooten had gotten careless. He should have known better. He had ridden these mountains since the summer of '29, and he had survived to the ripe old age of sixty-two simply because he'd always kept his nose to the wind and his eyes peeled for Injuns. There weren't many who lasted as long in the mountains as Slim had before the odds went against them. He had made it through more scrapes with hostiles than he could remember. But this time he was thinking that his number had finally been called. He'd made a bad mistake, and he was afraid he was going to have to pay for it with his life.

If he had kept to the ridges and worked his way along the hills to the west and north, he most likely would never have been spotted. But he had let himself get in a hurry, spurred on by the urgent nature of his mission and the knowledge that he had already taken too long to find Trace McCall. Desperate to save time, he had cut across the wide flat that led to the river. And like a damn greenhorn, he had been caught in the open. He had no choice now but to ride like hell and hope his horse was up to it.

They were Blackfoot. He was sure of that. A war party, out looking to raid the Crows maybe, and by pure coincidence—and his bad luck—they had flushed him out alone. He had already started across the flats when the war party emerged from a low draw to the south. Too late to avoid being seen, he at first continued along at a fast walk, hoping the Blackfeet would have no interest in him, though he knew better. The Sioux, the Cheyenne, and the Arapahos had been on the warpath all summer. They were getting testy, what with the ever-increasing numbers of white settlers passing through their territory on their way to the Oregon and California territories—and the Blackfeet were always at war with damn near everybody. He was praying that since he was obviously not a settler, this bunch might pass him by and continue on to wherever they were heading.

In years past, Slim had been on quite friendly terms with the Sioux and the Cheyenne, even traded with them as recently as last fall. But this summer had brought an entirely different atmosphere for white men in this part of the territory. A year ago he might have ridden over to greet them, even if they were Blackfeet, swap a few polite greetings, maybe trade for a little tobacco or coffee. But not this year. This year he was just one more unwanted white man trespassing on their hunting grounds.

He looked back in their direction. They had veered from their original path and were now riding on a line to intercept him. He kicked his horse into a faster pace, almost a trot, and set a course for a long string of cottonwoods lining the river. He thought that if he could reach the safety of the riverbanks, he might be able to discourage them with his rifle. He looked back again to see the war party loping along now, steadily increasing their pace. Glancing back at the trees, he judged them too far away for him to hold to his present speed. Knowing that it was always unwise to show fear in the presence of a party of Indians, he had hoped to keep to a seemingly casual pace. But the war party was rapidly closing the distance between them. *So much for bluffing*, he thought. *Time to run for it.*

As soon as he broke for the river, he heard the whoops and yells behind him. He didn't have to look back to know that the war party was in full gallop after him. Lying low on his horse's neck and holding his packhorse's lead line, he begged for all the speed the beast could give him. It didn't take long to see that it wasn't going to be enough. The Blackfeet were rapidly overtaking him on their swift little ponies. He could hear the wild shrieks and taunts above the thundering of his horses' hooves as he rode hell-bent for leather across the rough prairie. An arrow landed with a smothered thump and embedded itself in his bedroll behind the saddle. He kicked his horse hard, but the already tiring animal was doing the best he could, and losing ground to the Indian ponies with every stride.

Desperate now, Slim dropped the lead rope and let his packhorse go, hoping the Blackfeet would break off the chase to go after it. No such luck. Two of the warriors veered off to chase the packhorse, but the rest, a dozen or more, never hesitated in their pursuit, their taunts and jeering yelps filling the dusty air around him. His horse was beginning to stumble with weariness. Still, Slim kicked his heels frantically, demanding more speed as an arrow whistled by him, followed by several more as the warriors closed the gap between them. In the next moment an arrow found its mark in the horse's flank, causing the crazed animal to kick and break his stride. Slim almost came out of the saddle as the wounded animal bucked and stumbled and came close to going down before regaining his footing. In that brief span of time, the pursuing warriors were able to close to within twenty yards.

At close range now, the Blackfeet filled the air with arrows. Slim tried to stay low on his horse's neck, but he could not avoid the hailstorm of arrows that swirled about him. He was no more than fifty yards from the banks of the river when the first arrow struck him in his lower back. It was like a solid blow from a man's fist, and he grunted as the wind was knocked out of his lungs. Although he could feel the burn of the arrowhead as it lay embedded deep in the muscles of his back, he did not let up on his frantic spurring of his exhausted horse, battering the poor animal's sides with his heels.

A second arrow struck his shoulder, causing him to curse aloud in pain. Still, he managed to pull the pistol from his belt and turn to fire at the warrior closest behind him. He spat out another oath as the startled warrior doubled up and rolled off his horse's back. A third arrow and then a fourth slammed into Slim's back and his thigh, but he remained in the saddle, refusing to go down. Still driving his stumbling horse toward the river, he was aware of a numb feeling beginning to creep over his entire body. All around him the river basin was filled with the angry shrieks of his enemies as he continued to feel the blows of arrows—too many to count now—stabbing at his body. The bright morning sun seemed to fade, although there were no clouds to block it, and his vision became blurred and strained.

Suddenly the ground before him seemed to roll as if the earth had suffered an upheaval. The last thing he remembered before he was suspended in midair was his hand gripping his rifle as his horse went out from under him. He landed hard, breaking the arrow shafts in his back, driving one of them deeper into his lungs. The sound he heard was his own scream of agony, followed by the discharge of his rifle. His impact with the ground had caused him to squeeze the trigger and send a rifle ball whistling harmlessly into the air.

"Damn," he swore, when his head cleared enough to realize that he had wasted the shot. He knew he was finished, but he fully intended to take one or more of the screaming devils with him. He fumbled with his powder horn, trying to reload for at least one good shot. But his fingers were stiff and numb, refusing to cooperate, and try as he might, he was unable to pour a measure of powder in the barrel. Letting his rifle fall, he pulled his long Green River knife from his belt and held it under his leg where it could not be seen by his assassins. He lay back and waited, the arrow in his back like a burning-hot iron, as big as a tree limb. It sent a lightning stab of pain through his body whenever he moved.

Pulling up around him now, the Blackfoot warriors continued to circle the fallen man, shooting arrow after arrow into his body. Soon Slim could not raise himself under the sheer weight of the many arrows that penetrated his bony frame. Still he would not die. Far beyond the threshold of agony, he did not beg for mercy nor scream out in pain.

Astonished by the white man's refusal to die, several of the warriors dismounted and stood over the mortally wounded man. Though he was bloodied and too weak to sit upright, his eyes were clear as they followed the movements of the warriors around him.

"What keeps this old buzzard alive?" the warrior closest to Slim asked. His question was met with only puzzled grunts from his brothers.

"It took enough of you," Slim answered him, speaking in the Blackfoot tongue, his voice strained and raspy.

Slightly taken aback, the warrior grunted and drew a long skinning knife from his belt. He held it up for Slim to see. "I will dance with your scalp tonight. In my song I will sing of the white man too stupid to die." There was a low murmur of laughter from his followers.

"Tell me your name, if you ain't ashamed of it," Slim forced through his painful grimace. "I wanna know who kilt me."

The warrior smirked. "I am Little Bull," he said defiantly, pounding his chest with his fist. "It is Little Bull who kills you, white man." Then he grabbed a handful of Slim's thin white hair and prepared to scalp him.

"Well, Little Bull, you heathen son of a bitch, I'll wait for you in hell," Slim rasped. With one last surge of will and defiance, he brought his knife up and struck Little Bull in the ribs, sinking it as deeply as his waning strength allowed.

The Blackfoot warrior yelped in surprise and staggered backward, stumbling over the feet of the warrior behind him and landing solidly on his backside. Astonished by the sudden counterattack, his friends could only gape in amazement. Little Bull roared in anger as he stared dumbfounded at the knife in his side. Though painful, the wound was not deep enough to penetrate his lung, the major damage having been done to his pride. Embarrassed before his friends, he scrambled to his feet and set upon the helpless white man, stabbing him repeatedly with the Green River knife. Infuriated by the insolent grin on the dying man's face, Little Bull struck again and again until he was too weary to continue.

Finally Slim slid into the gentle darkness that awaits all men. His final thought was one of regret that he had been unable to find Trace McCall and tell him that Jamie Thrash and little Polly Tyler had been stolen away by Kutenais.

There was barely enough light to see when Buck left his rough shack in Promise Valley, crossed the river, and turned his horse toward the mountain pass to the east. It was a long shot, but he had a vague notion where his young friend might be. There was a camp high up in the Bitterroots, near a waterfall where he, Trace, and Frank Brown had found the streams filled with beaver—so many, in fact, that they were certain that they were the only trappers to have found it. After Frank died and Buck settled himself in Promise Valley with Reverend Longstreet's flock, Trace returned to the mountains, often wintering in the camp by the waterfall. The market for beaver plews had long since died out, but it was still a good place to hole up if a body desired solitude. And that seemed to be the frame of mind Trace McCall was in since his mother died.

Thoughts of the young mountain man filled Buck's mind on this chilly morning in late summer as he guided his horse along an old Indian hunting trail that led to the buffalo country. Buck took some credit for introducing Trace to the life of a trapper. He had taught Trace how to set a beaver trap and how to skin the critter and dry the plew. But he could take no credit for the unexplained craving inside a man that pulled him toward the mountains. That had to be put deep into a man's soul by his Maker, and Trace McCall was as much a part of the Rocky Mountains as the sheer wall of stone that defined the trail up through the pines ahead.

Buck's thoughts turned to the purpose of his journey. He could not entertain much hope for Jamie Thrash. The girl had a lot of spunk, he had to admit, but she was likely to suffer more abuse at the hands of the Kutenai braves than her spunk could handle.

If she was lucky, one of the warriors might take her for a wife—not a great deal of consolation, but better than if she was taken as a slave. The youngster, Polly Tyler, might have an easier time of it—if, in fact, the Indians had stolen her, as it appeared. Indians were right fond of children, and little Polly would more than likely be adopted by one of the Kutenai women—especially if that woman had lost a child to sickness or accidental death. It was Jamie he was worried about. She was a fair-looking young lady, and if Buck had to guess, he'd bet she was a virgin—and virtuous young women were highly desirable among any Indian tribe.

"It's a damn shame," Buck lamented to his horse as he followed the trail higher up among the pines until they gave way to a treeless meadow strewn with craggy outcroppings of sharp, jagged rocks and weather-polished boulders that seemed to be only momentarily stable, as if at any moment they might start tumbling down the mountainside. *Grizzly country*, he thought as he took a long, sweeping look across the open expanse of grass before him. It was the time of year when grizzlies were adding fat for the coming winter, a time of year when they were even more irritable than usual.

Satisfied that he and his horse were the only critters in the meadow, he nudged the animal forward, veering off to the south in order to strike the narrow pass that would take him across the ridge and down the other side of the mountain. He wasn't worried about Indians—he didn't expect to encounter any this high up on the ridges. Elk and deer hadn't left for the lower ranges yet, but most of the tribes would most likely be down in lower country, following the buffalo herds to replenish food caches and take skins to turn into winter robes.

The thought of elk meat was enough to cause Buck to lick his lips as he recalled the aroma of a sizzling chunk of freshly killed elk, roasting over the coals of a warm campfire. Moments like these were when Buck regretted his decision to settle down with Reverend Longstreet's little gathering of pilgrims. "Damn, I miss the mountains," he moaned. The brief span of years when beaver pelts were bringing top dollar had been the happiest years of Buck's life, and every once in a while, when he was taken with a melancholy mood, he would mourn the passing of the old days, when he and his old partner, Frank Brown, rode the high country, free as a couple of eagles, enjoying the bounty offered by the streams and rivers from the upper Missouri to the western side of the Rockies. "Damn, it was a good life," he blurted as his eyes moistened with emotion.

As if to taunt him further, a bull elk emerged from the trees below and disappeared through the narrow pass that Buck was heading for. The temptation to taste elk meat again was almost overpowering, but Buck reminded himself of the urgency of his journey. Still, the couldn't resist a little teasing of the lovesick bull, which was no doubt searching for a cow to mate. Buck followed the elk through the pass and descended the slope beyond, making his way through the boulders and stunted trees toward the taller pines below.

There was no sign of the elk when Buck emerged from the ring of pines and entered a small grassy clearing. To his left was a steep cliff that rose more than a hundred feet; to his right, a thick forest of pines and fir trees. Straight ahead, the game trail he had been following cut through a broad thicket that was a tangle of high brush and vines. "Huh," Buck snorted softly. "Now, which way did he go?"

He decided to see if he could call the elk to him. Cupping his hands before his mouth, he pursed his lips and issued his best imitation of a comely young elk cow looking for a beau. There was no response, so he called again and paused to listen. There was still no answer to his mating call. He had no intention of lingering for long—he had no time to hunt— it was just in his nature to have the satisfaction of calling up an elk.

He was about to give it up when he tried one last time. Still there was no answering grunt or bugle to his love call. But as he started to ride on, he heard a noise on the far side of the thicket. Buck grinned. *Maybe I ain't lost my touch after all,* he thought, and cupped his hands to his mouth once more. *Come on, sweetheart. Come on and meet this sweet little honey.* Again he heard the rustling of branches, and then he spotted the movement of the brush and small trees as the would-be suitor made his way through the thicket. He couldn't see the animal as yet, but from the disruption he was causing, Buck knew he was a big one. Buck could not contain a chuckle as he thought about how angry the elk was going to be when he discovered the source of the love calls. *Lucky for you I ain't got time to shoot you and butcher you.*

He rode to a position at the edge of the thicket where he could watch the elk when he came out into the open. He sat and waited by a clump of berry bushes that he deemed to be at a safe distance from the point where he figured the elk would emerge— elk were not especially sweet-tempered, and Buck intended to give this one plenty of room. It was simple enough to follow the big animal's progress by the wake of bending limbs and shaking bushes. Buck was thinking that he should have been able to see the bull's antlers by this time. No sooner did the thought occur than the bushes stopped cracking and trembling and it was suddenly dead quiet. Buck waited for a few minutes, but still there was no further movement in the thicket.

He laughed and mumbled low, "What's the matter, lover boy? You ain't gone bashful on me, have you?" He nudged his horse a little closer, but the animal was reluctant to obey. He was about to give the horse a kick in the slats when the thicket seemed to explode before him, and suddenly he had an angry grizzly almost in his lap. The horse reared back on its hind legs, catching Buck by surprise and causing him to drop his rifle. He tried to wheel the terrified horse around, but the grizzly was too quick for him. The giant beast slashed out with one huge paw and caught the horse at the base of its neck, knocking it over on its rump and separating man from mount.

Buck came out of the saddle and hit the ground hard, rolling in an effort to get away from the raging bear. Having lost his rifle already, his only weapons were his pistol and his knife. He drew them both from his belt, even before he stopped rolling. Buck saw his horse scramble to its feet, eyes wide with terror, and bound across the little clearing, bucking and kicking all the way.

The grizzly hesitated a moment to consider the fleeing horse. Then he looked back at Buck, who was now inching slowly backward. Infuriated, the great beast reared up on his back legs. Standing at least eight feet tall, the monster bared his fangs and roared out his anger. The leaves on the bushes shivered in response, and Buck knew that he was about to meet his Maker. The grizzly dropped back down on all fours and started advancing toward the helpless man, slowly at first, but steadily increasing speed, his fangs bared and gleaming in the morning sun.

Buck had no options left. He tried to back away slowly, hoping the bear would be content to see him retreat, but the grizzly was intent upon having a meal. There was no longer any time to be afraid. Buck played his only card. With the bear practically on top of him, he fired his pistol, aiming for the cavernous mouth of the monster. The slug hit the bear on his lower jaw, and while causing him to pause for a moment, it only added to his rage. With no more now than his knife and his bare hands, Buck prepared to fight for his life.

With blood dripping from the wound in his jaw, the furious grizzly reared up again on his back legs and prepared to lunge. Buck looked up at what could only be certain death. Thoughts flashed through his mind—he had always known his life might well come to a violent conclusion, but he would have hoped for some ending less terrifying than the one he now faced.

The great beast's constant roar filled the air with a sound so loud that Buck never heard the crack of the Hawken rifle behind him. In fact, he was stunned, unable to understand what had happened when he saw the bear's left eye suddenly explode, a result of the rifle ball expertly aimed for an instant kill shot. The grizzly's roar ended with a bellow of pain, and then there was silence as the bulk of the great carcass settled in a heap at Buck's feet.

Buck could not move for a long moment, stunned by the glimpse of death still lingering before his eyes. He just sat there on the ground, staring at the monstrous hairy mound that was no more than a few inches from his feet. Weak and unsteady, he finally got to his feet and looked behind him to see his rescuer walking toward him, leading two horses. If

Buck had been afforded the time to pray when the bear started to make his final lunge, he would have prayed for the appearance of the very man who now was walking tall and confidently toward him—Trace McCall.

"When did you start hunting grizzlies with a pistol?" Trace said, a wry smile on his lips.

"Trace . . . damn, " Buck replied, suddenly out of breath and weak in the knees. He sat down on the ground again, landing heavily on his bottom like a sack of grain. "I'm gittin' too old for this."

"I found your horse running like hell on the far side of that slope back there—figured you might need a little help." Trace led the horse up to where Buck had settled and held him steady when he tried to pull away from the carcass of the bear. "He's got a nasty slash on his neck—oughta heal all right, though. I figured it to be a grizzly."

Buck was so happy to see his young friend, and so relieved to still be alive, that he almost forgot that he had been on his way to find Trace. The traumatic encounter with the bear over, he remembered why he was on this trail in the first place. "Trace," he blurted, "I come lookin' fer ya. Injuns run off with Jamie Thrash and Polly Tyler!"

He could not have stunned Trace more if he had hit him with a club. The tall young mountain man had already started to skin the grizzly when Buck's statement stopped him cold. *Jamie, stolen!* The thought hammered at his brain, numbing it with shock. He stepped back from the carcass, his skinning knife already bloody, his eyes staring but not focusing on anything in the present. After a long moment of silence, during which he attempted to collect his emotions, he questioned Buck, asking for all the details of the abduction. He listened without comment while Buck recounted the events that had brought him to this mountain pass.

His emotions under control now, Trace said, "Well, we'd best get started." Glancing at the still-warm carcass, he said, "I reckon we'll leave this one for the wolves." As an afterthought, he added, "I've got a packhorse loaded down with buffalo, anyway."

They started out up the ridge to retrieve Trace's packhorse, then rode back on the trail Buck had just come up. As they made their way back down through the pines, Buck asked about Slim Wooten. "Slim Wooten rode out toward Three Forks about two weeks ago to tell you about Jamie and little Polly Tyler. I reckon he didn't find you."

"I reckon I found him," Trace returned softly, "at least what I think was him."

This caused Buck to cock his head around abruptly. "Gone under?" he asked, looking directly into Trace's eyes.

Trace nodded. "Blackfeet. I never saw so many arrows in a body before. When I found him, he was getting pretty bloated, and his face was cut up so bad I wasn't sure who he was. It sure didn't look like Slim, but I reckon that's who it was, all right."

"Damn," Buck muttered, almost under his breath. "There ain't many of us left from the old days. Dammit, Trace, we used to ride free as birds over these mountains. Most of the Injuns were right hospitable, except the Blackfeet and the Gros Ventres, and maybe the Utes, but even they was friendly when it come to needin' somethin' they could trade for. Now all the tribes is gittin' stirred up. I tell you the truth, Trace, I'm too old to traipse around these hills anymore. I can't half see—I'm even gittin' to where I can't hold my water anymore." He stopped abruptly as soon as he made that last statement, realizing that he was confessing things he'd had no intention of admitting to anyone.

Trace had no answer for his old friend. He felt compassion for Buck while realizing that no one could fully appreciate the anguish and frustration every man must experience when his days in the sun were nearing an end. Knowing Buck as well as he did, Trace decided it was best not to comment. On other occasions, Trace would have probably chided Buck about being too old to cut sign. But he sensed that Buck's brush with death on this day had had a sobering effect on the old trapper, and he knew Buck was embarrassed to have admitted to human frailty.

There was not a great deal of conversation on the ride back to Promise Valley. Both men were deep in their thoughts—Buck bemoaning his own mortality

and Trace troubling over the distressing news Buck
had brought. He wasn't sure how old Polly Tyler
might be—seven, eight, nine—he wasn't good at
guessing the age of children. But he felt deep compassion for the child. She was too damn young to
have her whole family murdered right in front of
her eyes. And he had a special feeling for Jamie, and
he knew she was fond of him. This ordeal might be
enough to destroy her mind. The thought of the two
girls in the hands of Kutenai warriors created an urgency in him that he needed to put out of his mind.
Otherwise he would not be able to keep his concentration on his business when it came time to track
their captors.

Early the next afternoon they rode down through
the lodgepole pines and out into the broad river valley that was the tiny settlement named Promise Valley by Reverend Longstreet. They went directly to
Jordan Thrash's place, where they found Jordan
working to rebuild his burned-out log house. When
he saw the two riders approaching, Jordan laid his
axe aside and went to meet them. He started apol-
ogizing immediately, not even waiting for the two
men to dismount.

"Trace, I swear there wasn't nothin' I could do.
There was too many of 'em. Buck'll tell you." He
looked at Buck, his eyes pleading.

"Jordan." Trace said, acknowledging the slight little man's presence. To him, it wasn't necessary for
Jordan to make excuses for not defending his daugh-

ter. Trace just naturally did not expect a man like Jordan Thrash to stand up to a raiding party. Together, he and Buck searched out what little sign remained after more than two weeks, and Trace could see why Buck was not optimistic about their chances for success in finding the girls.

"Not much to go on," Buck said.

Trace nodded, then said, "You say the Tyler place was hit. Anybody else?"

"No," Buck replied. "They left here and went upriver till they come on the Tyler place. Killed both brothers and Rosemary, too—and burned their cabin. Then, from what I could see, they followed the river on up the valley. I reckon they figured they'd done enough mischief and decided to head for the mountains."

Trace looked back at Jordan, who was wringing his hands and fidgeting nervously. "And the Tyler girl ain't been found yet?"

Jordan shook his head vigorously. "No. Nobody's found poor little Polly yet."

"Well, I'm going after them," Trace announced quietly, "but I don't know how much chance I've got of tracking them. Sign's pretty old. Maybe I'll have better luck when the tracks clear the valley and I can find out what trail they're following."

"Reckon I'll go with you," Buck said.

"I appreciate it, Buck, but I guess I druther go alone if you don't mind." Before Buck could protest, Trace quickly added, "I reckon the folks here in the valley will be needing to have you around in case there's more trouble—they'd feel a whole lot safer." He didn't want to hurt his old friend's feelings, and he was glad when Buck responded in agreement.

"Maybe you're right, pardner. These folks is already a little jumpy. Besides, it's a lot easier for one man to stay outta sight." Buck was relieved to find that Trace didn't expect him to go.

"I expect I'll be gone for a spell," Trace said. "That raiding party's got a pretty good start, and it'll be getting cold before you know it. I'm hoping to catch sight of 'em before the first snow, but chances are mighty slim." He saw the pain in Jordan Thrash's eyes when he said it, so he added, "'Course I could catch 'em before they get back to Kutenai country if they ain't in a hurry. Anyway, I'll do the best I can."

It was a clear and pleasant morning when Trace left the ruins of the Tyler cabin and rode off upriver. Still, there was a bite in the morning breeze that warned that summer would soon be only a memory. Trace knotted a neckerchief loosely around his neck to ward off the chill. He checked the lead rope on his packhorse, glancing back at the roan as he did. He would have preferred to take only one horse—the paint he was riding—but he had a feeling that this task might take a while to accomplish. With winter coming on, he was going to need all the buffalo meat he had dried, plus the hide for warmth. The prospect of wintering alone in the mountains held no dread for Trace. He found that at this stage in his life he welcomed the solitude of the mountain meadows and forests. He had discovered at an early age that he was born to roam the high ridges, dependent upon no one but himself, his rifle, and his horse. This was the reason it troubled him that Jamie hinted of a future for the two of them beyond the close friendship that Trace envisioned. He did think a lot of Jamie, but each time he tried to imagine settling down with her as a wife, it seemed more like marrying his sister. Jamie represented domestic imprisonment to his spirit, yet he could not shake the girl's grasp on his emotions. And here he was, he told himself, thinking about her again when he was supposed to be looking for sign.

High above the ridge before him, a hawk wheeled on the fresh morning breeze. When he glanced up and saw it, Trace smiled. It was a sign to him, an omen that told him his path would be a good one. For the hawk was his kindred spirit. When still a boy, he had spent four years with Red Blanket's band of Crows. His adopted father, Buffalo Shield, had taught him the importance of identifying his kindred spirit in the animal world. He had never thought to question the truth in Buffalo Shield's words, for he could sometimes feel himself as one with the hawk. And when he heard the high, lonesome cry of the hawk drifting across the valley, he could feel its wild spirit trembling deep inside his own veins. He could not speak of such things to other white men—only Indians understood. When he thought of these things, he could not help but appreciate the irony in the fact that the Blackfoot band had given him the name of Mountain Hawk.

Buck was right. The raiding party had ridden hard by the river to a point where the mountains closed in to wall off the valley. Then they turned to the east, following a long, narrow draw that led into the higher hills. The sign was old, but there had been no rain for weeks, so it was not difficult to follow the Kutenai raiders. Trace was able to make good time on the trail, since when sign became scarce, there was usually only one path through the steep passes. He simply took the only route available to him and picked up the Indians' trail on the other side.

After crossing the mountain ridges east of Promise, he came down into a seemingly endless stretch of rolling hills where the grass was still green, and here and there a fading patch of yellow flowers remained, stubbornly defying the coming winter. The war party had camped here, close by a restless stream. Trace took a few minutes to study the few signs remaining—ashes from the fire, some patches of grass that were still matted down, some bones from a rabbit. *Not much fresh meat for a party this size*, he thought. *They must have a supply of dried meat or pemmican.* He wondered how Jamie and little Polly had fared here.

A short ride of no more than two hours brought

him to the beginning of an old Indian trail that led into another line of mountains, higher than those he had just left behind. He was in the land of the Nez Perces now, and he knew that this was one of the trails Nez Perce hunters used to go to the buffalo hunting grounds on the eastern side of the mountains. He had often traded with the Nez Perces when he was trapping with Buck, and they had always been friendly. Trace did not, however, relax his sense of caution. These were unsettled times, and any tribe might get their dander up for the most insignificant of reasons.

As he expected, the party of Kutenai warriors followed the hunting trail through the mountains toward Flathead country. Trace made his way up the slopes, following the winding trail as it sought out the passes and draws, until it crested and started down the far side. He paused for a few moments to scan the peaks around him. The sheer majesty of the Bitterroots never failed to impart a feeling of calm to him. He filled his lungs with the cold mountain air before nudging the paint with his heels. He would sharpen his eye when the trail descended the high ground and crossed the valley below him. If Jamie's captors were intent on returning to their homeland, as he suspected, then they would have left the trail and struck out due north at some point in the valley.

He crossed the entire width of the valley, riding slowly, searching the ground on each side of the Nez

Perce trail, but he found no sign that indicated where the Kutenai had left the trail. Yet he felt certain that they had. The sign was too old, and the trail too well traveled for Trace to determine if the war party had continued on into Flathead country. His intuition told him that they most likely turned north, so he went back and searched the trail again, concentrating his efforts on the ground around the stream that bisected the valley. Maybe they had become cautious and decided to cover their trail. They had been careless and unconcerned to this point. Maybe there was bad blood between them and the Flatheads. Whatever the reason, they had definitely decided it was best to hide their tracks.

It was pretty difficult to disguise the trail of a party this size, even tracks as old as these. Trace figured the only way it could be done was to ride up the stream, so he guided the paint into the water and walked him slowly up the streambed. There was no sign of any disturbance in the rocky stream bottom, but he was firmly convinced that his hunch was right, so he continued doggedly up the stream toward the northern end of the valley.

Finally his patience paid off, and he saw what he was looking for. It was only a flat stone the size of a dinner plate, but it looked somehow out of place. He dismounted in the shallow water and stooped to examine it. It had been dislodged and tilted up on edge, the result of being stepped on by a horse, he figured. His hunch confirmed in his mind, he stood up again and looked at the valley before him. Kutenai country was to the north and west. Blackfoot territory was also north, but farther to the east. The valley where he now stood was crossed by parties from several tribes—Kutenai, Blackfoot, Nez Perce, Flathead, even Pend d'Oreille and Gros Ventres. This perhaps explained the Kutenai warriors' caution.

Climbing aboard the paint again, he continued up the stream, studying the banks on either side. The Kutenai left the streambed where a group of willows bordered the low bank, and headed in a general northwest direction. The trail was easy to follow until it led up through a narrow draw and out onto a flat, rocky slope. There it ended. He searched in vain for a hoofprint, a disturbed rock—something—but there was nothing. The slope was too rocky and the trail too old. After a long while, during which he dismounted and scanned the ground, he stood up straight and sighed. *I reckon this is where the tracking ends and the searching begins.*

# CHAPTER 5

Left Hand stood over the white woman while he studied her thin features. Jamie stared back at him defiantly. He was unmoved by her show of courage, being more interested in her value as a possible trade. This white woman was very skinny. She didn't look like she could do much work, but he supposed he would keep her as a slave unless someone showed an interest in her as a wife. He knew a Flathead man who had taken a white captive for a wife, and it had turned out very well for him. She had made a good wife. He was not so sure about this one. She was pretty enough, but her body was frail, her hips were thin, and he wondered if she would have a problem birthing a child. Maybe one of the younger men in the village might be interested in her. Left Hand himself was content to have just one wife, although he sometimes wondered if Red Leggings might wish he would take another wife to help her. Maybe he would give her this white woman for her slave.

The child was another matter. Eight or ten summers, she could more easily be taught the Indian ways. He would cut her bonds as soon as they reached the village. His good friend Black Elk had already expressed an interest in the child. Black Elk's wife had been unable to bear him a child. So when they had killed the two men and the woman at the last cabin, Black Elk spared the child.

Though determined to show a brave face to her captors, Jamie was terrified inside. She got to her feet when the gruff-looking Indian motioned for her to get up, a somewhat difficult task with her hands tied behind her. The gruff one, with the help of another Indian, picked her up and put her on the back of one of Tyler's horses. Polly Tyler was likewise deposited on another of her father's horses, and they were once again on the trail.

Heartsick and despairing, Jamie had no idea how far they had come from her father's log house. She only knew that she was weary from the long days on horseback and the meager allotment of food. Her captors were not overly abusive to her, although their handling of her was far from gentle. Aside from the lump on the side of her face, received as she had tried to run when they had first descended upon her house, she was none the worse for wear physically. She was horrified when first captured, though, and the first night on the trail she had not slept at all. Having witnessed the merciless slaughter of Bradley and Bentley Tyler, she was too terrified to close her eyes, fully expecting to be raped and then murdered. It had not happened, however, and now after so many nights that she had lost count, she still had not been threatened with undue violence. She might receive a stinging blow across her backside from one of the warriors' whips if she didn't move smartly enough, but that was about the extent of the abuse. It was far more difficult for her to endure the absence of privacy when it came to taking care of nature's call. She was never allowed out of her captors' sight, not even to urinate, and she was forced to do her business in public as well, humiliated by the watchful gaze of one or more of the men, observing her like farmers at a stock show.

In an effort to put on a brave front for Polly's sake, Jamie forced a smile as she caught the girl's eye. Polly gave no indication that she noticed, simply staring straight ahead. The little girl had cried almost constantly for the first two days on the trail. Now, her tears seemingly exhausted, she made not a sound—just stared at the horizon as if trying to look beyond the terrible tragedy she had witnessed. At night Polly was permitted to sleep close to Jamie, and she would snuggle up as close to Jamie's body as possible, cringing whenever one of the Indians would approach. The child was never threatened with physical harm, but Jamie feared that the traumatic events of her capture might destroy Polly's mind. She did the best she could to talk to her, hoping to restore some stability to her life. It was a difficult thing to do in the presence of such obvious savagery. The gruff one was especially terrifying— standing over them, admonishing them in strange guttural tones that Jamie could not understand. The fact that she had not been physically harmed up to this time was not enough to reassure her that she would not be abused once the war party reached its destination.

Three more days' travel brought them to the edge of a large lake surrounded by mountain peaks. Left Hand led the party around the western shore of the lake, and as they progressed farther and farther around the expanse of water, Jamie detected an air of excitement among the warriors. Soon she saw the reason for it. When they filed over a small rise covered with fir trees, she saw the lodges by the water's edge. It was Left Hand's village. Now the warriors restrained themselves no longer. Calling out with whoops and loud greetings, the younger men in the party raced their ponies toward the village. The people in the village returned the greetings, and women and children could be seen running to meet the returning warriors. In the excitement of the war party's return, Jamie considered making a run for freedom, but Left Hand, his perpetual stoic demeanor in place, pulled his horse up beside hers and paced her, shoulder to shoulder. It was just as well, she thought, for she would surely not have gotten far before they ran her down.

As she rode into the Kutenai village, her hands

tied in front of her, her horse led by Left Hand, she was at once frightened by the upturned faces that stared at her; some jeering, but most displaying open curiosity. Some, mostly women, tugged at her legs as if testing the muscle. Left Hand did not stop until he reached a skin lodge where a short, stout woman stood, her hands on her hips, watching her husband's progress through the gathering of her people.

"So," Red Leggings said, "my husband has brought home another wife." She was not pleased.

Left Hand's stoic expression did not change as he ignored his wife's sarcastic tone. "I captured a white woman. I have no need for another wife." He shrugged his shoulders. "I thought you might want her to help you with your work. If not, maybe I can trade her."

Somewhat mollified to find that she was not to have competition in her lodge, Red Leggings nodded her head while she thought it over. She considered the prospect of having a slave for only a few moments before she decided. "I don't need anyone to help me in my duties. Trade her."

Left Hand responded with a grunt. His wife's curt command, with many of his friends standing around listening, was degrading and embarrassing to him. After all, he thought, it was a man's place to decide if he would take another wife. After a moment, he said in his gruff voice, "It may please me to keep her. I'll think on it some. In the meantime she can help you in your work."

So Jamie's fate was decided on the whim of an obstinate husband. Red Leggings huffed her disapproval but made no reply, her lips pursed in an expression of silent protest. She walked up beside Jamie, who was still seated on her horse, and cocked her head to one side, then the other, thoroughly scrutinizing this unwelcome addition to her lodge. "Huh," she finally grunted and grabbed Jamie's ankle. Before Jamie knew what was happening, Red Leggings suddenly shoved Jamie's leg up, dumping her on the ground.

With her hands still tied, she had no time to try to break her fall, so she landed hard, the wind knocked out of her. As she struggled to catch her breath, she was only vaguely aware of the laughter of the people gathered around. Although she was afraid and confused and gasping for air, she somehow understood that she must not cower before the ill-tempered Indian woman. Jamie got unsteadily to her feet, then strode directly up to Red Leggings. With her face thrust nose to nose with the Indian woman's, Jamie glared defiantly into Red Leggings's eyes. Somewhat surprised, Red Leggings took a step backward while shoving Jamie away with her hands. Emboldened, Jamie took a step forward and again thrust her face into that of Red Leggings. When this brought another wave of laughter from the onlookers, Red Leggings blinked, exasperated. Then her anger took hold. She grabbed a handful of the impudent captive's hair and yanked her sideways, off her feet. Again Jamie fell to the ground, and Red Leggings received a roar of approval from the people. So encouraged, Red Leggings administered a kick to Jamie's bottom before the stricken white girl could recover.

"Enough!" Left Hand commanded and pulled his wife away. "She will be of little value if you beat her to death." He looked down at Jamie, who was struggling to get to her feet. "Get up," he ordered.

She did not understand his words, but from his gestures, she guessed what he had said. On her feet now, and trying to maintain a defiant posture, she was aware of a child crying behind her. She realized then that it was Polly. A warrior, whose name was Black Elk, she would learn later, lifted Polly off her horse and held her at arm's length, closely examining the child. When Jamie looked around, she saw the warrior leading Polly away, toward the center of the camp. Her heart went out to the child, but she was powerless to help her. Polly looked back at Jamie, pleading with her eyes, but she did not resist.

The first several days in the Kutenai village were a nightmare of endless chores for Jamie, from dawn until dark. Scraping and stretching hides, gathering wood and water, picking chokecherries and serviceberries—all at the beckoning of the ill-tempered Red Leggings. The woman stood over her, con-

stantly scolding and chastising in her shrill voice,
screaming words that were only a collection of
grunts and hisses to Jamie. Frequently, if Jamie did
not understand the commands of the overbearing
Indian woman quickly enough to satisfy her, she
would administer a few sharp raps across Jamie's
back with a willow switch that she constantly carried. Jamie soon learned the Kutenai words for
"bring," "wood," "water," "come," "carry," and a
few other terms that required instant compliance.

Left Hand seemed impervious to his wife's treatment of her slave and showed very little interest in
Jamie beyond occasional curiosity, as when she
would attempt to clean herself at the edge of the
lake—before Red Leggings jerked the rawhide
thong around her neck and dragged her back to the
task at hand. Jamie was thankful for Left Hand's
lack of interest in her. She had feared that he might
be intent on forcing himself upon her, even taking
her as a wife. At least she was spared that. She told
herself that she could endure the harsh treatment
at the hands of Red Leggings as long as she was
not sexually attacked. She even hoped that somehow her salvation might yet come.

In the days that followed, Jamie saw very little
of Polly Tyler. When she did catch glimpses of the
child, she was surprised to see her seemingly content in the company of other little girls her age.
Most of the time she saw Polly with her new mother
close by, teaching the child how to prepare animal

skins, how to cook and sew, and how to do other women's chores. In the Kutenai camp, the little boys were free to run and play nearly all of the time, but with the girls, it was a different matter. They were trained at a very early age to do the chores that Kutenai women did all their lives. Polly appeared to respond well to her new life. After a few days she no longer seemed to notice Jamie toiling under Red Leggings's doleful eye.

During these dreadful times, especially when left to sleep at night, Jamie often thought of Trace, and sometimes she cried herself to sleep. She had always nourished the thought that Trace would one day return to Promise Valley and to her. Now she wondered where he might be, and if he even knew she had been abducted. If he did know, would he come to find her? To hang on to her sanity, she would pretend that Trace wanted her as his wife and was even now on his way to rescue her.

As time passed, Jamie's thoughts of rescue faded. Soon she no longer contemplated escape at all. Resigned to her existence, she abandoned all thoughts of the future. Her world was only the work she did from sunup to sundown. Finally a day arrived when Red Leggings did not draw the rawhide loop around her neck but merely beckoned for her to follow. Accustomed to the taunts of the other Kutenai women as she went about her tasks, Jamie realized that the verbal abuse had gradually subsided until now she was generally ignored. Apparently

no longer amused with holding a tyrant's hand over
her white slave, Red Leggings even abandoned her
switch. After the cessation of abuse, life was almost
tolerable, with no more than her daily work to
worry her.

The village awoke one morning to find a heavy
frost on the grassy banks of the lake. The men of
the camp gathered in the council lodge, and after
a short discussion they agreed that it was time to
strike the camp and move into the mountains. Winter would soon arrive, and the winds that swept
the open plain around the lake would be cold and
hard. The men had made a good hunt and the
women had worked hard, drying the meat and
skins necessary to keep them warm and well fed.
It was time to go into winter camp, where there
was shelter from the winds and plenty of wood for
the fires.

Jamie's grasp of the Kutenai dialect was sufficient by now for her to understand Red Leggings's
instructions when it was time to take down the
lodge and prepare a travois with the lodgepoles to
carry it. While she was busy with this chore, she
noticed that a warrior called Beaver Tail came to
their fire and sat down to talk with Left Hand. This
was not unusual—many of the men of the village
came by periodically to talk with Left Hand. But
Beaver Tail had come on several occasions during
the past three days, and Jamie could not help but

notice that his gaze often fell upon her. Though mildly curious, she didn't find the matter interesting enough to dwell on—until Left Hand approached her and bade her pause in her work while he talked to her.

"Willow Switch," he called, using the name the people had given her because of the frequency of Red Leggings's switch across her back, "we will talk a little." He waited for her to stand and look into his face. "You have worked hard. Red Leggings is pleased with your work and says that you have learned well. Others in the village have said that you have learned many things from Red Leggings's teaching." His voice was gruff even when he was not chastising, but now he chose his words carefully, pausing often between statements to make sure she understood what he was saying. "One who has noticed your good work is Beaver Tail. He has come to me and said that he thinks you might now make a good wife."

Jamie had been concentrating on following Left Hand's words, listening carefully lest she miss the meaning of his statements. Though she was much improved in her knowledge of his language, some of the words escaped her. But she was well aware of the word for "wife," and when she heard it in connection with Beaver Tail and herself, she must have blanched, for Left Hand quickly continued. "I think it would be a good match. Beaver Tail is well respected by the people. He is a brave warrior and has counted many coups. His wife is barren and cannot give him a son. He does you great honor in offering to trade for you."

Jamie was dumbfounded, unable to speak. The horror of the proposition stunned her for a moment. The possibility of this dilemma coming to confront her had been on her mind for some time now. She didn't even know if she had anything to say about the decision. She was a slave, yet Left Hand seemed to be making a case for Beaver Tail in an attempt to persuade her. She was aware then that Left Hand was carefully studying her reactions.

"Beaver Tail has some concern," Left Hand continued, hesitating in his effort to phrase his speech so he was sure she understood. "He wonders if you are ready to become one of the people, or if you will try to run away someday." Left Hand paused, looking at Jamie with a question in his eyes. "Will you?" he finally asked.

Jamie found it astounding that Left Hand would ask her such a question in childlike innocence, as if he expected a frank and honest answer . How could she answer truthfully? She had no doubt that if she told him the truth—that she would certainly escape if the opportunity presented itself—he would resume the practice of tying her up at night. She did not want to lose that small measure of freedom she had worked so hard to gain. One thing she was sure of, however, she did not want to be Beaver Tail's—or any other brave's—wife, even though such an arrangement would certainly make her life easier.

Reluctant to return to the cruel conditions of her early captivity, she reconsidered the proposition. She sneaked a long look at Beaver Tail, who was sitting solemnly by Drags Him's campfire, apparently awaiting an answer. Staunch and dignified, he sat there, a man of average height with less-than-striking features. She suddenly formed an image of him in a state of passion and knew at once that she could not endure it.

Left Hand pressed for her answer, so she decided to risk his anger, for she could not consent to Beaver Tail's proposal. Averting her eyes so as not to meet his glare, she finally said, "I do not want to be Beaver Tail's wife. I want to stay with Red Leggings."

To her surprise, Left Hand did not erupt in anger. Instead he simply gazed at her for a long moment before nodding slowly, as if giving her words serious consideration. "You may go back to your work," he said and turned away without showing even the slightest hint of irritation. Jamie returned to the task of packing up the lodge. As she busied herself with the travois, she stole glances at the two men now talking by the fire. Beaver Tail nodded as Left Hand talked to him. Then, after a polite word on parting, he turned and walked away, never sending another glance in Jamie's direction. Later, Left Hand apparently told Red Leggings the girl's decision because Jamie noticed an almost immediate change in Red Leggings's disposition. She was evidently pleased that Jamie had expressed a desire to stay with her. *Maybe my life will take a turn for the better after all*, Jamie thought.

Trace McCall made his way through mountain passes that he had not traveled since trapping the east slopes with Buck Ransom years before. When the trail of the Kutenai war party had finally petered out on the rocky slopes of the Bitterroot Mountains, he had no choice but to search out every favorite Indian camping spot he could remember—and that was more than a few. Bands of Indians were camping in several of these sites, but none of them were Kutenai. As he scouted each camp, getting as close as he thought safe, he saw preparations being made to go into winter camps. He hoped to find the Kutenai war party before they traveled back into some secluded valley, making it even more difficult to find them. As each day passed with no sign of them, he began to think his chances of finding Jamie were growing slimmer and slimmer. "Dammit!" he muttered, "that war party came from a village somewhere." Maybe the village was on the western side of the mountains. It didn't figure, he decided, and determined to continue on north, keeping in mind that he was now skirting Blackfoot territory and had best keep a sharp eye.

\*     \*     \*

Jamie wasn't sure what had caused her horse to rear back, almost breaking the lodgepoles that formed the legs of the travois. Moments later, she was amazed to discover the arrow protruding from just above the animal's chest. At almost the same moment, the terrifying whoops of the Blackfoot war party echoed throughout the valley as a screaming hoard of warriors swept over the low hills that framed the lake.

Left Hand's village was taken completely by surprise. Since all the people were busy preparing for the move to winter quarters, there were no scouts watching for enemies and none of the men were out hunting. So there was no notion in anyone's mind that a Blackfoot war party had approached, making ready to attack the unsuspecting Kutenais.

For a moment Jamie was frozen. Her heart racing, she was too terrified to move. Over the crazed scream of her wounded horse, she heard the shrill cries of the women and children of the village as a general panic set in. People were running everywhere, women trying to herd their children to safety, men dashing for their weapons. And all about her, people were falling—wounded or dead, she couldn't tell. It was like a dream to her, as if she was not a part of the melee, but only an observer. Suddenly Red Leggings ran past her and yelled for her to run. Jamie simply stared at her, still too confused to move. And then Beaver Tail was by her side. He opened his mouth to say something to her, but before he could speak, a rifle ball split his forehead and he slumped to the ground. As if just realizing at that moment that the terrifying wave of painted warriors sweeping through the village was real and she was not exempt from the slaughter, she finally registered the signal from her stunned mind to flee.

Her first reaction was to jump on the horse to escape, but the poor animal was finished. He crumpled as soon as Jamie jumped on his back, and she was barely able to dive out of the way and avoid being pinned under his weight. She picked herself up as quickly as she could and started running after Red Leggings and some of the other women, who were trying to gain the cover of the willows by the lake. Gasping for air, she dared not slow down, although her lungs were aching. On all sides of her people were falling. It seemed the air was thick with arrows and rifleballs, and the ear-shattering noises of the massacre combined to make a nightmare of sound. Her mind barely noted a vague recollection of Left Hand and Black Elk, their weapons in hand, running to try to defend the horse herd. She glanced up just in time to see Left Hand stopped suddenly by an arrow in his chest. Unaware of her own screaming, she ran harder.

Anticipating the stinging bite of an arrow in her back at any second, she followed the women into the willows and flung herself on the ground, seeking any protection she could find. The thicket was filled with frightened women and children, huddled together in little groups, hugging the ground in desperation. There was no place to run. The thicket offered the only protection, scant though it was. Beyond the willows lay nothing but open ground. She could no longer see the battle, but the sounds of slaughter were still very real, even though she covered her ears with her hands, trying to block it all out.

The women had been hiding in the thicket no more than half an hour when the continuous clamor of the attack subsided, giving way to only occasional rifle shots and cries of triumph as the Blackfoot warriors finished off the wounded and took scalps. Some of the women began to weep and soon the low moans of songs of mourning drifted through the willow branches.

"Hush!" a voice scolded. Jamie recognized it as that of Red Leggings. "Our only chance is that they did not see us run here to hide. They are Blackfoot—they will kill us if they find us." There was quiet in the thicket again.

Trembling with fear, Jamie tried to dig herself deeper into the roots of the willow with her hands. "Listen," someone cautioned. There were no longer any sounds from the village beyond an occasional word shouted between members of the raiding party. Jamie looked to each side, trying to see other women around her in the thicket. The vines that laced through the willows shielded them from her sight, and she felt that if she could just see someone else, she might not feel so all alone. Then the rustle of some willow leaves in the gentle breeze caught her eye and she saw a small Indian girl huddled close to the ground, like a rabbit when a wolf is too close to run. As the wind moved the leaves again, she realized it was Polly Tyler. The girl did not see her, and Jamie could not risk calling out to her. She waited, listening, praying.

Now voices could be heard approaching the thicket. Jamie held her breath, afraid to move. In a few minutes there were voices on the far side of the thicket—the Blackfeet had surrounded them. Jamie crouched lower, her hands trembling with fright. A moment more brought a crackling sound to her ears, and then the smell of smoke drifted to her nostrils. They were going to burn them out!

Although there had been no rain for many days, the willows and vines were green still, leaching water from the lake to sustain them. Consequently, the thicket did not blaze easily, but generated clouds of thick gray smoke. The Blackfoot warriors brought burning limbs from the Kutenai cookfires and threw them into the brush and vines. The willows refused to ignite completely, but the smoke had the desired effect upon the women and children hiding there.

In no time at all, the thicket became unbearable. Crying and coughing, trying not to breathe the acrid smoke, they were finally compelled to abandon their hiding places and make their way toward fresh air. "The lake," Jamie heard Red Leggings whisper. "Go to the water." Jamie followed her lead, and one by one, everyone struggled through the tangle of vines and willows.

The Blackfoot warriors had anticipated their escape route and were waiting by the water's edge. As the women and children stumbled out of the smoky tangle, they were ruthlessly slaughtered. Red Leggings was one of the first to be struck down by a Blackfoot axe, as she was leading the doomed Kutenais out of the thicket. Some of the other women, and many of the children that followed, were able to slip between the line of warriors and plunge into the chilly lake, swimming as hard as they could to escape. They were easily overtaken by the strong Blackfoot warriors, who slit their throats, their blood forming small red pools in the water.

Jamie, still fighting her way out of the now blazing thicket, could see the carnage taking place on the lakeshore. She stopped for only a moment and realized there was nowhere to go but forward. She saw a young girl she was certain was Polly swimming as fast as she could toward the center of the lake. A warrior swam after her. A strong swimmer, the Blackfoot toyed with the child, swimming right behind her, taunting her. He played with her as a cat plays with a mouse until she was too exhausted to swim any farther. Then, laughing, he caught her by her hair and held her head under the water until she drowned. Jamie was sick with fear. She decided her only chance was to run along the shore once she cleared the thicket. She tried to hold her breath while she waited for an opportunity to spring out of the willows and run, but the smoke was burning her eyes and choking her. Finally she could wait no longer. Dashing out of the trees, she managed to dodge a waiting warrior and sprint toward the rocky shoreline. She was overtaken almost immediately, and tripped from behind. Down she went, slipping and bumping over the stones. As quickly as she could manage, she scrambled to her hands and knees and tried to crawl. Her head was violently jerked back by a hand in her hair, and she saw the steel blade of the knife flash in the morning sun as it was held poised before her throat.

"Stop!" Little Bull ordered. "She is white."

Two Kills paused and took a closer look at the woman, still holding Jamie by her hair, his knee placed in the small of her back while she held on to his other wrist with both of her hands. "So she is white," Two Kills said. "What difference does that make? She is living with Kutenais." He began to force his knife hand down toward Jamie's throat. She strained against him but could not hold him off. She could feel the sharp edge of the skinning knife against her windpipe.

"Wait!" Little Bull insisted. "She is also young. Plum will give three horses for a young white girl."

Two Kills was filled with bloodlust and eager to

kill. "We have plenty of horses now. These Kutenai dogs have seen to that."

"Since when does a man have too many horses?" Little Bull asked. "Plum will give three good horses for this worthless woman."

Two Kills relented, but not before giving Jamie a taste of his knife. He drew the blade lightly across her throat, just enough to draw blood, then he slammed her to the ground, where she lay sobbing. "Maybe you are right," he said and cleaned his knife on Jamie's skirt.

Little Bull turned Jamie over with the toe of his moccasin and grinned down at her. "I make your talk . . . you hear?" Jamie nodded. He continued. "Maybe we let you live if you don't cause trouble . . . you hear?" Tearfully, she nodded a second time. "Good," he said, "you stay there. If you try to run, I'll shoot you." He poked her in the stomach with the barrel of his rifle. Jamie lay back, pulling her knees up to her chest in a protective position. She was no longer sobbing, but her tears continued to pool in her eyes. Satisfied that she was subdued, Little Bull got a length of rawhide from one of the captured saddles and tied her hands and feet, then left her and joined the other warriors appraising the spoils of their raid.

Shivering uncontrollably, Jamie looked around her at the bodies of the Kutenai women and children. It was difficult for her to believe that she was still alive, for she was certain she had been facing death only minutes before. The cold, lifeless lumps lay everywhere, for this Blackfoot raid was not simply to steal horses. This was a scalping party, bent on slaughter, with no notion of taking prisoners. She thought of little Polly Tyler and wondered if the child might have been spared if the Blackfeet had known that she was white. *Poor Polly*, she thought, *the Kutenais turned her into an Indian*. Maybe it had cost the child her life.

# Chapter 6

Jack Plum sat on his horse, a dappled gray with white stockings on his back feet, and watched while his Blackfoot friends rounded up the last strays of the Kutenai horse herd. His sharp, chiseled face wore a sneer, which was the closest Plum ever came to a smile. *It was a damn good raid*, he thought. The Kutenais' camp had accumulated a great many horses, and in the Blackfoot camp, horses meant wealth. *Ol' Left Hand had himself a pretty good summer*, he thought. The fact that he had often traded with the Kutenai chief in the past had no effect on Plum's conscience, for the simple reason that the wiry mountain man did not possess a conscience.

He spotted his partner at the far end of the camp, piling buffalo hides on a travois. Plum's grin widened as he saw Crown pause to drag a small child's body over to the fire. Crown liked the smell of roasting flesh. Plum almost laughed out loud when he thought about his partner. Even the Blackfeet were afraid of Crown. The only man who did not fear the dark and brooding Crown was Plum

himself—and that was because the two renegade
trappers had a mutual respect for each other's
venom—much like two rattlesnakes.

Plum turned his horse and rode slowly toward
the upper end of the camp, where the other two
members of his little gang of white renegades were
searching the bodies of the dead for anything of
value. Plum was satisfied with the results of the
sneak attack on the Kutenais. There was plenty to
go around for his men, as well as for Little Bull's
warriors. And later on, when they returned to the
Blackfoot camp and Plum brought out the whiskey,
most of the Indians' share of the plunder would end
up in Plum's hands anyway.

He pulled up before the two white men searching the bodies. "Find anything?" he asked.

Sowers looked up at Plum and shook his head.
"Nothin' much worth a shit." He motioned toward
the other man, a huge bear of a man who now stood
grinning foolishly at Plum. "Ox got a gold ring offen
one of them squaws—looks like a weddin' ring or
somethin'. Musta belonged to a white woman."

Plum looked at Ox, and the big man nodded his
head vigorously as he fumbled in his possibles bag
for the ring. When he found it, he held it up for
Plum to see. Plum reached out and took it from him.
"Now, that shines, Ox. You done right good." He
felt the weight of the ring. "Yessir, you done good."
He handed it back to Ox. "You can keep it till we
get back to camp. Just mind you don't lose it."

He was about to say something to Sowers when he heard his name called. He turned in the saddle to see Little Bull motioning to him. He and Two Kills stood waiting while Plum rode up. What Plum thought was another body turned out to be a live woman. Before he could ask the Blackfoot why she was still alive, Little Bull spoke, his face a picture of smug satisfaction.

"She is a white woman . . . a young white woman," Little Bull said.

As Little Bull had anticipated, this captured Plum's interest right away. "A white girl, you say? Let's have a look at 'er." He dismounted while Little Bull grabbed Jamie's bound hands and pulled her upright. "Well, I'll be . . ." Plum started, looking into the face of the frightened woman. "Ain't this somethin'?" His dark, deep-set eyes peered out from under heavy eyebrows and roamed up and down her body, a sinister leer plastered on his face. "That there's prime stuff, all right." He looked quickly at Little Bull. "I'll trade you one of my horses for her."

Two Kills promptly spoke up. "She belongs to both of us."

"All right," Plum shot back, "I'll give both of you a horse."

"Two horses each man," Little Bull replied.

"She ain't worth that much," Plum protested, then quickly went on, "I'll give you three horses for her. Now that's a fair offer."

Little Bull glanced at Two Kills and smiled. He

had predicted that Plum would give three horses for the white woman. But now he had seen the lust in Plum's eyes when the white man looked at the slender girl at his feet, trembling like an aspen leaf in the wind. Looking back at Plum, Little Bull said, "Four horses, and we pick 'em."

Plum looked pained, but he didn't prolong the dickering. "All right, four, and you can pick 'em outta my string—but that don't include the gray here."

Little Bull grunted his satisfaction with the deal, and grasping the thong that tied Jamie's hands together, he dragged the helpless girl over and dumped her at the gray's feet. "Now we both have something to ride," he said, and laughed at his own joke.

"I reckon we have," Plum said, talking to himself as he dismounted to take possession of his prize. Jamie tried to back away from the leering renegade, but was unable to do so with her hands and feet tied—a fact that appeared to amuse Plum. He stood over her, a thin, wiry man, his buckskin britches and shirt shiny black from the grease and smoke of many campfires. Though hatchet-thin, his face reflected an evil strength, warning that he was not a man to be taken lightly. Jamie wished she could return to her life with the Kutenais—it had been a paradise compared to what she feared lay ahead for her.

Plum reached down and took hold of the rawhide thong that bound her wrists, just as Little Bull had, and slowly pulled her up on her feet. He kept his eyes locked on hers, like a man pulling a badger out of a trap, wary of a sudden attack, ready to strike out if it became necessary. "There, now, little missy, let's have a look atcha." She tottered back and forth, trying to keep her balance with her feet still tied together, while Plum walked around her, appraising his new possession. "You ain't got a helluva lot of meat on ya, have ya?" He reached down and placed a hand on her buttocks, and squeezed hard.

Jamie's reaction was automatic. She whirled and swung her bound hands at Plum, aiming at his face. She missed, but the suddenness of the movement caused her to lose her balance, and she fell heavily. Plum, having nonchalantly dodged her intended rebuff, moved to stand over her again, a crooked grin on his sharp features. "You know, little missy, you're some lucky I'm the one what bought you. Now if it'da been Crown what got you, I expect you'da been half used up by now. But me—why, hell, I'm gonna be the sweetest stud that ever rode you. Now, lemme help you up." He held out his hand and grasped the thong again. When she was on her feet once more, he said, "First, I reckon you and me better have a little understandin'." Before she could move, he suddenly struck out with the back of his hand. The blow caught her squarely on the side of her face, knocking her down again.

Jamie screamed in pain. While she lay at his feet, quivering in fear, he reached behind him and pulled a rawhide whip from his saddle. Without hesitation, he began whipping the helpless woman. She cried out with each welt that was laid across her back and buttocks until finally she could no longer make a sound. Expert with a whip, and having beaten women before, Plum stopped short of doing permanent damage to his goods.

"Now, just so's you understand," he snarled, his face only inches above hers, "I own your ass— bought and paid for." He placed a rough hand on one of her breasts. "These is mine." His other hand pawed at her crotch. "And this is mine. Four damn good horses I give for you, and if I don't git my money's worth outta you, I'm gonna cut your nose off and give you to Crown to play with."

Jamie was devastated. She felt that she was barely alive after the terrible beating, and the prospect of what lay ahead for her was even more terrifying. Afraid to make a sound, afraid it might ignite his rage again, she nevertheless could not control her crying. How, she wondered, could God let this happen to her? Before she had been stolen by Left Hand, she had resolved never to show fear in the face of savage Indians if she ever was called to confront them. It was better to show defiance, she was convinced. But this— she had never imagined anything like the situation she now found herself in. She had been afraid many times since she and her father had left Grand Island on the Platte and started the trek west. But she had never experienced the horror she felt at the hands of this demon in dirty buckskins. It was then she realized that she had been the unfortunate one in Left Hand's camp. The lucky ones were those who had been killed.

"Get up," Plum ordered, after cutting the bonds off her ankles. Jamie did as she was told, and stood trembling while Plum tied a rope to the thong that bound her hands. He then climbed in the saddle and led her toward the center of the Kutenai camp, where his partner was now appraising a bay horse that had once belonged to Black Elk. When Crown looked around and saw Plum coming, he paused and squinted his eyes.

"What you got there?" he demanded to know.

Plum smirked and replied, "I got me a tender young rabbit. Meet the new Mrs. Plum." Then he laughed hard, as if that was the funniest thing he had ever heard.

Crown did not join in the laughter, but continued to stare at the captive girl walking dutifully behind Plum's horse. Jamie could feel the man's gaze upon her body. Cold, emotionless eyes roamed over her body, seemingly peering through her clothes and examining her naked body. Jamie shivered involuntarily and immediately hung her head to avoid his gaze. "I fancy her myself," Crown said, his words slow and measured.

Plum laughed. "I figured you might."

"Whadaya want for 'er?"

"I ain't lookin' to trade 'er," Plum replied, no

longer laughing. "I bought 'er from Little Bull for four horses, and I reckon she's my property and nobody else's."

Crown scowled as he looked first at Jamie, then back at Plum. "That don't hardly seem fair," he said. "I figure we're partners in all the plunder." He gestured toward the stack of buffalo hides. "We share everything we take."

Plum's eyes narrowed. "Not this piece we don't," he replied, giving the rope a jerk, which made Jamie lurch forward a couple of steps. He studied Crown's scowling face for a few moments, then said, "Maybe when I'm through with 'er. We'll see."

Crown was obviously not pleased. He continued to stare unblinkingly into Plum's eyes for a long minute before looking back at the girl again. He moved a few steps closer to Jamie and took a closer look at her face, and the welt left there by Plum's backhand. He reached out as if to touch the bruise, and Jamie drew back from his hand. Her reaction almost brought a smile to his expressionless face. He turned back to Plum. "I'll buy half of 'er from ya."

"No, dammit, Crown. I told you she ain't for sale, none of 'er." He pulled Jamie up closer to his horse. "And you can forget any notions about sharin' 'er. The last time I let you share a woman was that little Pend d'Oreille gal up on the Missouri. I reckon you remember what happened to her—you killed 'er."

"She didn't move to suit me," Crown responded coldly.

"Yeah, I reckon," Plum said. "But you ain't gettin' your hands on this'un till I'm done with 'er."

Crown didn't say anything for a few moments, his eyes never leaving his partner's. After a long silent moment while the two men locked gazes as if measuring each other, Crown growled in a low voice, "Maybe I might just take 'er."

"You might," Plum growled back, "but you know I'll cut your damn gizzard out and feed it to the dogs."

This was not the first time the two had gone at each other, and like other times, the confrontation amounted to no more than a standoff. Crown was fully capable of carrying out any threat he made— Plum knew that to be a fact. But he also knew that Crown realized that it was Plum who was in bed with Little Bull and his band of Blackfeet. They merely tolerated Crown and the other two white men for Plum's sake.

Little Bull had already questioned the need for Plum's three white partners, but Plum had insisted they were necessary. He and Crown had ridden together since the early days with the Hudson's Bay Company. The two of them had decided it was a sight more lucrative to trap the trapper than to trap the beaver. After they spent two years bushwhacking hardworking company men, the Hudson's Bay people finally found them out, and they were

branded outlaws. Their salvation lay in Plum's relationship with a Blackfoot woman—Little Bull's sister. Plum remained with the Blackfoot band after the
woman was supposedly killed when her horse
bucked her off and stomped her to death. Only
Crown knew that she was dead before Plum rigged
the accident, beaten to death by Plum's fists. Little
Bull's band, like most Blackfoot bands, was not
friendly with many white men, and if Little Bull tolerated Plum it was only because the man was a
source of weapons and whiskey.

When Little Bull questioned the presence of Sowers and Ox, Plum explained to him why they were
vital. Since Plum and Crown were outlaws, they
would certainly be hung, or possibly shot on sight,
if they showed up at any of the trading posts on the
upper Missouri. That was why Plum had persuaded
Sowers to cast his lot with him. Sowers was a thief,
but not a well-known one, so his role in Plum's little ring of cutthroats was to take the stolen hides to
the fort to trade for powder, shot, blankets, knives,
hatchets, and the other essentials. Ox was a simpleminded stray that Sowers had picked up at a trading post. His only contributions to their cause were
his size and his strength. He always accompanied
Sowers when he went to the fort to trade the pelts.
None of the other three knew, or cared, where Ox
had come from. He just showed up at the fort one
day when he was a child, and nobody ever came to
claim him. Sowers happened to be there trading

some pelts that he, Plum, and Crown had stolen from a free trapper on the Milk River, and Sowers offered Ox some food if he would help load his mules. Ox gratefully accepted the handout and then, like a stray dog, took up with Sowers and followed him back to Little Bull's village.

High above the rocky peaks of the Bitterroot range, a red-tailed hawk circled effortlessly on the breast of the wind that swept up the steep slopes. Far below, on the eastern side of the ridge, the hawk could see the smoking remains of the Kutenai village and the band of Blackfoot warriors as they skirted the shore of the lake. Wheeling on its broad wings, it cried out its shrill *kreeee* as if to alert the lone white man making his way along the steep western slope—searching. If the hawk cared at all about man's struggle against man, it could have appreciated the irony of the situation—the lone scout was no more than twenty miles from those he searched for—as the hawk flies.

Trace left the old game trail and skirted another deadfall that blocked his path. He was no longer tracking the band of Kutenais. The only things he counted on now were instinct and blind luck as he worked his way along the treeline toward a low slot in the mountains that looked to be a likely place to cross over to the east slope. If his memory served him, there was a lake in the next valley where several tribes sometimes camped, the Kutenais among them. It was late in the season now, but maybe there were still a few who had not abandoned the higher elevations to find a protected valley for the winter. It would take two days of careful traveling, however, before he reached the valley and the lake that was its crown jewel.

It had been a cold night, and the morning broke chilly and cloudy. A few scattered snowflakes drifted past his face as he coaxed the flames of a small fire to life. Squinting up at the slate-gray sky, he wondered if this day might bring the first real snow of the winter. It could get rough this high up if he got caught in a heavy snow. It wasn't his own well-being that concerned him—he could survive just fine. But if it snowed hard enough, it would close the mountain passes, and he would lose more time to the party of Kutenais he searched for. Warming his hands by a healthy fire now, he told himself there was nothing he could do about the weather. "If it snows, it snows," he said to his horse. "We'll just do the best we can. Won't we, boy?"

Although the prospects of poor weather failed to panic him, still Trace did not linger over the fire. After a breakfast of dried buffalo meat warmed over the flames, he saddled the paint and picked up the trail once more. It was close to midday when the trail broke free of the pines and he got a clear view of the southern edge of the lake.

It had been a year since he had first seen the lake, but he recalled the circumstances that had caused him to discover it. He had followed an elk down from the hills on the northern tip of the lake. As he made his way through the fir trees that covered the low hills near the water, he discovered he was about to ride into a Flathead village. He had to smile when he thought about it. The elk had seemed surprised, too, and it stood rigid as a statue at the edge of the trees. Trace had to think the situation over—he was sorely craving some elk meat, but there was the Indian village, no more than three hundred yards away. At that point Trace was uncertain what tribe they were, whether they were friendly or not. He looked at the village, then back at the elk, still standing like a stone, just begging to be shot. Maybe the elk was smart enough to think the man wouldn't risk taking a shot this close to an Indian camp. Trace smiled again as he remembered the scene. He had followed that elk for more than two miles, and he didn't want to give up on it. *What the hell*, he finally decided. He put his rifle away and reached for his bow. Leaving his horse tied to a fir tree, he stalked the still frozen elk on foot, making his way downwind of the animal until he had closed to within about thirty yards. He knelt on one knee to steady himself, notched an arrow, and stuck a second one in the ground beside his knee. It had to be a kill shot—he didn't want to merely wound the animal and chance the possibility that it might bolt out into the open and alert the Indian camp of Trace's presence.

Trace was good with a bow, and that shot was

one of the best he had ever made. The first arrow found its mark, behind the animal's front leg and low enough to puncture the lung. The elk reared up on its hind legs, then came back down, its front legs folding when it landed. The first arrow was still in the air when Trace notched the second. When the elk came down, the second arrow found its mark some twelve inches behind the first. The elk staggered no more than ten or twelve yards before crumpling.

Trace had butchered the elk right there, listening for any hint of movement in the trees behind him and watching the Indian camp by the shore of the lake. He took his time, removing the hide and packing the meat. He knew that if it was a hostile village and they discovered his presence, they would be on him like a swarm of yellow jackets. When he was finished, and his meat safely packed on his horse, he decided to work his way a little closer to the camp to identify the tribe. Much to his chagrin, he recognized them as Flathead, at that time a friendly tribe. *Hell, they would most likely have helped me butcher the animal.* He laughed at the memory, but it would have been hell to pay if they had turned out to be Gros Ventres or Blackfeet and had discovered him making meat right on their doorstep.

On this cloudy day in late September, Trace saw no Flathead camp as he came up from the south end of the valley. Something caught his eye, though, and he paused to scan the western shoreline of the lake.

He stared hard at a long, grassy flat near the upper end of the water, not sure if he had seen something or not. It was difficult to determine against the cloudy gray sky, but after a few moments he realized the movement that had caught his attention was a thin column of smoke. A campfire? Maybe, but if it was, it was a mighty puny one. Every fiber in his body instantly became alert.

Returning to the cover of the trees on the low hills that circled the little lake, Trace made his way carefully around to a point opposite the source of the smoke. After he had tied his horses in a shallow ravine, he checked the loads in his rifle and pistol, then started toward the lake on foot. Before crossing the last little rise that shielded him from the open flat before the lake, he stopped and listened. There were no sounds that would indicate a human presence.

On his belly, he pulled himself to the top of the rise. Before him was the aftermath of a massacre. Bodies lay everywhere, like droppings from a herd of giant buffalo. Here and there a burned-out tipi still smoldered, sending up the thin spirals of smoke he had first seen. It had been a slaughter. He did not move for a long time while he searched the camp with his eyes, making sure he was the sole living man there. When it was obvious that whoever had done this deed was long gone, he stood up and scanned the scene once more.

Before going down into the camp, he returned to

the ravine to fetch his horses. He had seen a lot of bear sign on his way down the slope that morning, so he didn't want to leave the horses tied to a tree while he investigated the camp. The paint was reluctant to enter the scene of the mass killings, and the packhorse pulled back on the lead rope so violently that Trace decided to hobble them near the edge of the camp while he proceeded on foot.

The bodies had already begun to bloat, and Trace figured the only reason the buzzards had not found them was that low gray clouds had settled in over the valley. It wouldn't be long, he thought, as he walked among the slashed and mutilated bodies. They were Kutenais, all right. There was enough left to determine that, and he was pretty sure the band he had searched for had been from this village.

He examined a broken arrow shaft. "Blackfoot," he muttered. The whole village had been wiped out by a Blackfoot war party. Now that he was certain he had found the Kutenai war party, he set about the grim task of looking for Jamie's body in this field of death. It was with a feeling of gut-wrenching dread that he began the grisly chore—closely examining each female body, turning over those that lay facedown. It was not a simple task because there were so many corpses. After checking all those in the open grass, he discovered more bodies near a scorched willow thicket. Some even floated in the shallow water near the shore. It was not difficult to paint a picture in his mind of the terrible thing that had happened here, and he feared the worst, but he did not find Jamie's body.

There was hope, then. But as soon as he thought it, he reminded himself that if she had been taken captive, she was now in the hands of the Blackfeet. That thought was none too encouraging. Now the feeling of urgency returned, and he told himself it was time to move on. He would have to scout the area to pick up the trail. He took one more look around him at the thicket, and as he started to leave, something caused him to take a closer look at the body of a child bobbing in the shallow water. Even though the body was swollen, he realized the face was white. He waded out a few feet from shore and pulled the body in so that he could take a closer look. There was little doubt that it was the Tyler girl. There was nothing he could do for the many bodies of the Kutenais, but he could at least commit little Polly to the ground.

The trail was not hard to find. The Blackfeet had left the same way they came. A big party, driving a sizable herd of Kutenai ponies, they left a wide track toward the northeast corner of the valley. Trace looked up at the sky. He was lucky that the snow had held off, although clouds still hung ominously over the mountains. He figured he had better not waste any time, since they had at least a couple of days' start on him. If it snowed heavily enough, it could cover a trail even as wide as this one.

# CHAPTER 7

Although the clouds had threatened all day, there was no more than a dusting of light snow, and most of that fell on the higher slopes. When Plum and his band of cutthroats and Blackfeet left the steep peaks behind and came out on the rolling expanse of prairie, there were even small patches of blue showing though the dingy clouds. From this point on, it was a matter of no more than a few hours' ride to reach the large Blackfoot village.

Plum and Crown rode at the head of the procession, along with Little Bull. Sowers and Ox rode on ahead of the main body, helping to drive the captured horses. Jamie, her body sore and aching from the beating she had received, rode slumped in the Indian saddle, her hands tied together. Plum kept her close behind him on a lead line.

Plum pulled his horse over close to Crown's. Speaking to his partner in a tone low enough that Little Bull could not overhear, he said, "Take Ox and ride on ahead to the cache." The four renegades had a secret hiding place in the bluffs by the river where their stores of trade goods were kept. Little Bull knew of its existence, but had been unable to locate it. There were two kegs of whiskey left from Sowers's last trip to Flathead Post, and Plum planned to use those two kegs to cheat his Indian allies out of their share of the horses and hides taken from the Kutenais.

"Why don't you go?" Crown answered.

"Because I told you to," Plum shot back. His tone softened as he added, "Besides, I need to stay here and make sure Little Bull don't git suspicious and send somebody to trail you." Crown always seemed ready to challenge Plum's authority. *One of these days I'm gonna have to kill that bastard*, Plum thought to himself.

Crown glared coldly at Plum for a long moment before grunting something under his breath and suddenly kicking his horse into a gallop to catch up with Ox and Sowers. Plum watched him as he rode away, wondering how long it would be before there was a showdown between him and Crown. Crown had been doleful and moody for as long as Plum had known him. Lately, however, it seemed he was getting more and more ill-tempered, and Plum had an idea it was because he was beginning to chafe under Plum's position of authority.

They had been partners for more than four years. Crown would be a good man to have on his side if his Blackfoot friends ever turned on him. And Crown had no conscience when it came to killing a man, or cheating the Indians. Little Bull's band feared the dark and somber man. They were convinced that an evil spirit dwelled in his heart. Plum wasn't worried about an evil spirit, but he respected the potential danger in Crown. And Plum was of a mind to strike first if Crown was approaching the point where he wanted to challenge him. But Plum figured if there was going to be trouble it wouldn't come until after they had cheated the Blackfeet out of their share of the plunder. If he'd thought otherwise, he probably would have simply shot Crown in the back right then as he rode away. At the moment, though, there were other things to think about.

He looked back at the sorrowful girl slumped in the saddle. "It won't be long now, darlin'. We'll be there in another hour, and then you can show me what I got for my four horses."

Jamie, her chin almost touching her chest, was in a state of total despair. Plum's treatment of her had not been particularly cruel since the terrible beating he had administered two days before, but the dread of what was to come had been devastating to her now fragile state of mind. There had been two nights on the trail with no sexual attacks—perhaps because of Plum's reluctance to perform where there was no privacy, although she doubted the man had any notion of modesty. Whatever the reason, she was grateful. There had been another argument with the man called Crown over Plum's refusal to share her. The thought of either man terrified her, and she was not sure she would be able to hold on to her sanity when it happened.

Too frightened to sleep, her hands tied and one ankle tied to Plum's ankle, she cried silently each night, afraid to make a sound lest she evoke Plum's anger. She prayed constantly for some miracle to save her. The only hope she had was Trace McCall, and she couldn't even be sure he knew of her distress. She had prayed for him to come when she was a captive of the Kutenais, but those prayers were never answered. She knew there was not much hope. No one was sure where Trace was. She had not seen him for a year. How could he know? What could he do against a whole band of Indians, anyway? She gave up her last shred of hope and resigned herself to her fate, horrifying though it promised to be.

They rode into the Blackfoot village amid a bedlam of war whoops and gunfire as the people celebrated the triumphant return of the warriors. The captured horses were driven through the middle of the village and out the other side to graze with the Blackfoot horses, and the warriors charged back and forth through the camp, yelling and firing their rifles into the air.

When Jamie was spotted, she was immediately set upon by a horde of angry Blackfoot women, clawing and pulling at her in an attempt to knock her off her horse. Plum shouted and cursed at the frenzied women, beating them back with his whip before they could pull her to the ground. He angrily informed them that this white girl was his property and was to be his wife. Properly chastised, the women reluctantly backed away.

Little Bull, having been an interested spectator of the attack, laughed at Plum's anger. "Your wife is not very popular, Plum." Still laughing, he wheeled his horse and rode toward his lodge.

Plum led his captive to a lodge on the outer ring of tipis. Unlike the other lodges, it was covered in plain skins without decorative pictures or symbols. Upon dismounting, he reached up and pulled Jamie off her horse. She landed on her side, crying out in pain from the impact with the hard ground. Plum showed no sympathy for her, merely jerking on the rope that bound her hands. When she did not get to her feet right away, he started dragging her toward the entrance of the tipi. Too frightened to resist, she begged the determined Plum for mercy. It only served to sharpen his sense of desire, which was already honed to a keen edge, and he continued to drag the screaming woman until they were inside the tipi. The horses stood where they were, neither hobbled nor tied, their saddles still on. Plum had only one thing on his mind, and it had been pounding away at him ever since he first had laid eyes on the girl.

Much of that first night in the Blackfoot camp remained a blur in Jamie's mind. But the one thing that stayed with her forever was the total horror of Plum's assault. Such was the magnitude of her terror that her mind tried to block out the details of that night of revulsion, leaving her with the feeling that she would never be clean again. She knew that she had fought him, scratching and clawing at his face as he forced himself upon her, until he began to hammer away at her with his fists. She didn't remember a great deal after that, for she had mercifully slipped into unconsciousness.

When she came to her senses again, she was alone in the tipi. It was dark inside the lodge, but the light of the many fires outside illuminated the skin walls of the tipi, and the sound of drums and warriors chanting in celebration reverberated around her. Her body felt as if it were on fire. Bruised and bleeding from the wounds on her face, she tried to sit up, but found she was tied down, her arms and legs spread. Her initial feeling was one of despair and disappointment that she had not died but had awakened to this world again. If she had not been staked down, hand and foot, she would have sought to take her own life—hell could be no worse than this hurt she was now suffering deep inside. She strained against her ropes, but it was to no avail. Plum had made sure of his captive. She looked down at herself and realized that her skirt was pulled up over her hips, leaving her exposed from the waist down. With her hands tied, she was helpless even to cover herself. She lay her head back down and began to cry softly.

After a time, she fell into a fitful sleep. Sometime during the night she was vaguely aware of the huge form of Ox standing over her, staring stupidly at her exposed body. Then someone, probably Plum, cursing and shouting, drove him outside. She no longer cared. Nothing mattered anymore.

Morning came, and once again she was sorrowfully disappointed to find that she was still alive. Her limbs ached, her head was throbbing, and her mouth was dry from thirst. She tried to get up, but discovered she was still held fast. Aware of a rank odor of sweat and tobacco smoke, she turned her head to the side and saw Plum sleeping a few feet from her. Her eyesight seemed somehow impaired, and she realized then that her left eye was swollen shut. Turning back, she was startled to find Ox hovering over her, barely inches from her face. She screamed involuntarily.

Ox grinned his brainless smile, then returned his gaze to her lower body. He reached out to pull her skirt down to cover her nakedness, but she misunderstood his intentions. Her scream roused Plum from his slumber. He threw his blanket aside and sprang up with a pistol leveled at the giant. "Damn you, Ox!" he cursed. "I told you to stay the hell away from her." He put his pistol down. "You damn near got your fool head blowed off. Now go on back outside."

Ox simply grinned at Plum. "I was just lookin', Plum. I wasn't touching nothin'." He continued to stare at the helpless woman before him. "You beat her pretty good. I don't think she wanted to git married."

Plum was too tired to exert himself. "Just go on outside like I told you."

"I'm goin'," Ox replied, then said, "Lookee here, Plum, she's done made a puddle."

Plum was already losing his patience with the overgrown man-child, and Ox's discovery that Jamie's long-ignored bladder had finally released on its own didn't help his disposition. "Git the hell outta here before I git my whip!" Ox retreated without another word.

Now Plum was fully irritated. He had been in his blanket barely an hour before Ox's intrusion brought him bolting out of a sound sleep. Little Bull's scalp dance had gone on all night, the celebration winding down only when the first rays of the sun penetrated the morning clouds. When Crown returned from their cache with the whiskey, Plum had made a present of the first keg to his friend Little Bull. After the Indians had emptied it, Plum and Crown drove a hard bargain for the second one. After the trading, things ended up as Plum had planned—he and Crown owned most of the plunder from the Kutenai raid—and Little Bull and his warriors were left with hangovers.

Thoroughly rankled, even beyond his usual sour disposition, Plum kicked his blanket away, laying aside the two pistols he always slept with, and got to his feet. He stood scratching himself for a few moments while he looked down at his bride, a look of disgust on his grimy face. Then he drew his skinning knife from the belt beside the tipi wall, and cut the thongs that tied Jamie down.

"Git your ass up from there and clean yourself up," he commanded. Then he stood back and watched her, making sure he stood between her and the two pistols he had set beside his blanket

Movement was slow and painful for her. Her limbs, once freed, were stiff and sore, and she almost cried out with the pain of moving them after they had been immobilized for so long. "Come on, dammit," he chided impatiently, reaching toward his rawhide whip. That motion caused her to hurry as best she could, and she struggled to her hands and knees. It was then that she felt the excruciating pain in her pelvis. Still, afraid of another beating, she pushed herself on up and finally stood on wobbly limbs. He took her arm and pulled her out the entrance flap.

Plum pointed to the creek at the eastern side of the Blackfoot camp and gave Jamie a shove to get her started. He followed close behind her as she stumbled along on legs that were weak and ached with every step as she made her way through the center of the circle of lodges. She kept her head lowered to avoid eye contact with the people moving about in the preparation of the morning meal, but she could nonetheless feel the stares that followed her every painful step. She realized at once why

Plum was unconcerned about cutting her bonds. Where could she run? There were at least two hundred pairs of eyes to watch her.

Little Bull, like most of the other warriors, did not leave his bed until the sun was high in the morning sky. The inside of his mouth felt as if it had grown fur during the night, and he had a terrible thirst for water. But after a long drink from the water bag, his head began to spin and he had to sit to let it settle down. After a while, he was able to stand again. Once he was convinced that he was steady enough, he left the lodge and made his way down to the creek, cursing the evil whiskey that Plum had brought the night before. Last night he had craved more and more of Plum's firewater, not caring what the cost was. Now he felt foolish and angry at the same time. This was not the first time Plum and the three other white men had cheated him. The more he thought about his dealings with the hatchet-faced trapper, the more it made his head hurt. He decided to put his anger aside until he could think more clearly.

Many of the men of the tribe were at the creek when Little Bull arrived. He peeled off his shirt and leggings, and wearing only his breechclout, plunged into the frigid water, thrashing his arms about and kicking his feet. It was a custom of the Blackfoot men to take a morning plunge, to clean themselves and to condition their bodies to withstand the bitter cold of the winter hunts. But this day found most of the men of the village seeking only to clear their heads of the cobwebs from the night of celebration.

When Little Bull felt he could stand the chilly water no longer, he climbed out and dried himself, then sat down on a flat rock beside the creek. In a moment he was joined by Two Kills.

"My wife said that Plum brought the white woman down to the creek this morning to make her clean herself," Two Kills said. "She said the woman had been badly beaten." Little Bull nodded, and Two Kills continued, "These white men are evil. They say they are our friends, but how many horses did you trade for the worthless firewater?" Little Bull did not answer. "No friend would cheat me to get my horses." There was a pause, then, "How long are we going to permit these white men to remain in our village?"

Little Bull did not answer his friend immediately. He was thinking about what Two Kills had said. He had no more fondness for Plum than Two Kills did. Yet Plum and his partners had supplied Little Bull's warriors with guns and powder, and Little Bull hesitated to cut off that source of supply. His Blackfeet were at war with every trading post in the territory, and Plum had been a useful supplier. Still, he was a filthy and treacherous man. Little Bull would like to be rid of him—and the dangerous one called Crown. He realized that he had not answered Two

Kills's question, so he said, "As long as they can bring us guns."

When Little Bull sat before the fire later that afternoon, eating the boiled meat that his wife, Red Sky, had prepared, he thought again of the four white men in his camp. Calling Red Sky to him, he asked, "Have you seen the white woman today?"

"Yes," Red Sky answered. "I saw her this morning when the hatchet-faced one led her to the creek."

"What are the people saying about her?"

Red Sky shrugged indifferently. "Nothing. She was badly beaten. I think he will kill her pretty soon."

Little Bull considered this for a few moments. It was of no concern to him whether the white woman lived or died. Still, it troubled him some that Plum would treat the woman so cruelly. Blackfoot men had occasionally captured white women and taken them as wives. These women were usually treated the same as Blackfoot wives. Little Bull did not understand why Plum didn't treat the woman as his wife—or just go ahead and kill her. He decided that Plum's chief interest in the woman was merely to satisfy his sadistic urges.

In the plain-hide lodge on the outer circle of the camp, Jamie was not certain whether this assault upon her was the second or third, for she had been unconscious for most of the initial night of terror. This time she had made only a feeble effort to resist, giving it up completely when he added a few fresh welts to her already battered face. In order to endure the nightmare, she tried to go totally limp, as if she were dead, her mind leaving her body and the present behind. This lack of movement on her part was infuriating to Plum, and he threatened her life if she did not respond. Still she made no response—death would only bring relief from her suffering. After a few minutes of mauling and pawing the helpless girl, Plum lost the edge on his lust and withdrew.

He went outside, where his three partners were seated around the fire, roasting some meat over the flames. Plum grabbed the willow limb that Ox was holding and pulled the strip of meat from it. Tossing the hot venison back and forth in his hands to cool it, he settled himself before the fire and proceeded to tear at the meat with his teeth.

"Ah . . . damn, Plum," Ox complained, "that was just about done."

"There's plenty of meat. Cook another one," Plum replied. The simpleminded giant puckered his lips as if about to protest but said nothing. He cut another strip of raw meat and held it over the flames.

Crown sat across from Plum and studied him with a cold eye. Plum had what Crown wanted, and Crown's mind would usually fester over something like that, knowing no peace until he got what he wanted. He considered simply killing Plum and taking the girl. As he sat there glaring at his partner across the coals of the fire, he thought about the consequences that might follow. There was the matter of Ox and Sowers—where would they stand? With him or with Plum? He had no qualms about killing all three, but he didn't like the odds if they decided to side with Plum. As far as the Indians were concerned, he doubted if Little Bull cared whether the white men killed each other off or not. There was a good possibility, however, that once the killing started, the Blackfeet might decide to go ahead and clear all the white men out. He made up his mind that it would be best to wait until they were away from the Blackfoot camp, but he scowled at the thought that he would have to bide his time.

"What are you lookin' so glum about, Crown?" Sowers asked, as he blew on a strip of sizzling deer meat.

"None of your damn business," Crown snapped back.

Sowers jerked his head back as if he were dodging a punch. "I swear! You've been cross as a she-bear for the last several days. Must be the cold weather settin' in."

Plum, watching the two with a hint of a smirk on his lips, said, "Crown's got somethin' else eatin' at his liver. Ain'tcha, Crown?" Crown didn't answer. Plum continued to goad his sullen partner. "Crown's been eyeballing my woman in there, thinkin' 'bout how it would be with a white woman."

Crown's face grew dark as a thundercloud as he continued to stare at Plum through eyes narrow with anger. Though he remained silent, he was thinking, *Keep talking, you son of a bitch. Talk yourself into an early grave.* He made up his mind right then that Plum was a dead man as soon as he caught him with his back turned.

Plum silently measured Crown with his eyes. He had read the signs in Crown's disposition since the raid on the Kutenai camp, and he had seen the man fester over something before. He knew Crown wouldn't let it go—he would let it build until he exploded. Only this time, Plum would be the object of his rage. Knowing that, Plum purposely continued to goad him, trying to bring Crown's anger to a head while there were plenty of people around. Crown would have to make a move or back down. Plum hoped he would make a move toward him. He had a cocked pistol under his leg, and he would settle his hash for him in short order. Crown's share of the plunder would make a right nice bonus for the three remaining partners.

But Crown was not as foolish as Plum had hoped. He had already considered his odds and decided that this was not the time for a showdown. In addition, the pistol almost hidden under Plum's leg had not escaped his notice. No, he told himself, the showdown would be on his terms, not Plum's. "I'm goin' to see to my horses," he finally stated and got up to leave.

Sowers breathed a little sigh of relief as Crown walked away. He was still holding a piece of roasted meat in his hand, having forgotten about it while he watched the war of wills between Plum and Crown. Unlike his sidekick Ox, who was happily chewing away, oblivious to the friction between the two cougars, Sowers could see a violent confrontation coming. It had been coming for a while now—Crown was getting more and more edgy every day.

The obvious way to defuse the situation was for Plum to let Crown share the woman. He had done it before, but that was with Indian women, and Plum must have wanted to keep this one around for a spell. Crown was hard on women. He had left two of them dead—the Cree girl up above the Medicine Line and a Pend d'Oreille woman near the Missouri. Sowers reckoned that Plum must be thinking about those two and he wasn't ready to have Crown fly into one of his rages and slit the white woman's throat. It was coming, though, the showdown between the two of them. When it happened, Sowers hoped they would kill each other off. He and Ox would be happy to take the leavings and bid farewell to this band of Blackfeet for good.

Inside the tipi, Jamie painfully forced herself to get to her feet. She felt dirty, and while she wanted to go to the creek to clean her body, she knew that she had been soiled inside her soul and would never be completely cleansed of that stain. Her head throbbing, her face marked by trails of countless tears, she determined to rid herself of thoughts of suicide.

For during the savage, bruising attacks on her body, her fright had turned into a numbing anger. She now had a reason to live—to somehow take revenge on the man who had so brutally destroyed her life. She resolved to withstand the beatings and the assaults and determined that Plum would pay for what he had done to her. What did it matter anymore what abuse her body endured? There were no more thoughts of Trace McCall and a possible future that might include him. Her mind had been scarred forever. This was no time to think of dying. This was a time to reach deep down inside her battered soul and summon any strength that remained there. Determined now, she straightened herself and threw the door flap back.

The three men still seated by the fire were startled to see Jamie suddenly appear in the doorway of the lodge, a blanket wrapped around her. Plum's eyes immediately narrowed as he looked for some sign of treachery from the girl. Sowers, a grin plastered across his chubby cheeks, leered at the battered woman. Even though he felt no sympathy for her misery, he was still mildly shocked to see the evidence of Plum's physical abuse. Ox smiled his foolish smile and said, "Good morning, Mrs. Plum." His simple greeting held no intent to be sarcastic.

Looking from Plum's suspicious glare, to Sowers's openmouthed smirk, and finally to the blank gaze of innocence on the huge man-child's face, she endeavored to maintain a fearless expression. Her eye caught sight of the roasted piece of venison in Sowers's hand and she felt a sudden pain in her stomach that reminded her that she had not eaten for two days. Plum watched her closely as she reached out toward the piece of meat.

"Git your own damn meat," Sowers snapped and pulled his hand away.

Ox immediately jumped to his feet. He pulled a piece of roasting deer meat off the willow branch that had served as a spit and offered it to Jamie. "Here's you somethin' to eat, Mrs. Plum."

Jamie cocked her head slightly to look into the simple giant's eyes, her own left eye still swollen enough to make sight difficult on that side. Reading no deception there, she took the piece of meat and began to chew it furiously. Ox smiled his satisfaction.

Plum watched the incident with suspicion, expecting some sudden attempt to escape. But Jamie seemed intent upon satisfying her hunger and nothing more. Finally he surmised that the woman's spirit had been broken and she was too frightened to do anything that might call his wrath down upon her again. He smiled to himself, amused that Ox referred to her as Mrs. Plum.

"I want to clean myself," Jamie stated boldly.

Plum's eyebrows raised in surprise to hear her speak. "Oh, you do, do you?" He stared at her while he thought about her request, considering the potential for any tricks on her part. He decided there was little risk in letting the woman clean up. She stood waiting for his permission. "All right," he said at last, "you can go down to the creek yonder." Then he pointed toward the flat expanse of treeless terrain between the creek and the hills. "You see that open land there? I can set right here and put a bullet between your shoulder blades before you ever get to them hills."

"I won't try to run," Jamie stated frankly.

"Damn right, you won't," Plum fired back. "Now, go on. Ox, you go with her." He was confident that Ox was no threat to try anything with his woman. "You watch her, but you keep your hands off her." Ox nodded eagerly.

Jamie looked from Plum's scowl to the open face of the bearlike Ox and came to the same conclusion that Plum had reached. This simpleminded hulk was probably no threat to her. She was thankful that his mind was like that of a child, for if he harbored any lustful thoughts toward her, she thought she would probably be crushed under his attack. She turned and started walking toward the creek, Ox following happily along behind.

The morning air was cold, and the water was even colder, but Jamie didn't mind. It felt good on her bruised face and arms, numbing the tender cuts that were too fresh to have started healing yet. Ox sat on the bank and smiled broadly as he watched her bathe. His smile turned to a frown when he saw the bleeding start again on her facial wounds.

"He beat you bad," Ox sympathized.

"Yes," she answered softly, then paused. "Turn around. I have to clean myself down there."

His smile returned. "Plum said I should watch."

She didn't bother to ask again. She could see that he had no intention of turning around. After what she had been through, it didn't matter a great deal, anyway. He had seen everything there was to see, and she supposed it was no different than exposing herself before a dog or a horse. To make it a little less public, she waded farther out into the icy water, until it was up to her thighs. Then she sat down and hurriedly completed her bath. When she came shivering out of the cold water, Ox handed her the blanket she had brought. She dried herself as best she could with it and returned to the fire, Ox following dutifully behind.

After that morning Jamie was granted a bit more freedom during the daytime when Plum was not concerned that she might escape. Still, he was wary enough to continue to tie her at night after he was finished with her. Jamie endured her nightmare, using the method that had saved her sanity before as she forced her mind to separate itself from her body. She prayed nightly that there would come a time when he did not tie her and she would have an opportunity to take her revenge.

The bad blood between Plum and Crown still simmered, and Jamie was aware that she was the cause of it. She shuddered to think of her fate if the two men finally fought over her and Crown was the victor. One evil might be as bad as the other, but Jamie knew that Crown lusted for more than satisfaction for his animalistic desires. He had a bloodlust. She was convinced that he would kill her.

Little Bull sat in front of his lodge, talking to Two Kills and Medicine Horse. His wife, Red Sky, brought a bowl of boiled meat and set it down before the three most influential men of the village. The discussion that was taking place was to decide if it was time to move into winter camp. Little Bull was of the opinion that it was past time to go. "This time last winter, we were already settled near the headwaters of the Yellowstone. That was a good camp. I think we should return there."

Medicine Horse, being the eldest of the three, nodded solemnly and said, "It would be good to return there—if the Sioux are not in the vicinity." He drew deeply from the clay pipe, then handed it to Two Kills. "The winter is late in coming this time, but I think the snow will come before two more sleeps."

Two Kills was about to comment when their talk was interrupted by a commotion near the outer circle of lodges. They paused while they looked for the cause. In a few moments they saw Black Otter approaching them. He was leading his daughter by the arm, and a small crowd was following them. As they neared the three men sitting there, Little Bull could see blood around the girl's mouth. He got to his feet to meet Black Otter.

Fully irate, Black Otter began railing at once. "Look at my daughter!" He grabbed her chin roughly and pushed it up so Little Bull could see the girl's bleeding mouth. Before Little Bull could ask what had happened to her, Black Otter exclaimed, "That white dog, the evil one, tried to force himself on her! Look at her mouth!"

Little Bull was immediately incensed. He did not have to ask which white man had assaulted Black Otter's daughter. "The evil one" could only mean Crown. He knew Black Otter had come to him for justice because of the fear that he, like most of the camp, had of Crown, believing the man to be an evil spirit.

When Black Otter calmed down to the point where he could relate the incident that had taken place, Little Bull learned the details of the story. Bright Cloud and some of the other women went to the creek to fill the water pouches. They saw Crown sitting on a log near the creek, but they paid him no mind until he started to talk to them. He said he would bring Bright Cloud gifts if she would lie with him. She rebuffed his advances, saying that she was a virtuous girl and had no desire to lie with one as filthy as he. Crown became angry and grabbed her. He tried to pull her into the bushes, but her friends came to her aid, pulling back on her arms and flailing Crown with sticks and pebbles. Furious, he lashed out at them, knocking one of them down while he kept his hold on Bright Cloud's arm. She struggled to get away, but he threw her down and got on top of her, trying to pull her skirt up over her leggings. When the other women continued to pelt him with rocks, he finally had to retreat. But before he did, he struck Bright Cloud hard across the mouth with his fist.

Two Kills didn't wait for Little Bull to respond before he demanded, "Now the white men show themselves for the evil dogs they have always been. I say we must kill these devils now. We have tolerated them in our camp for too long."

Black Otter proclaimed his agreement with Two Kills, and the people who had gathered quickly joined in the cry for the white men's scalps. Little Bull alone was not ready to pronounce the death penalty. "Wait," he commanded, "let us talk about this before we act." He, like the others, longed to see the last of the likes of Plum and Crown, along with the other two, but he had a grudging respect for the firepower of the four white men. He knew that his braves could overcome the four, but not without paying a dear price in lives. Also, Plum had been married to Little Bull's sister before the accident took her life. He must think about that as well as the guns and powder Plum had supplied to them for over two years.

He talked directly to Bright Cloud. "I know this man Crown struck you, but he was not able to violate you, was he?" When she answered that he had not, he said, "These are dangerous men. They have many guns and use them well. Only one of them has committed this outrage, but if we kill him, his friends might fight us. I think it is best to drive them from our village, and let them go unharmed. After all, they have fought with our warriors in many battles. It is only right that we let them go in peace."

His statement was met with obvious disappointment from the crowd gathered before his lodge. To further placate the injured parties, he added, "To pay for this insult, we will not permit them to take the horses and skins they traded for their whiskey. Black Otter shall have ten horses for himself to pay for the wrong they have done to Bright Cloud." This seemed to placate the incensed Black Otter somewhat, and the rest of the people were satisfied just to be rid of the white men. The prospect of regaining the plunder they had been cheated out of was enough to satisfy the others.

"What the hell happened to you?" Plum asked when Crown walked up to the fire and sat down. Crown had a knot beside his eye that was still swelling. A trickle of blood was drying upon his face.

"One of them damn squaws hit me with a rock," Crown growled.

Plum laughed. "You been tryin' to go courtin' again, ain't you? Your style's a little rough for these

Blackfoot maidens, Crown. Maybe you oughta go back to them Cree women you're so popular with."

Crown only glared at him. He didn't appreciate Plum's banter, and he was still in a foul humor from the confrontation that morning. "I've had just about enough of your . . ." That was as far as he got before he was interrupted by a warning from Sowers and the sound of Little Bull with a group of warriors coming up behind them.

Plum, seeing the delegation approaching, smelled trouble, "Well, now," he said, "what's this here?" Seeing the grim expressions on the Blackfoot faces, he glanced at Crown. "What've you been into?" He didn't wait for Crown's answer. "You damn fool, I oughta shoot your sorry ass."

"You oughta try," Crown stated coldly.

The two locked eyes for a moment, but there was no time to take it further. Little Bull was already before them, his warriors forming a circle around the four men. Plum took notice of the fact that the warriors were armed. Those who owned guns had them, and the rest carried war axes and bows. He didn't like the look of this. He glanced at Crown and noticed that he had picked up his rifle and laid it across his knee. Plum's hand came to rest on the handle of his pistol.

"Welcome, friend," Plum started, his eyes darting back and forth between Little Bull and Two Kills. "Why have you come to the lodge of your friend with so many armed warriors?"

Little Bull wasted no time with polite talk. "Plum, you and these others are no longer welcome in this village. If you are still here when the sun comes up again, we will kill you. You must never again come to this camp."

Plum was stunned. "Well, that's a helluva note," he exclaimed in English. Then he responded in the Blackfoot tongue. "I don't understand. Why does my friend talk to me this way?"

Little Bull related the incident that had taken place at the creek that morning and informed Plum that the general mood of the people was to punish the white men by death. It was only through Little Bull's intervention that the four of them would be spared and permitted to leave in peace.

Listening to the Blackfoot war chief's words, Plum struggled to keep his anger under control. He cast an accusing glance in Crown's direction. *You had to do it, you son of a bitch.* It had taken more than two years to gain the trust he thought he had established with the Blackfoot band. It was a lucrative arrangement—like having his own private army of raiders. True, they were not his to command. But Little Bull had been easy to manipulate, what with the Blackfoot's natural tendency to be warlike. To have it all destroyed because of Crown's lustful urges infuriated Plum. *Maybe,* he thought, *there's an easier way out of this.* Knowing Crown had been too lazy to make any effort to learn the Blackfoot tongue—he recognized only a few basic terms—Plum made an appeal to the chief's sense of justice.

"If what you have told me is true," Plum said, "then my heart is filled with shame." He glanced at Crown with a slight grin, and Crown smirked in return. Plum continued. "This thing Crown has done is a bad thing, and he must be punished." He searched Little Bull's face, expecting to see some change in the stony countenance, but there was none. Plum pressed on. "I will turn this man over to you to punish as you see fit. My white friends and I will not interfere." Again he paused to see if there was any sign of appeasement in Little Bull's face. As before, Little Bull maintained an unyielding facade. "Crown is sorry for the insult to Bright Cloud and is ready to pay for it with his life." Plum glanced at Crown again and whispered in English, "Nod your head to let him know you're sorry." Crown shrugged indifferently, but nodded his head several times, never suspecting the fatal significance of his gesture. When Plum looked back at Little Bull, he knew the sacrifice was not going to be accepted.

The Blackfoot warriors had stood silently watching the four men while their war chief talked to Plum. There was a sense of restlessness among some of the younger braves, making it necessary for the elders of the village to restrain them. Plum was aware of the tinderbox that threatened to ignite if he demonstrated even a spark of anger. So he attempted to maintain a calm disposition as he made one more plea.

"We have fought side by side for many moons. Your enemies are my enemies. We should not let this one evil man destroy our friendship." He gestured toward Ox and Sowers. "These two and I will help you kill Crown." Sowers, who could understand enough to know what Plum proposed, nodded agreement. Ox sat there with his perpetual smile of amazement on his wide face, waiting for Sowers to explain what was going on.

Little Bull had held his tongue until Plum had finished speaking his peace. He now gave his final decision on the matter. "It is no good, Plum. You call yourself friend to the Blackfoot, but what kind of friend are you? What you say is true—we have fought side by side—but you and your white friends grow rich from the spoils of our battles, while my people have gained nothing. We are tired of being cheated by you. Go now, and be thankful that I hold my warriors back."

Plum scowled inwardly. His plan to appease the Blackfoot chief while also getting rid of Crown hadn't worked, so now he needed Crown, and Crown's guns, for his own protection. Plum knew he was finished here. Accepting his defeat, he sought now to cut his losses. "It will be as you say. We will pack up our hides and round up our horses, and leave you in peace."

Little Bull slowly shook his head. "You will take

no skins. You will each take two horses, nothing more."

Plum recoiled slightly. "Surely you would not steal our property," he replied.

A hint of a smile creased the stern features of the Blackfoot war chief. "No, I would not take anything that truly belongs to you."

"So that's how it is, is it?" Plum muttered in English. But noticing the increasing impatience of the young warriors, he said nothing to the chief. He turned to Sowers and said, "Looks like we ain't got much choice if we wanna keep our hair. Saddle up and let's git the hell outta here before some of these young studs go off half-cocked."

Sowers didn't have to be told twice. He had followed the conversation, wondering the whole time if it would suddenly ignite into a massacre. He, like Plum, knew that if the shooting started, they might kill half a dozen of the Indians, but then they would all four be rubbed out. He nudged Ox on the shoulder and said softly, "Git your stuff packed and saddle your horse." Ox smiled and did as he was told.

Crown, who had sullenly watched the discourse between Plum and Little Bull—his hand never off of his rifle—now looked at Plum and then Sowers. "What the hell is goin' on?" he demanded. "Are they throwin' us out? Are we lettin' these damn Injuns chase us off over a little innocent fun?"

"Shut up, Crown," Plum snapped. "Git your damn stuff together. It was you got us into this mess.

Now keep your mouth shut before you git us all kilt." Crown started to get his back up, but one look at Plum's face told him it was not the time to push it.

Inside the lodge, Jamie had crept up close to the entrance flap to listen to the confrontation taking place outside. She didn't understand what the dispute was over, but she could tell by the tone of the voices that it didn't bode well for Plum and his friends. The last statements in English finally told her that the Indians were ordering them to leave. She felt a flutter of excitement with the hope that she might be left behind. She was certain that her treatment at the hands of the Blackfeet could be no worse than that she received from the cruel and sadistic white men. After all, she thought, her time spent as captive of the Kutenais had been a pleasant experience compared to the hell she now endured.

Outside, Plum made another appeal to Little Bull for a bigger share of the horses, which was again denied. "One horse to ride, one horse for pack," Little Bull stated.

"What about her?" Plum asked when Jamie stepped out of the tipi.

Little Bull looked at Jamie for a few seconds, then said, "Take her with you. She is your wife."

"I get a horse for her?" Plum quickly asked. Little Bull shrugged before nodding yes.

"Please, I want to stay with you," Jamie suddenly

cried out to Little Bull. "I can work hard. Don't make me go with him!"

"Shut your mouth," Plum warned.

Little Bull didn't understand, but he assumed the woman was pleading for her life. "You go," he said, using the few words of English he knew.

"Damn right, you go," Plum growled under his breath while squeezing Jamie's arm in a viselike grip. "You're gonna pay for that bit of sass, bitch." He shoved her back toward the tipi.

Jamie stumbled, and almost fell, but she grabbed onto Ox's arm to regain her feet. The oversized brute steadied her and, gazing intently into her bruised face, asked, "Don't you wanna go with Plum?"

She looked up at him. The confusion written on his face was genuine, and in spite of her own hopeless plight, she almost felt sorry for the simple giant. "No, I don't want to go with Plum." She could see that this only added to his consternation.

Correctly gauging the temperament of the Blackfoot camp, the four white men wasted no time getting ready for the trail. A cold wind swept down the length of the valley as the train of five riders and nine horses filed through the lower end of a rocky canyon. Plum was in a hurry to make his way downriver to Three Forks. There wasn't much time to set up a winter camp, so he figured it best to return to a favorite campground. He pushed them along, keeping the horses to a steady pace until they reached a sheltered ravine with a trickle of water running down to the river. Here they made camp for the night.

During their travel that day, Plum had allowed Jamie to ride without being tied, but she rode in the middle of the string with Sowers and Ox behind her. If she had entertained any notions of escape, she quickly discarded them, for there was no place for her to run on the narrow trails. Resigned to her fate, she still could only wonder why God would sentence her to such misery. There was to be a slight reprieve, however. As before, when they had left the Kutenais' camp on their way to Little Bull's village, Plum did not assault Jamie that night. She did not escape his ire altogether, for he laid into her with his whip as punishment for her outburst to Little Bull. Her cries of despair were of no concern to the other men, with the exception of Ox, who pulled his blanket over his head in an effort to block out her screams. After what seemed an eternity to the tortured girl, Plum was finally satisfied with the punishment and hobbled her ankle to his own with a rawhide cord. Then he rolled up in his blanket and went to sleep.

Jamie was awakened by the gentle touch of a huge hand on her shoulder. Even though still in a half-dream state, she automatically cowered, expecting to be struck. When that did not happen, she blinked her eyes open, straining to see in the darkness. She almost cried out when she became alert enough to discover Ox's wide face only inches from her own, the faint light from the dying coals of the fire flickering across his rough features.

"Shhh," he warned, placing his hand across her mouth. "Don't make no noise." When she nodded that she understood, he took his hand away and whispered, "Come on, before Plum wakes up."

Jamie hesitated for only a second while she weighed the likely consequences if she blindly did as she was told. Ox, although his physical appearance was terrifying, had actually been the only one of her four captors who had never really harmed her. Realizing that the cord binding her to Plum had been cut, she scrambled up as quietly as she could and followed him out of the circle of firelight. As she stepped over the sleeping form of Sowers, and around Crown's prone body, she considered the possibility that Ox might simply be planning to try to make love to her. She discarded the thought almost as soon as it occurred to her. Ox was deathly afraid of Plum, although Jamie knew that the giant bear of a man could crush the smaller Plum if he was of a mind to. So she tiptoed out of the firelight into the darkness of the moonless night, following the hulking form before her.

After some thirty yards or so, Ox stopped so suddenly that Jamie bumped into his broad back in the darkness. When he turned to face her, she caught a glimpse of a horse standing before them on the narrow trail. Straining to see in the pitch-black of the ravine, she realized that it was the horse she had been riding, saddled and tied to a low bush.

Ox placed his hands on her shoulders and asked, "You don't want to be married to Plum, do you?"

Astonished by his innocence, she answered, "No. I'll never be his wife."

He hesitated then, his huge hands still holding her by the shoulders, while he sorted it out in his child's mind. Finally satisfied with his decision, he said, "If you ain't really Plum's wife, it ain't right for him to beat you, is it?"

"No," she replied softly.

He nodded his head several times. Then he suddenly lifted her off her feet as easily as he might lift a puppy. He sat her on the horse and, still holding her shoulder said, "Ride as far as you can before daylight, so Plum can't catch you and beat you no more."

He stepped back and suddenly inhaled sharply, his hands reaching for the horse as if stricken. Puzzled by his strange behavior, Jamie was about to ask if he was all right when he began to stumble. He grunted in pain as Plum withdrew the long skinning knife from his side. Before Ox could recover from the attack, Plum plunged his knife into his stomach and slashed a long rip in his gut. Ox crumpled to the ground.

Jamie screamed as Plum grabbed a handful of her shirt and pulled her off the horse. As she lay helpless at his feet, he slapped her several times.

"Thought you was gonna run off, did you? Maybe now you know what happens to anybody who tries to steal my property."

"What's goin' on?" Crown yelled as he came crashing through the underbrush, alerted by Jamie's scream. Sowers was right behind him.

"Ain't nuthin' goin' on," Plum answered calmly. "Ox ain't gonna be with us no more, that's all."

Crown, panting from his exertion, almost tripped over Ox's body in the dark. "What the hell?" he blurted out. Then, seeing Jamie quietly crying at Plum's feet and the saddled horse behind them, he quickly added it all up. "Huh," he grunted, "we could sure use Ox a helluva lot more than we need that damn woman out here in Blackfoot country. Why did you have to go and kill him?"

Plum reached down and cleaned the blade of his knife on Ox's shirt. "That's what happens to anybody that crosses Jack Plum," he said, the warning in his tone unmistakable.

"Ah, damn," Sowers whined. "Ol' Ox didn't know what he was doin'." He knelt down to examine him. "He ain't dead yet." A faint moan was heard from the wounded man. Getting closer, Sowers said, "Damn, Plum, you opened his gut. He's tryin' to hold his insides in with his hand."

"Let him lay!" Plum commanded.

Sowers shook his head sadly, but got to his feet again. He had kinda liked ol' Ox. He would miss having the big bear around. He knew that Ox was too stupid to realize the gravity of his actions. To Ox, it most likely amounted to the same as letting a squirrel out of a trap. *Well*, Sowers thought, *I reckon you learned the hard way not to cross a snake like Plum.* Stepping back from the body, Sower asked, "Whaddaya want to do with him?"

"Let him lay," Plum repeated. "See if he's got his pistol on him."

"He ain't," Crown replied. He had already checked. Crown, though not indifferent to Ox's early demise, wasted little sympathy for his oversized friend. His only regret now was that there would be one less gun to fight any hostile Indians they might encounter. If they had to come up one man short, Crown would have preferred that it was Plum lying there dying.

"Come on," Plum ordered. "It's a while yet to daylight, and we'd best git some sleep." He reached down and pulled Jamie to her feet. "Git that horse and lead him back to camp." He gave her a shove toward the animal. "I oughta make you walk tomorrow."

They left Ox to die there in the middle of the cold, dark trail. It was a horrifying experience for Jamie and left her cold and shaking inside, even after all the violence she had been a witness to in the weeks since she had been abducted from Promise Valley. She felt a deep sadness for the unfortunate innocent left to suffer and die alone. Ox, in his simpleminded compassion, had tried to release her from her prison.

The price he paid for his kindness was far out of proportion to the crime he had committed. She would certainly have taken the opportunity to escape—she had nothing to lose but her life, and that had become considerably less dear to her. But logic told her that it would have been a futile attempt. Even if she had been fortunate enough not to ride off a cliff in the darkness, Plum probably would have tracked her down within a day's time. As for Ox, a whipping with Plum's rawhide whip would have been ample punishment to prohibit his trying to help her again.

The morning broke cold and clear. An icy wind swept through the ravine, threatening to scatter the glowing coals from the fire. Sowers dragged a dead log up to the fire to act as a windbreak while Jamie, at Plum's instructions, filled the coffeepot from the spring. She turned her head when Crown took a few steps away from the fire to urinate, making no effort to hide himself.

"Hurry up with that coffee," Plum growled, still sitting by the fire, his blanket wrapped around his shoulders. Though the command had been directed at Jamie, his attention was not focused on the girl. He was glaring at Crown instead. It was evident to Jamie that Plum was irritated by Crown's tendency to expose himself in front of her. *Maybe,* she thought, *they will finally kill each other, and I won't have anybody but Sowers to deal with.*

A confrontation between the two might seem inevitable, but it was not to come that morning. After Plum had had his coffee, he and Crown divided Ox's belongings among the three men, and then they saddled up. Ox's two horses were tied on a line behind Jamie's horse, and Plum led them all down through the brush to strike the trail they had followed the day before.

When they reached the place in the trail where Ox had been left to die, there was no body! *Ox was gone!* His three former partners were surprised but only mildly concerned, surmising that he had dragged himself off to die.

"We shoulda put him out of his misery last night," Sowers moaned.

"Shut up, Sowers," Plum snapped. He could not abide the waste of a bullet on a man who was going to die anyway.

Leaving Jamie to hold the packhorses, they broke from the trail and scouted within a short radius of the spot where bloodstains still remained as testament to the previous night's crime. Because of the steepness of the slopes on each side of the trail, the search did not last long. None of the three reported any sign of the dying man.

"Well, he won't git far before the wolves git him," Crown said with a smirk. Not wanting to waste any more time on a dead man, they got under way again, leaving Ox to the wolves, or the vultures—whichever found him first.

# CHAPTER 8

Trace studied the open plain before him. The Blackfoot war party had followed the river through a narrow valley that led out of the mountains. The path they had taken was an old hunting trail. Trace was now in familiar territory, for the war party had led him back to the country he had summered in. It was not far from this place that he had killed a buffalo cow, just before he rescued Buck Ransom from the grizzly. He found it ironic that he might have simply stayed where he was and waited for the Blackfeet to come to him, for they were evidently headed for the Blackfoot encampment on the Missouri—Little Bull's village.

This country was dangerous for white men. No one appreciated that more than Trace. The mountains now behind him had been his summer home, high on the upper slopes where he had been sought out and challenged three times by young Blackfoot braves who sought to gain big medicine by killing the Mountain Hawk. But now the Hawk was in Blackfoot domain, and Trace was well aware of a

need to sharpen his senses. Knowing where the trail
led now, he decided it would be best to travel at
night from here on.

With the setting of the sun, the nights turned cold
and brisk on the open prairie, and Trace pushed his
horses hard to cover as much ground as possible
while there was a three-quarter moon to light the
way. The threat of snow that had hung over the
mountains had given way to clear skies once he
reached the rolling plains, and thousands of tiny pin-
pricks of light dotted the pitch-black sky. His intention was to reach the Missouri by daybreak. Once
he reached the safety of the trees by the river, he
would stop and rest the horses, maybe catch a few
hours' sleep himself. When his horses were fresh
again, he would push on in the daylight, following
the river east to Little Bull's village.

Long and cold, the night seemed reluctant to release the darkened prairie, but at last Trace saw the
welcome outline of the trees bordering the Missouri.
The first rays of sunlight were just beginning to
spread across the rolling hills when he led the horses
down to the water. He stretched his back and shoulder muscles while he stood there waiting for them
to drink, stamping his feet to get some feeling in his
toes. He had made good time during the night, and
he was eager to go on to the Blackfoot village. But
he knew the horses needed to rest. Looking around
at the many gullies that etched the banks of the river,
he figured that this was as good a place as any to

make his camp. He found a hollowed-out depression underneath a tree-covered bluff and decided it was a suitable spot to spread his buffalo-hide bedroll.

It was late morning by the time Trace was in the saddle and under way again, carefully avoiding the patches of frost that remained in the shade of the trees. He knew that the likelihood of his keeping his scalp depended upon his ability to traverse this territory unseen and without leaving a track. Constantly scanning the horizon for signs of a Blackfoot hunting party, he stayed close to the river, following its meandering course even though he knew he could reach the village quicker by riding on a straight bearing northeast. It would do Jamie very little good if he were caught out on the open plain by a large hunting party.

The thought of Jamie caused his mind to linger. He had been searching for her for weeks now, and he could not rid himself of the nagging fear that she might be beyond his reach. He permitted himself to worry about her for only a few brief moments, then forced himself to push those thoughts out of his consciousness. The only option available to him was to continue searching until he found her—dead or alive.

The presence of many trails—most of them old—alerted Trace that he was getting close to the Blackfoot village. Still, he had seen no riders, and as the sun began to sink behind the mountains to the west, it looked more and more as if Little Bull's village might have moved. He was certain that he was within a mile of the Blackfoot camp, yet there was no glow of cookfires. He made his camp by the river and waited until sunup to confirm what he already knew.

As he suspected, Little Bull's village had packed up and left, seeking a more sheltered camp to wait out the winter. Trace scanned the horizon carefully before riding into the abandoned camp. As there was no sign of anyone else, he guided the paint into the water, crossed the creek, and rode to the center of the campsite. Dismounting, he studied the ground for sign. From the freshness of many of the tracks, it appeared that it had been only a short time since the village was dismantled. Raking through the ashes of one of the cookfires, he discovered that the ground underneath was still warm. *They're only hours ahead of me*, he thought. The village must have moved out the day before. His heartbeat quickened slightly with the realization that he might overtake the Indians before sunset the following day.

The wide trail left by the departing camp was easy enough to see, but Trace deemed it wise to scout the perimeter of the camp for any fresh tracks. After quickly covering the circumference of the circle of lodges, he determined that the entire village had moved out en masse—with one exception. He stood and considered the one fresh trail that departed from that of the rest of the village. A party of at least four or more, with twice that many horses, had veered off toward the mountains, following the river to the southwest. Curious, he knelt down to study the tracks more closely. Though fresher than most of the old tracks that covered the banks of the creek, he decided they were slightly older than the wide trail left by the many horses and travois. Was this smaller trail important to him? He could only guess, so he decided that it was more than likely a hunting party that would, no doubt, circle back and rejoin the main camp at some point. Trace wasted no more time at the abandoned campsite. Eager now to overtake the Blackfoot village, he set out after them.

Medicine Horse's son, Crooked Leg, guided his pony through the fir trees that covered the eastern slope of a low line of hills paralleling the trail his tribe had taken the day before. As a Blackfoot warrior, his responsibility on this day was to scout the backtrail in case an enemy might be following to attack the rear of the camp.

Crooked Leg was respected in his village for his courage in battle and the many scalps on his lance. Most of the other young warriors scouted in groups of three or more, but Crooked Leg often rode alone, confident in his ability to prevail over any danger he might encounter. This past summer, he had ridden alone up into the high mountains, searching for the legendary Mountain Hawk, on a quest to establish himself as the most powerful warrior in his village. It was with great disappointment that he had been unsuccessful in his search for the man Little Bull had seen transform himself into a hawk. All

Crooked Leg had found was the remains of Two Horses at the base of a steep cliff. His friend had been missing for ten sleeps after announcing that he was going to seek out the Mountain Hawk. Crooked Leg brought back the unmarked arrow that had killed Two Horses. Medicine Horse had said that the Mountain Hawk made no marks on his arrows, and he was certain that Two Horses had been killed by the Hawk. Medicine Horse's words had filled his son's heart with an even stronger desire to find the Mountain Hawk—Two Horses had been his friend, and his death should be avenged—but revenge was not the sole reason Crooked Leg had searched for this white devil. Two Horses had enjoyed a reputation as the most fearsome warrior in Little Bull's camp. If Crooked Leg could succeed where Two Horses had failed, he would bring great honor to himself.

Approaching the edge of the trees, Crooked Leg suddenly pulled his pony up hard. On the flat below him, a lone rider leading a packhorse followed along the trail left the day before by the Blackfoot camp. From his appearance, he seemed to be one of the crazy white trappers that wandered the land. Crooked Leg wondered why any white man would be foolish enough to follow the Blackfoot village. *I will ride down and kill him*, he thought, and turned his pony to intercept the rider. Still puzzled that this intruder boldly trailed his people, Crooked Leg watched the rider closely as he converged upon the point where their paths would cross.

Lower down the slope now, Crooked Leg could see his prey more clearly. The trapper sat tall in the saddle. He carried a rifle in front of him, resting across the saddle, but he had a bow strapped to his back. Crooked Leg realized at that moment that his prayers to Man Above had suddenly been answered—*it was the Mountain Hawk!* It had to be! No other white man would be fool enough to follow the Blackfoot village alone. It made sense to him now: When the people of the village had left, the Mountain Hawk had come down from the upper slopes looking for them.

Crooked Leg could feel the tension in every muscle as he fought to contain his excitement. He would have preferred to pray and make medicine, paint his face and adorn his pony for battle, but there was no time. He must quickly prepare for his ambush, striking like lightning before the man could turn into a hawk and escape.

Leaving his pony in the trees, Crooked Leg shed his heavy buffalo robe and made his way down to the bottom of the slope on foot. He left the musket that Jack Plum had sold him with his pony, taking only his knife and his axe. This kill must be hand to hand in order to gain the greatest honor. As he moved silently through the low brush near the bottom of the hill, he watched the progress of the mountain man as the man approached a dry streambed.

The paint tossed his head and snorted, causing Trace to become immediately alert. He pulled the nervous pony to a stop while he looked hard at the trail ahead. His eyes searched the trees on the hill to his left, but he could see nothing that could possibly have spooked his horse. He listened. The constant wind whispering in the fir trees was the only sound he heard. To his right, there was no sign of life on the treeless hills that rolled toward the horizon. After a few moments, he decided it was nothing and nudged the paint gently with his heels. Ahead was a streambed—dry now with the absence of winter runoff—and he guided his horse toward it.

The attack came silently, so swift that Trace was taken completely by surprise. He had no hint of the danger until he suddenly found himself in midair, frantically trying to brace for the impact with the hard ground and at the same time struggling with his assailant to protect himself from the slashing thrusts of a knife. Upon impact with the ground, they separated, both men rolling quickly to break the fall and then scrambling to their feet.

Trace found himself facing a determined Blackfoot warrior, a knife in one hand, a war axe in the other. He realized his heavy buffalo coat had saved him serious harm from the Blackfoot's knife. There was no time for additional thought, for Crooked Leg charged into him, anxious to attack before the mountain man transformed himself into a hawk. Screaming a bloody war whoop, the Blackfoot warrior lunged at Trace and swung his war axe at Trace's head. Now encumbered by the heavy coat that had saved him moments before, Trace nevertheless managed to jump back, the blade of the axe missing his face by inches. Fumbling, furiously to get his coat open, he finally got his hand on the handle of his pistol and drew it from his belt just in time to aim it and fire. The lead ball smacked squarely into the center of Crooked Leg's chest as he charged into Trace once again. Though mortally wounded, Crooked Leg was only slowed by the bullet, and he continued to lunge at Trace. Again, Trace was quick enough to avoid the war axe, stepping aside at the last instant, then cracking the back of Crooked Leg's skull with his empty pistol.

The Blackfoot crashed to the ground and lay still, dazed by the blow to his head, dying from the bullet in his chest. Trace quickly picked up his rifle from the ground where it had fallen when he was knocked off his horse, and stood over the prone Indian. When Crooked Leg did not move for several seconds, Trace took his foot and rolled him over on his back. He could see then that his bullet had finished the Indian. Crooked Leg's eyes fluttered open momentarily and gazed into the face of his executioner before they closed for good.

Trace stood there for several minutes, looking around him for signs of additional warriors, glancing down occasionally at the corpse lying at his feet. He was in luck—the warrior was alone. It had been a close call. He took his coat off and counted three rips in the hide, then he looked at the long skinning knife still in the dead man's grasp. *That coulda been it right there*, he thought. Thinking it unwise to linger any longer, Trace took the corpse by the wrists and dragged it into the brush. *No need to advertise it*, he thought. That done, he rounded up his horses and, knowing that the Blackfoot would have had a horse nearby, started back up through the trees.

He was not halfway up the hill when the paint whinnied and was answered by the Indian's horse. Trace found it in a thicket of smaller trees, well out of sight. The Blackfoot's buffalo robe and a musket were lying on the ground beside the horse. Trace picked up the musket and examined it. *One of the old ones from the Hudson's Bay Company*, he thought. *No doubt it came from his friend Jack Plum.* It was loaded, and Trace knew the Indian could probably have killed him from ambush if he had used the musket. But having lived with the Crow Indians when he was a boy, Trace knew the significance of Crooked Leg's attempt to kill him in hand-to-hand battle.

Trace had thought at first to cut the Blackfoot's pony loose so that it wouldn't starve to death tied to a tree. Traveling as he was in hostile country, he wasn't keen on the prospect of leading an extra horse—one was trouble enough. But after examining the Indian pony, a powerfully built bay about fifteen hands high, he decided the Blackfoot had been extremely well mounted, and he was reluctant to leave such a fine piece of horseflesh to go free. He strapped the buffalo robe on the back of the Indian saddle and secured the musket on his own pack-horse. That decision made, he set out on the trail of the Blackfoot village once again.

After another half day's travel, Trace examined the trail carefully. It was fresh, no more than a few hours old. Already cautious, he would have to be even more watchful. He had steadily gained on the moving village, and now he must be mindful of over-taking a rear guard. Another worry was the warrior he had killed. Certainly by nightfall, they would be-come concerned that he had not returned and might send a scouting party to search for him.

The trail had steadily led toward the north, and Trace figured Little Bull's planned destination was the Milk River. There were several spots along the river where the Blackfeet and the Gros Ventres had wintered before, and if Trace's memory served him, the Milk was no more than forty miles away. That meant at least one more day on the trail before the village would strike the river. Little Bull would prob-ably make camp early today and reach the Milk to-morrow. Since the sun was already low in the sky, Trace could overtake them any time now. To be on the safe side, he decided to wait until dark before going any farther. Spotting a grassy draw that would afford him shelter, he led his horses in, dismounted, and waited for sundown.

He started out again when the last rays of sunshine began to flicker out behind the mountains to the west—in a matter of minutes, it would be totally dark. It was not difficult to find the Blackfoot camp however. The glow of cookfires in the dark, cold night could be seen from more than a mile away. Trace rode steadily toward the fires at a leisurely pace. He was no longer in a hurry, for if he did find Jamie he would have to wait until the camp was asleep before he could attempt to go in after her. Finding her was the first priority. Only then would he have to figure out how best to rescue her.

When he was within a quarter of a mile of the camp, Trace tied his horses in a ravine dotted with low bushes and continued on foot—it wouldn't do to let his horses get too close to the Blackfoot pony herd and start whinnying back and forth. Little Bull had camped in a broad valley that connected two converging ridges, forming a low box canyon at the southern end. After looking over the layout of the camp, Trace decided the south end of the canyon was the best place from which to watch. The Indians had settled near the closed end of the canyon, taking advantage of the shelter from the icy wind. Their position placed them directly under the gaze of anyone who might be watching from that cliff— an indication to Trace that Little Bull was unconcerned about caution. So Trace returned to collect his horses. He took them south of the hostile camp, then doubled back to a position behind the boxed end of the canyon and tied them in the trees on the southern slope. When he was satisfied that they would be concealed even in daylight, he made his way back over the ridge and down to a cluster of rocks some fifty feet above the Blackfoot camp.

From his position above the camp, he found that he had an excellent view of the entire village. He might have been concerned for his safety if this was a more permanent camp. But the Indians were only stopping overnight. They had set up no lodges, and the people would simply wrap up in warm furs and sleep before the fires that night. Trace thought there would be little likelihood that any sentries would bother to scale the cliff he was watching from, so he left the cover of the rocks and worked his way closer to the edge of the cliff.

A relaxed and carefree atmosphere enveloped the Blackfoot camp. The men sat in small groups, laughing and talking while the women were busy tending the fires and preparing meat for supper. Trace caught the aroma of roasting antelope as it wafted up the face of the cliff. It reminded him of his own hunger, and he reached into a pocket and pulled out a piece of buffalo jerky. As he chewed the tough, leathery strip, he constantly scanned the camp below him back and forth in an effort to find Jamie. He saw no one who resembled her. His eyes darted from one cookfire to the next, from one small gathering of women to individual girls fetching wood or water. She was not there.

Discouraged, he told himself that it was a large camp and it was very dark. It was quite possible that his visual survey could have missed her. Besides, she had been a captive for several weeks now—she would most likely be dressed in skins and moccasins, making it more difficult to recognize her. He would wait until daylight when he could see better. After the Indians had settled down to sleep, Trace made his way back over the ridge to check on his horses, then returned to his perch above the Blackfoot camp and waited for dawn.

The new day broke cold and clear, the threat of snow that had hung over the mountains for the past week having faded away. Trace was jolted awake from a series of fitful catnaps by the sounds of breakfast preparations below him. It was early yet, and the Blackfoot women scurried around in the crisp morning air to revive the dying fires and prepare for the day's march. Trace strained to see everyone in the camp, his eyes darting back and forth, searching as he had done the night before, but his luck was no better in the light of day. It was a large camp, with close to three hundred people, but he was certain that he could not have missed Jamie if she was there. As he watched, a group of warriors met near the center of the camp and appeared to carry on a serious discussion. Immediately after, three braves jumped on their ponies and rode out of the canyon, heading back along the previous day's trail. *Looking for the missing warrior,* Trace thought. He watched them until they had ridden out of sight to make sure they weren't going to circle around behind him.

Reluctant to admit to his failure to find Jamie, he remained in his position above the camp until the village had packed up and moved on. He watched every preparation, looked hard at each family group as they took to the trail, hoping to catch a glimpse of Jamie. When the last Blackfoot rode out of the canyon, Trace reluctantly rose to his feet, watching the column of Indians disappear. Stiff and cold, he stood there for a few minutes while he decided what to do. He had been certain that Jamie was traveling with Little Bull's band. Yet now he was certain she was no longer in the camp. He did not want to consider the possibility that obviously presented itself— that they had killed her. He decided to rule that out, simply because he did not want it to be so. There were other possibilities, such as the trail that he had guessed to be that of a hunting party. Now that he thought about it, those five riders leading extra horses never rejoined the main village. Unwilling to give up on the belief that he would eventually find Jamie, he resolved to return to the river and pick up that trail to the south. Knowing that he was now at least four days behind the smaller party, he hurried back to his horses and started back.

After leaving the cover of the mountains, Trace veered away from the wide trail left by the Blackfoot village and looked for an alternate route on the western side of the ridge, thinking to keep the ridge between himself and the three warriors searching for their friend. It was much slower returning that way, for there was no trail—not even a game trail, and he constantly had to climb or descend when suddenly confronted with a cliff or chasm. Still, he preferred that to the possibility of a confrontation with the three Blackfoot warriors. When he reached a point that was well past the dry streambed where he had been ambushed, he crossed the ridge and descended to the valley floor where he could make better time.

He arrived at the site of the former Blackfoot village in early afternoon of the second day. He had seen no sign of the three warriors, so he was confident they had returned to their village. After watering his three horses, he studied the trail of the small party that had left the main body of Indians— this time more closely. He came to the same conclusion he had made before: four, possibly five, riders, with five extra horses. *Jamie could be on on of those horses*, he thought.

Four days south of where Trace stood, Jamie knelt before a fire, boiling some meat from a deer that Sowers had killed that morning. They had been out of fresh meat for three days, and Plum finally ordered a halt in their travel to hunt. The actual hunting was done by Sowers. Plum did not trust Crown to be left alone with his woman, and Crown was reluctant to let Plum out of his sight. That left only Sowers who could be trusted out of the sight of both men.

The atmosphere among the three men had deteriorated to one of deadly suspicion. Plum was still furious with Crown for destroying his relationship with Little Bull's band, while Crown was growing increasingly bitter with jealousy about Plum's refusal to share his spoils—specifically, Jamie. Sowers remained in a state of nervous fidgeting, watching them both, hoping that when the explosion came, he would not get caught in the crossfire. His fears were not enough to persuade him to tuck tail and run, however. He still entertained the possibility that the two might kill each other, leaving him to inherit all the spoils, Jamie included. It was an uneasy partnership, but one that Plum found necessary since he no longer enjoyed the protection of Little Bull and his Blackfeet.

"Gimme some of that meat," Crown demanded, walking up behind the wretched girl tending the pot. He reached down and put his hand on her shoulder. She immediately flinched, causing him to smile a wicked, lopsided grin. He continued to crowd her as she attempted to move away. "What you squirmin' away fer? I ain't gonna hurtcha." His eyes seemed to burn right through her clothing, his smile turning to a sneer. "I ain't like Plum—I know how to treat a woman."

Jamie said nothing in response but continued to cower before the evil-smelling renegade. She feared Crown more than Plum. Plum was cruel and brutal, but she had become hardened to his rough treatment. Crown was sadistic. She didn't have to hear about the two Indian women he had killed to know this. One look into those dark, calculating eyes told of his passion for causing pain.

"You can git your damn hands off my wife now," Plum spat as he came out of the trees behind Crown. He walked up to face his partner, his hand resting on the handle of his pistol. "I swear, a man can't go take a piss without you gittin' your hands where they don't belong."

Startled at first when Plum came up behind him, Crown snorted defiantly, taking his time to remove the offending hand.

"Your wife?" he scoffed. "I don't remember seein' you stand up in front of no parson with this bitch."

"You heard me," Plum said, his fingers tightening around the handle of his pistol.

Crown considered the advantage Plum had and decided the odds were not in his favor. "All I was after was somethin' to eat," he said. "You wouldn't shoot a man for tryin' to git somethin' to eat, would you?" They glared at each other for a long moment before Crown shrugged and took the bowl of boiled meat that Jamie held up to him. *One of these days I ain't gonna back down*, Crown thought as he favored

Plum with a smug smile and moved to the other side of the fire to eat.

For Jamie, another moment in a lifetime of tense moments had passed without bloodshed. Her existence was punctuated by one threatening situation after another. In her agony she wondered why she did not simply lose her mind. Beyond despair now, she no longer had thoughts of suicide. She yearned only to live for the chance to punish those who had destroyed her soul. If she could be granted that one opportunity for revenge, she did not care what happened afterward.

"One more day oughta find us at Three Forks," Sowers offered as a change in conversation. He, like Jamie, had felt the tension in the confrontation between Plum and Crown and wondered if this was going to be the showdown. He had mixed emotions about the potential face-off. While he enjoyed the thought of the two of them killing each other and leaving him to take the plunder, he didn't particularly relish the notion of wintering alone in this territory—not even of wintering with the woman. It would have been fine if Ox hadn't crossed Plum and gotten himself killed. There was going to be a great deal of hard work building a rough lean-to, wood to cut for the fire, gathering enough food to last the winter, Ox would have come in handy. *Too bad the simple bastard was so softhearted*, Somers thought. *I reckon he got what he deserved.*

# CHAPTER 9

Trace moved out from the abandoned Blackfoot village early in the afternoon, finding the trail left by nine horses easy to follow. He made good time, covering a lot of ground before darkness forced him to make camp for the night. The night sky was clear when he bundled up in his buffalo robe and went to sleep, planning to get started again as soon as it was light enough to ride.

He awoke to a stark white world. A good four inches of snow covered his buffalo-hide bedroll already, and it was still falling, so thick that the trees around him seemed to have vanished behind a frosty veil. It had been coming for days now, but Trace had hoped it would hold off until he found this small party he had been trailing. "Dammit!" he swore as he roused himself from his bedroll and hurried to saddle the paint. "Pretty soon, there ain't gonna be no trail to follow," he complained to his horse. Not taking time to eat or make coffee, he started out.

He picked up fragments of the trail whenever it led under trees where the snow had not completely covered the ground, but he was able to make barely a mile before every trace of hoofprints disappeared beneath a blanket of white. Discouraged and frustrated, he could do nothing but guess where the party was heading. It could be anywhere, but so far they had stayed close to the river, so he assumed they would continue to follow it. He prodded his horse and started out once again.

The snow continued for the greater part of the morning but tapered off at a depth of about ten inches, making travel a little difficult in some places. Bundled against the cold, Trace pushed on, keeping a sharp lookout on the way ahead while periodically checking to the rear to make sure nobody was trailing him. Behind him, his packhorse and the Blackfoot's bay followed patiently along, their breath like puffs of smoke on the frigid air.

Before noon, the clouds began to dissipate, and soon the sun burned through scattered holes in the overcast sky, creating towering shafts of brilliant light as it reflected off the snow. Trace was almost forced to close his eyes when passing through these patches of blinding sunshine, and he felt extremely vulnerable to anyone who might be waiting in ambush. It was with a great deal of relief that he welcomed the thickening of the clouds during the afternoon, which shut out the direct rays of the sun once more.

He had not stopped since leaving camp that morning, so he decided it was time to rest and feed his horses. His own belly felt the need for something hot as well. He continued on until he came to a wide stream that emptied into the river. A thick stand of willows on the bank of the stream would afford him some shelter for a fire, and a scattering of cottonwoods would provide feed for his horses.

In a matter of minutes, Trace had a healthy fire going, fed by a pile of dead branches that he dug out of the snow. Once that was taken care of, he cut off a bundle of green cottonwood branches and stacked them by the fire, using the buffalo robe of the slain Blackfoot for a ground cloth. Pulling one of the burnt ends of the deadwood from the fire, he fashioned it into a handle by sticking the point of his Green River knife into it. Then, using that as a drawknife, he skinned the sweet, tender bark from the cottonwood limbs. Soon, he had enough bark shavings to feed all three horses. He watched them eat for a few moments before seeing to his own supper.

The next morning he was relieved to find that there had been no additional snowfall during the night. The morning was cold and gray, however, and he studied the sky while he waited for his coffee to boil. It didn't look like it would snow again anytime soon. He had not made coffee the night before because his supply of coffee beans was nearing depletion. *Three or four more pots and that's about it*, he thought. His buffalo jerky was just about gone too. Soon he would have to hunt for fresh meat.

Under way once again, he had ridden no more than a mile when he pulled the paint up short, for he heard something on the wind. He listened and soon recognized the unmistakable sound of a pack of wolves attacking. *They probably jumped a deer or an elk*, he thought, *maybe a bear. Maybe they'll share a little of it.* He nudged the paint forward and rode toward the sound, keeping a cautious eye out to make sure he discovered the wolfpack before they discovered him.

Topping a low ridge, he pulled up again when he spotted the source of the sound. Below him, near a treeless gully, he counted six wolves attacking an animal that had gone down but was still making an effort to defend itself. Trace strained to identify the wolves' prey. After a moment he realized what he was looking at. "Damn!" he muttered. "That's a man!"

Kicking his horse firmly with his heels, Trace checked his rifle as the paint immediately responded, galloping toward the snarling pack of wolves. Intent on attacking their prey, the beasts were unaware of the mountain man charging down upon them until the Hawken rifle spoke, knocking one of their number down. Reloading on the run was difficult with half-frozen fingers, but Trace had done it before. By the time he was within twenty yards of them, another wolf was lying dead in the snow. The remaining four scattered, snarling and yelping as they fled.

Trace pulled up and dismounted. The victim—Indian or white, Trace couldn't tell at that point—lay back in the snow, exhausted. Trace moved quickly to his side, pausing to assess the situation before kneeling down to see what help he could provide. He was a white man, apparently a trapper. Trace had not realized how big the man was until he knelt beside him. *No wonder I couldn't tell if it was an elk or not,* he thought. The man's eyes were closed, but he was breathing, so Trace tried to determine how badly he was hurt.

There was blood on the man's hands and arms, but it was from superficial wounds, not serious enough to cause a man to be in the state this one seemed to be in. Then he noticed the crusted stains of an old wound in the man's side and another across his belly. Odd, Trace thought, that he was wearing no heavy coat or robe in weather like this. It was a wonder that he hadn't frozen to death. Upon closer examination, Trace determined that the wound in the man's side was a puncture wound, while the other was a long slash. Someone had done a fair amount of work on him with a knife.

After a few more moments, the big man's eyes flickered, then opened wide. He looked into Trace's face, and managed a weak smile. "Thanks, mister. I thought them wolves was gonna eat me," he rasped.

"Where the hell did you come from?" Trace asked. He looked around him, expecting to see a horse. "What happened to you? Indians?"

It was with a great deal of effort that Ox tried to answer Trace's questions. Already barely hanging on to life, he had been further weakened by his efforts to defend himself from the wolves. "T'warnt no Injuns," he forced out. "T'was my friends."

"Your friends?" Trace responded incredulously. "Mister, you better find some new friends." He looked again at Ox's wounds. "That cut on your belly looks pretty bad. We're gonna have to see what we can do about that. What the hell are you doing out here, anyway? Ain't you got a horse?"

Ox shook his head. Then taking a deep breath, he said, "They left me to die, but I ain't dead yet." There was no trace of defiance in his tone, just a simple statement.

Trace shook his head, amazed. "No, you ain't dead yet, but you're pretty damn close to it. Who left you to die?"

"Plum . . . and Crown," Ox answered weakly.

"Plum!" Trace shot back. "Jack Plum? How the hell . . ." he started but at once realized what should have been obvious before. "Were you riding with that scum?" Ox nodded, and Trace continued. "Did you just ride out from Little Bull's camp?" Ox nodded again, and Trace realized for the first time that it had not been a party of Blackfeet he had been trailing. Anxious now, he asked the question that had been burning his brain. "Was there a white woman with you?"

Ox didn't answer immediately. He swallowed

hard and exhaled, then took a deep breath. "Yessir. That's the reason Plum cut me—I tried to help her git away."

Trace was stunned for a moment. Jamie with Jack Plum—and Crown! This was devastating news. If anything could possibly be worse than being a prisoner of the Blackfeet, it was to be captured by those two murdering renegades. Trace was sick inside at the thought of it. "Is she . . ." he stumbled over his words. "Is she all right?"

Ox was growing weary, but he tried his best to answer Trace's questions. "Yessir," he rasped, "she's all right. She don't wanna be Plum's wife is all." He looked up at Trace, an earnest look in his eye. "She told me so, so I untied her and helped her run, but Plum caught us." He closed his eyes then and mumbled, "I'm hurt bad."

Trace remained there on one knee for a long time, a multitude of thoughts racing through his head. He was inclined to ride as fast as he could, right then, to find Jamie and save her from the hell she must be enduring. But he had to force himself to think rationally. If he went charging downriver now, he would just be like a dog chasing its own tail—he still had no trail to follow. Then his thoughts returned to the unfortunate wretch before him. He couldn't just ride off and leave him like his "friends" had done. He should at least see what he could do for his wounds, and maybe ease his dying. After all, the man had suffered his wounds in attempting to help Jamie.

Even if he was riding with Plum and Crown, Trace owed him for that.

"Come on," Trace finally said. "Let's get you up on a horse and see if we can fix you up. We'll go back to where I camped last night. There's better cover there from the cold."

Ox tried, but he could not get to his feet. Even with Trace's help, it was obvious that if Trace was able to get Ox on the horse's back, the giant was still too weak to stay on. So Trace got his hand axe from his pack and cut a couple of poles for a travois. He took the buffalo hide he had taken from the Blackfoot warrior and cut slits along two sides. Then with strips of rawhide, he laced the hide to the poles. When he was done, he tied the travois onto the bay pony and with a great deal of effort managed to pull Ox onto it.

It was almost dark by the time they made it back to the willow thicket by the stream. Trace hustled to make a fire and settle Ox close to it. "The first thing we gotta do is get you warm," he said as he struggled to move the big man's body. "Damned if you ain't a big boy," he groaned.

After he had taken care of the horses, Trace took his axe again and went to work building a rough windscreen. Once that was finished, he boiled some of his precious coffee and ladled it slowly down his patient's throat. Ox gulped the hot black liquid greedily. Trace then took a look at Ox's wounds to see if anything could be done to help him.

After the coffee was finished, Trace took his only pot and melted some snow over the fire. When the water had warmed enough, he began to soak the encrusted shirt away from the stomach wound. It was a painful process, but Ox did not complain, registering his discomfort only by a flutter of his heavy eyelids. When the wound was clean enough for Trace to estimate the seriousness of it, he wondered if he wasn't just wasting his time. The gash was long and deep—he had seen men die from less serious wounds than this. Although there was little he could do for Ox, Trace hoped that at least he would feel better knowing it was cleaned up a little. The puncture wound in Ox's side had almost closed, but it was still a blue hole in the center of a gray-green bruised area.

"Well, I reckon that's about the best I can do for you now. Maybe I'll find some fresh meat in the morning, give you something to chew on besides that jerky." He stepped out of the firelight to take another look at the horses. Looking back at the stricken man lying beside the fire, he did some heavy thinking. *That poor bastard won't make it till morning. He's lost too much blood. He oughta been dead a long time ago. I guess the only reason he ain't is because he's half froze and it kept that wound from festering.* Trace was anxious to go after Jamie, and he had already lost this entire day. But what else could he have done? Then he wondered if he had really done the poor devil any favors, for he might feel more pain when his wounds had thawed out. *Hell, at least he'll die warm.*

To Trace's surprise, his oversized patient was still alive the next morning, which put Trace in somewhat of a dilemma. He had already counted on going after Jamie that morning, but the wounded man was still breathing. It would be unthinkable to abandon him, even if he was sure to die at any time. Trace made up his mind—he would wait a little longer. In the meantime, he would climb up in the mountains to see if he might run up on a deer or an elk.

After assuring Ox that he would return, Trace set out to find meat. When he had covered most of the western slope of a long ridge and found no sign of a living thing, he began to wonder if he might have to resort to eating wolf—if the scavengers hadn't found the carcasses yet. He was about to give up the hunt when he caught sight of three elk nibbling on the bark of some berry bushes in a thicket some fifty yards below him. Not waiting to be selective, he raised his Hawken and brought down the animal nearest to him. The other two elk jumped but did not bolt, staring in wonder at their fallen brother. Only when Trace appeared on his horse did the animals bound off through the snow. Trace bled and gutted the carcass where it had fallen, then tied a rope around it and dragged it back to his camp to butcher.

He cut some strips of meat, and placed them over the fire to roast as soon as he got back to camp. The aroma of the cooking meat was enough to entice his patient to open his eyes. Trace cut him a piece of the liver to chew on while the meat was roasting. Seeing Ox's ravenous appetite for the liver, Trace was amazed by the huge man's will to live. "Damned if you ain't tough as an ox," he commented.

Ox managed a feeble smile, and replied, "That's my name . . . Ox."

"Ox?" Trace replied. "Is that how you're called? Ox?"

Ox grinned and nodded. It was a fitting name, Trace decided. When the strips of flesh were done, he divided them equally and the two men ate. After Trace completed his butchering, he rolled up the elk hide and tied it onto the bay. When Ox had eaten his fill, he promptly fell asleep. Trace stoked the fire, then rode out to dispose of the remains of the elk away from his camp, so as not to attract any wolves that might still be lingering.

Trace sat on the paint high up on a ridge, looking out toward the west at snowy mountain peaks as far as he could see. He looked back at the river below him, following its course until it vanished in the hills. Somewhere out in that wilderness, five, six, maybe seven days ahead, Jamie was waiting. He hoped to God that she was still sane after enduring harsh treatment he did not dare to imagine. He felt the urgent need to go after her, and he thought of the stubborn giant who refused to die back in his camp. His emotions were in turmoil as he decided

what he must do. After laboring over the quandary
for several minutes, he decided his first responsibility was to Jamie. That decided, he turned the paint
back toward his camp.

Trace stood over the big man for a long minute,
studying his face. There was no sign of life as he lay
there, his eyes closed, his body still. Trace was about
to kneel down to make sure he wasn't breathing
when Ox's eyes opened, and seeing Trace standing
over him, he smiled. *Damn!* Trace thought. *What in
the hell am I gonna do?* He returned Ox's smile. Saying nothing, he turned and went to cut more cottonwood limbs to peel for horse feed.

As each hour passed, Trace became more and
more anxious. He could not rid his mind of Jamie's
desperate situation. Telling himself that she was still
alive and that the worst of her treatment was probably over now didn't help. Though her situation
might not be any worse today than it was a week
ago, it still had to be a living hell. He had to go to
her.

His mind made up, Trace started getting Ox set
up as best he could. He gathered a huge stack of
firewood and placed it within easy reach of the prone
man. When he had piled up enough to last for several days, he then stored a generous supply of elk
meat in the snow near the end of the windbreak. Ox
watched him, only his eyes moving as Trace moved
back and forth before him, busy with the prepara-

tions. When Trace was all done, he sat down beside the fire and ate some of the roasted elk.

"Am I gonna die?" Ox suddenly asked, his voice clear and strong this time.

Trace wished that he could encourage the poor simple brute, but he could not. "I don't rightly know, Ox. I reckon that's somebody else's call."

Ox's deep-blue eyes searched Trace's, pleading like an injured animal for some assurance. "Are you gittin' ready to leave me?" he asked, childlike and innocent.

The earnest question made Trace uncomfortable. He didn't want to lie to a dying man, but he hated to tell him the truth, too. "Hell, Ox, I don't know ... maybe ..." he struggled. "I might have to leave for a bit." He hastened to add, "But I got you all fixed up here so you can take care of yourself till I get back."

Ox's gaze, steady and unblinking now, locked on Trace. He had watched Trace's preparations to leave, and he knew the tall mountain man was not coming back. He would be alone again. He thought about the days after he had dragged himself away from the place Plum had left him to die—days of terrifying cold and gut-wrenching pain. He thought of the frigid nights when he had lain under a creekbank, covering himself with dead leaves, trying to keep warm. And he thought of the wolves. He was frightened, and he didn't want to be left alone to die in the freezing mountains. But he did not give voice to his fears. Instead he looked away and said simply, "Thank you fer doin' fer me."

The huge man's simple offering of his thanks hit Trace's conscience dead center, and he felt like a dog for leaving him to die. *Dammit,* he thought, *I've got Jamie to worry about now. There's nothing I can do to keep you from dying.* He made no reply to Ox's thanks, other than a curt nod of his head. Every man who challenged the mountains knew the odds were better than even that he would most likely die a cruel and lonely death—even a man as simpleminded as Ox knew that. It was a hard fact of life, but it was fair. Trace had always accepted this, now it was time for Ox to accept it.

It was barely sunup, another cold, gray day like the day before. Trace had already saddled the paint, and he was struggling with the decision as to whether or not he should leave the bay in case Ox pulled through. If he didn't leave the horse, it was a surefire signal to Ox that Trace didn't expect him to make it. The other side of it was that it made little sense to leave a dead man a horse to ride. *I might need that horse for Jamie,* he thought. He stood there for a few moments, the lead rope in his hand, deliberating. *Damn you for a softhearted fool,* he cursed himself and tied the rope to a willow.

When he was ready to go, he knelt down to examine Ox's wounds. Ox gazed up at him silently, but the pain was evident in his eyes. The puncture wound in Ox's side appeared to be healing, but there was no improvement in the more serious stomach wound.

"You rest up," Trace said. "There's food and firewood within easy reach, and I'm leaving you a horse in case you feel well enough to ride before I get back." The wounded man's eyes told Trace that Ox knew the score.

Ox gazed intently into Trace's face, a serene expression replacing his mask of pain. "Are you the one the Injuns call the Mountain Hawk?" he asked.

Trace shrugged. "I reckon," he answered, then quickly added, "but I ain't no hawk. My name's Trace McCall."

Ox smiled and nodded, then said, "Plum and Crown aim to set up camp at Three Forks."

Trace had considered that possibility, for Three Forks had been a frequently used camping area for trappers for years. He himself had wintered there with Buck Ransom before the beaver trade went dead. Years before that, Buck had wintered there when he and Frank Brown were in the employ of the Rocky Mountain Fur Company. Now that Ox had confirmed his suspicions, Trace was ready to ride. One glance at the doleful face of the huge man lying almost helpless before him brought his thoughts back to the decision he had already made. *Best to get on with it*, he told himself and rose to his feet, avoiding the melancholy eyes that now followed his every move.

Without another glance at the man lying by the

fire, Trace guided the paint across the little stream
and followed the river south. He wasn't comfortable
with his feelings, which refused to dissipate even
though his rational mind kept trying to tell him that
there was nothing he could do to stop Ox from dying.
He forced himself to concentrate on the task ahead.
To rescue Jamie, he was going to have to deal with
two of the meanest snakes in the Rocky Mountains.
He would have to keep his wits about him as well,
for Plum was known to be as cunning as an otter.
The third man—Ox had called him Sowers—was unknown to Trace, but if he was riding with Plum and
Crown, Trace had to consider him just as dangerous.

A light snow began to fall as Trace approached
the gully where he had found Ox fighting off the
wolves. He paused a moment to consider the two
carcasses still lying in the snow, as yet untouched
by scavengers. That surprised him, for he would
have expected the other four wolves to have returned. *Maybe they're already stalking some other helpless prey*, he thought, and the picture of Ox lying
before the rough windbreak returned to his mind.
*That's what comes with riding with the likes of Plum and
Crown*, he told himself. *He shoulda known better than
to throw in with varmints like them*. But the picture of
the pathetically simple man-child refused to leave
his mind. "Dammit to hell!" he exclaimed and turned
the paint around.

Although food was within his reach, the stricken

man had had no desire to eat. For the second time in a matter of days, he had been abandoned—and this time, he was sure to die. His simple mind had sensed a decency in the tall mountain man that he had not seen in other men he had encountered. And like a stray dog, he had longed to follow at Trace's heels. Ox had not expressed his fears when Trace prepared to leave, but he had no hopes of ever riding out of there on the horse Trace had left for him.

Lying before the fire, looking up at the cheerless gray sky, Ox tried to think back over his brief life. There was not a great deal he could remember about his early childhood—in fact, he found it hard to concentrate on anything for long periods of time. His mind seemed to want to flit about from one thought to another, like a butterfly in a field of summer flowers. He did recall his brothers, and his father, but when he tried to remember his mother, he drew a blank. He couldn't really recall a woman living in his pa's shack near the river.

One memory that endured in Ox's mind was that there was never enough to eat in his house—and he, being the youngest, was left with the scraps. He remembered the beatings, administered by his pa as well as his older brothers. Sometimes he would wonder why everyone resented his presence. He never tried to cause trouble. He couldn't help it if thinking came hard for him, and he never could understand why that inability caused his family to ridicule him.

One day stood out in his sketchy memory, however; the day his pa took him to work with him. Ox was placed on a stump near the loading dock and threatened with a severe beating if he moved from it while his pa helped some other men load a large riverboat. It was near dark when the job was finished and the boat was ready to depart the following morning. After the other men had left to go home for supper, his pa took his young son aboard the boat. Telling Ox that he was going to play a game with the captain of the boat, he untied a canvas flap on one of the cargo boxes and placed the frightened child inside. Ox could still remember his pa's words: "You stay put in this box and don't make a sound. 'Cause if you do, the captain'll whup you good. You be quiet and you'll be all right. There'll be somebody waiting for you at the other end." He gave the boy a piece of cornbread wrapped in a paper sack and tied the flap back down over the box. The last words he heard from his father were, "You go on to sleep. You'll be all right."

He cried—he remembered that—but he soon fell asleep, and he didn't wake up until he felt the boat moving away from the dock the next morning. Terrified that if he made a sound, he would be yanked out of the box and beaten, Ox tried to keep as quiet as he could. All that first day he lay quietly in his wooden cage, listening to the sounds of the men working the boat as they constantly walked their poles to the stern, then tromped back to the bow again. Ox had no idea how long he remained in the cargo box before he was discovered. One day one of the boatmen discovered a spreading stain with the distinct odor of urine at the corner of the box. Suspecting that some varmint, possibly a raccoon, had managed to get aboard, the crew untied the canvas and, to their bewilderment, pulled out a half-starved, thoroughly terrified boy.

His pa had been right about one thing—the captain was infuriated to find Ox stowed away in his cargo. His first thought was to throw the unwelcome passenger overboard, but at the intervention of some of the more benevolent members of the crew, he reluctantly agreed to permit the boy to remain on board until they reached Fort Union, above the mouth of the Yellowstone. The condition was that Ox was to stay out of the crew's way.

Upon arriving at their destination some six weeks later, Ox was unceremoniously parked on the dock at Fort Union, and he was still sitting there when the boat had been unloaded and pulled away again. It was at this juncture in his young life that Mr. Henry Clyde entered the scene. Much like the boat captain, Mr. Clyde was equally bewildered to find the abandoned youngster on his dock.

Possessing a somewhat kinder disposition than the captain, however, Henry Clyde took the boy home with him, where he presented the waif to Mrs. Clyde. Being of a Christian spirit, Louella Clyde embraced the undernourished orphan and took him into her fold. It was not to last, however. For just when it appeared that Ox had at last found a welcoming haven, Mrs. Clyde discovered the boy's lack of wit, and her enthusiasm for raising another child waned almost immediately. When there was no doubt that the stray youngster was decidedly slow in things cerebral, Louella Clyde made it plain to Henry that she had no intention of playing nursemaid to a half-wit. All Ox knew was that he had somehow displeased another grownup and was no longer welcome in the house. By this time it was not an unfamiliar feeling for him, so he was not surprised—he was only at a loss as to what he had done to earn Mrs. Clyde's displeasure.

Ox was promptly carted back to the trading post the next morning. Henry Clyde, however, possessed a heart made of somewhat softer material than that of his wife, and he could not bring himself to put the child out to find his own way. So Ox began life in a new home, the back storeroom of the trading post, where he remained until a sudden spurt of growth caused Mr. Clyde to question the wisdom in keeping the hulking young man in his storeroom any longer. Unknown to Ox, when a mountain man named Sowers showed some interest in him, Henry encouraged him to approach Ox with an offer of employment.

His thoughts returning to the present, Ox considered the man who had just ridden off to try to overtake Crown. Trace McCall was a good man, Ox felt certain about that. He wished that he had met Trace instead of Sowers. Then he wouldn't be in this mess. Trace had left him here alone, but Ox understood why Trace needed to go. He only hoped he got to Jamie before Crown killed her.

Weary of lying on his back, Ox forced himself to turn over on his side, a movement that always caused his stomach wound to send fiery stabs of pain through his abdomen. This time, however, the pain was decidedly less intense—a sign that might have been welcome had he not been so despondent over being alone. Now, facing the fire, he wondered if he might as well let it die out. Why prolong his dying? He had heard Sowers say that freezing to death was about as good a way to die as any; just go to sleep and never wake up. Then, like a child alone in the dark, he felt his heart quicken and an instant glow of joy when he suddenly heard horses padding softly through the snow behind him. The look of gratitude on Ox's face made Trace feel more guilty than ever for even thinking about leaving him to fend for himself.

During the next couple of days, Trace often berated himself for lingering with a dying man while Jamie was held captive by such dangerous renegades. But he could not justify leaving Ox, especially after spending more time talking with him and coming to realize what an innocent mind he was dealing with. He questioned Ox about Plum and Crown and the treatment Jamie had received. What Ox told him made his heart ache for Jamie, but he also was able to surmise that she had become hardened to her ordeal. Since he didn't know anything about Sowers, he questioned Ox about the man in order to have a fair idea of what he was dealing with.

"How did you hook up with those three in the first place?" Trace asked as he put a fresh cloth on Ox's wound.

"I was workin' fer Mr. Henry Clyde at Fort Union, and Sowers come in with a load of plews to trade," Ox explained. "He had six mules loaded with all kinds of plews—buffalo, beaver, deer, bear—everything. I helped him unload, and he asked me if I wanted to go with him and help him all the time. He said I could git rich, so I went with him."

"Did you get rich?"

Ox grinned. "No, sir, I didn't."

Trace shook his head thoughtfully. "Ox, how old are you?"

Ox thought a moment, then shrugged. "I don't know."

"Have you got any family? Ma and pa?" Trace asked.

"No, sir. My pa put me on a boat upriver, and when they was finished unloadin' it, they left me settin' there on the landin'. Mr. Clyde let me stay there in the back of the storeroom."

"And then you threw in with Sowers," Trace commented.

"Yessir. I wanted to git rich. Mr. Clyde said I growed too big to stay in the storeroom anyway."

Two more days passed, and Ox's condition made a drastic change. Contrary to what Trace anticipated, the huge man took a turn for the better. Instead of dying, he began a rapid recovery, and within a week's time he was able to sit up and move about. Trace was astounded by his capacity for healing, never suspecting that Ox's will to live had been rejuvenated by his return.

One morning Trace awoke to find Ox towering over him, a wide grin plastered on his face. Trace blinked a few times to rid his eyes of sleep, then asked one simple question. "Can you ride?"

"I think so."

They were in the saddle that same morning, following the river toward the place where the Missouri forks into three rivers, where, if providence favored them, Jamie was waiting.

# CHAPTER 10

On his hands and knees in the snow, Sowers backed away from the top of the rise and came plowing down to the edge of the pines where Plum and Crown waited. Jamie, huddled next to a tree trunk with a buffalo robe pulled over her head, tried to protect her face from the brutal cold. They had spent days on horseback in the bitter weather, in stinging cold that burned every inch of exposed skin. Her fingers were stiff and red, and she feared that her toes might be frostbitten.

"Well, what is it?" Plum barked, too impatient to allow Sowers time to catch his breath when he reached the trees.

Sowers grinned, still puffing. "Cozy as can be," he said. "They got 'em a nice little cabin built. I figure they's no more'n three of 'em—maybe four. I ain't shore, but they only got six horses out back."

Plum stroked his chin whiskers while he considered this. He hadn't expected to find anyone at one of his preferred campsites, especially since the beaver trade had all but disappeared. To find that someone had not only camped in his favorite spot, but had put up a permanent structure, galled him more than a little. On the other hand, it appeared to be just the setup he needed.

"No sign of any more cabins?" he wanted to know. When Sowers answered that there were none, Plum nodded and said, "I expect we'd best ride on in, and pay 'em a call—maybe thank 'em for building us a nice cabin."

Inside the crude log cabin, Boss Pritchard sat playing two-handed poker with Jake Watson. Neither man had any money, so they were playing just to while away the hours. Shorty Whitehead had become bored with a gambling game that involved no money, so he got up to put another log on the fire. He and Boss had built the fireplace of stone, and he was not shy about bragging on the success of it. It needed a little additional clay around the outside edges, but it kept the little cabin warm.

After Shorty was satisfied that the fire was burning steadily, he decided to go outside to take a look at the sky. He was still standing in the open doorway when he sighted a small party making their way across the snowy rise to the north. "Danged if we ain't got company," he called back over his shoulder, whereupon his two partners jumped up from the keg they had been using as a table and reached for their rifles. Shorty quickly assured them that the visitors were not Indians. "Looks like some trap-

pers," he said as he was joined by Boss and Jake a
the door.

"Whadaya make of 'em?" Jake asked, straining t(
see if it was anyone he knew.

"Don't know," Boss replied. "Don't recollect seein
'em before. Best keep your rifle handy till we se(
which way their stick floats."

"Hallo, there in the cabin," Plum called out whe▶
they had closed to within fifty yards.

"Hallo, yourself," Boss replied. "Who be ya?"

"Jack Plum's the name. Me and my little family
here is just passin' through, lookin' fer a place to se
up winter camp." They continued to approach. "
reckon we'll go on down a ways since you boys i!
camping here."

Realizing now that the fourth rider was a woman◀
Boss suddenly remembered his manners. "Well, sir
you got a few good hours of daylight left, so th(
lady might like to come in and get warm for a while.'

Plum smiled. "That's right neighborly of you, si▶
It is mighty cold, and we've been travelin' a spell.'
He pulled up close to Jamie's horse and issued {
low warning. "One peep outta you and I'll cut you▶
gizzard out." He signaled Crown with a slight no(
of his head and received a smirk in return. Crow▶
knew his part without being told.

Boss stood aside and held the door for the travelers to enter. "Come on inside, miss," he said a!
Jamie followed Plum through the door. "We shor(
didn't expect to see no white folks out this way i▶

this kind of weather." Jake and Shorty propped their rifles in a corner of the tiny cabin and stood aside to let their visitors get to the fire.

"Be careful," Jamie whispered as she passed by Boss, but he was unable to understand what she said.

"Beg pardon, ma'am?"

Though it was whispered, Plum overheard the attempted warning and quickly answered Boss. "She said it's best to be careful in this kind of weather." A quick glance in Jamie's direction promised the girl that harsh retribution was coming her way. Putting on a friendly smile for Boss's benefit, Plum said, "It's a nice cozy little place you got here."

"It's passable, I reckon," Boss replied. Motioning with his head toward his two partners, he said, "Me and Shorty and Jake here put it up this fall."

"Any Injun trouble?" Crown asked.

Shorty answered. "Not so far. There was a band of Crows camped 'bout fifteen miles below the fork. They was friendly enough. Anyway they moved out before the first snow."

This news pleased Plum. He wasn't any too popular with the Crow Indians, since he had cheated them on several occasions. "What are you fellers doin' up this way—trappin? This place was trapped out years ago, warn't it?"

"Yeah," Boss agreed. "We're just holed up here for the winter. Come spring, we'll head on down to the Snake, maybe go on through to Fort Hall."

"Well," Plum replied, assuming as friendly a ton as he could contrive, "I don't reckon I have to te you how long and hard the winters are out here. hope you laid in a good supply of stores to carr you to spring." He shot Jamie a stern glance whe he noticed the urgent look in her eyes as she sough to attract Boss's attention.

Unaware of the silent warning the girl was try ing to give him, Boss replied, "Oh, this ain't the firs winter we've spent in the mountains. I reckon we'r fixed about as good as we need."

"We ain't got much to spare, but I reckon we g enough to git by," Jake Watson interrupted. He wa a bit leery of the line of questioning Plum had em barked upon. He shot Boss a sideways glance.

Boss, picking up on Jake's caution, quickly adde "Not much, but maybe we'll git by."

Plum smiled. *I know you got some meat packed awa somewhere outside*, he thought. *It'd make it a lot easie if you'd just tell me where you buried it.* To Boss, h said, "Well, sir, me and the boys appreciate you git tin' this here cabin ready for us—saves us a lot c work."

Boss looked puzzled. "Beg pardon?"

Jamie was about to break her silence and war the unsuspecting trappers, but she was too late. Plur threw back his heavy buffalo coat to reveal a pisto in each hand. He stuck one of them right into Bos Pritchard's belly and pulled the trigger. While Bos doubled over, Plum turned and fired his other pis tol, the shot splitting Jake Watson's forehead. Shorty made a move for his rifle, but Crown already had a pistol aimed at the back of his head.

It had all happened so quickly—three sharp cracks from the pistols—that Jamie was still screaming when the shooting was over. Plum gave her a rap across her face with the back of his hand, silencing her. Horrified by the merciless slaughter of three innocent men, she stood in the center of the cramped little room, her body shaking uncontrollably. She looked around at Sowers as the acrid stench of gunpowder lingered on the air, filling her nostrils. He was smiling broadly, his pistol out even though he had not fired.

"All right, let's drag these bastards outta here," Plum ordered. He reached down to take hold of Boss Pritchard's feet, and the mortally wounded man grunted in pain. "This'un's still kickin'," he said. To Boss, he snarled, "Gut-shot—could take a while before you finally die. To show you I ain't a hard man to git along with, I'll put you outta your misery." He turned to Sowers. "Gimme your pistol, Sowers."

"Lemme do it," Sowers whined.

Plum smirked. "How about that, mister? Ol' Sowers here didn't git to shoot nobody. Where do you want it? In the ear? In the mouth?"

"You go to hell," Boss rasped, seconds before Sowers gleefully shot him point-blank in the face.

"Drag him the hell outta here," Plum commanded, and Sowers cheerfully obeyed. Turning to see Jamie

still shivering in fear, Plum aimed a foot at her backside and ordered, "Quit that damn sniveling and git
over there and see what's in that pot. Git us somethin' to eat."

Shaken out of her temporary paralysis, Jamie did
as she was told. There was a large iron pot hanging
over the fire with some meat cooking inside. Her
mind still stunned by the brutal murders, she forced
herself to go through the motions of stirring the dark
meat boiling in the pot while the three men rum-
maged through the belongings of the three murdered
trappers.

"Hell," Crown spat, "they was poor as church
mice." He threw an empty parfleche aside after he
had dumped the contents on the dirt floor.

"Don't matter," Plum said, "we got us a cozy little shack, and plenty of wood cut—and we can use
them rifles." He cocked his head in Sowers's direction. "Sowers, go outside and dig around some.
They're bound to have some meat laid aside."

"Ah, hell, Plum, lemme git my feet warm first,"
Sowers whined. "It's cold out there, and I ain't et
nothin' yet."

Plum fixed him with a chilly stare. "Git your lazy
ass out there—and after you find that meat, take care
of them horses."

"All right, dammit, I'm goin'," Sowers grumbled.
"I could use a little help. Why can't Crown help
me . . . or her? She could dig around in the snow
good as me."

"She stays here where I can keep an eye on her," Plum answered, starting to lose his patience.

"And I ain't gonna help you 'cause I don't want to," Crown said, a snide smirk on his face, as if he dared anyone to object.

Sowers knew when he had pushed it as far as was healthy for him, so he got up from the fire and dragged out the door, mumbling noisily to himself. Plum and Crown took the bowls Jamie had filled from the pot, sat down on opposite sides of the fireplace, and filled their bellies. While the men were preoccupied with their supper, Jamie cautiously sampled the dark, greasy meat. She wasn't sure what it was, but upon tasting it, decided it was better than it looked. It was the first time she had tasted bear meat.

Amused by her apparent fastidiousness, Crown grunted, then said, "Better eat all the fat part you can. It'll help you keep warm." He wiped the grease off his chin with his sleeve and grinned lasciviously. "Maybe Plum ain't able to keep you warm. I reckon *I* could keep you hot enough."

"I reckon I could keep *you* hot enough too," Plum shot back, "with a little gunpowder up your ass."

Crown's eyes narrowed, although his smug smile stayed in place. "Now that might be more'n a day's work fer you, Plum."

Jamie shuddered inwardly at the thought of sleeping with either of them, and as evening was drawing near, she began to dread the nightmare that most nights brought. Maybe, she hoped, Plum would rein in his lust since the four of them were obviously going to share the tiny cabin, and he was usually reluctant to assault her under the watchful eye of Crown. He was always careful about rendering himself vulnerable when Crown was around, so he might content himself with simply pawing her crudely.

Trace pushed the horses as hard as he thought reasonable through the steady snowfall. Every mile or so, he checked on Ox, riding behind him on the Blackfoot's bay pony. The big man was able to remain upright in the saddle, but it was obvious the ride was taking its toll. Trace knew it was too soon for Ox to travel, but he had let the urgency of his mission overrule his better judgment. Ox had insisted that he could ride, and Trace wanted to believe him because of his desire to catch Plum and Crown. Now he could see that he was going to have to stop and let Ox rest. The wound in the huge man's belly had begun to bleed again, and Ox had been reluctant to tell Trace about it. When Trace discovered it, he immediately began looking for a suitable place to camp.

A few feet up the side of a pine-covered slope, he spotted a rock overhang that would provide shelter from the snow. It was not big enough to cover the horses too, but the thick stand of pines would be shelter enough for them and would buffer the chilly wind that swept through the river canyon.

As soon as he helped Ox dismount and settled

im under the overhang, Trace took his axe and
tarted chopping some limbs from a deadfall. There
vas plenty of firewood from countless past light-
ing strikes, and soon he had a sizable stack under
he rock. After the fire was blazing, Trace went about
•reparing some of the elk that was left. Ox apolo-
ized profusely for being a burden, but Trace as-
ured him that when he was well enough he would
lo his share. Ox thanked Trace again and again for
tot leaving him to the wolves—so excessively, in
act, that Trace finally told him that if he thanked
im one more time, he was going to leave him right
vhere he was. Then, seeing the look of alarm in Ox's
yes, he hurriedly reassured him that he was only
)king and had no plans to leave him.

"You've got to help me find Jamie," Trace told
im, "so I want you to get your strength back. All
ight?"

Ox nodded his head, his eyes shining with ea-
;erness. "I'd like that, Trace." Then he frowned, his
·yes squinting with the seriousness of his thoughts.
'Plum and Crown are gonna have to pay for what
hey done to Jamie . . . Sowers too. He didn't tell me
hey was bad men, or I'da never left Mr. Clyde." His
·hin dropped to his chest and he said softly, "I
vouldn'ta let 'em treat Jamie that way if I'da knowed
he wasn't Plum's wife."

Trace, busy tending the strips of meat roasting
•ver the fire, paused and turned to look at Ox. *Poor
imple bastard,* he thought. *Big as a mountain, and as*

*naive as a ten-year-old.* Trace could have felt vengeful toward Ox simply because he had been a part of Jack Plum's gang. But in the short time since he had found Ox fighting off the wolves, Trace had discovered no natural mean streak in him. Ox's only crime was that he was too guileless to realize he was in with an evil bunch. Trace sensed a desire in this gentle grizzly to do the right thing now that he felt he had stumbled onto the proper path.

Ox again demonstrated his amazing ability to recover, for the following morning the wound appeared to be healing nicely with no sign of any more bleeding. By his cheerful attitude as he volunteered to help pack up their camp, Trace could see that his new partner was feeling much stronger.

On their way again, Trace and Ox rode in silence as the horses padded slowly through the snow-covered valleys and draws. Constantly scouting the slopes on both sides of them, Trace kept a steady course toward Three Forks. Ox, more alert than the day before, sat up straight in the saddle and, following Trace's example, scanned the hills right and left. Looking back at him, Trace could not help but find the sight amusing. Ox's tremendous bulk made the Indian pony appear no bigger than a dog—and the bay was at least fifteen hands high. The Blackfoot saddle was a snug fit for Ox, and it rode closer up toward the horse's withers. Ox's long legs jutted straight out, making it look as though the horse had four front legs. Trace shook his head, and turned his ttention back to the trail ahead. *What in the world ave I gotten myself into with this one?* he thought. If e could have read the childlike mind behind him, e might have been concerned indeed. For Ox had aken to him like a stray dog takes to a butcher— nd no dog could be more faithful to his master than Ox would be. In Ox's mind, Trace McCall was a man mong men, the Mountain Hawk, and Ox's personal avior.

Ox's improved condition allowed them to travel auch farther that day than the day before. They rode arough numerous snow showers, stopping only riefly at midday to rest the horses. Shortly before ightfall, they came to one of Plum's campsites, and race stopped to examine it. The tracks of the horses nd the imprints of bedrolls were still evident, al- hough they had been covered with a light layer of now. Ox had told him that there were four in the arty, counting Jamie. Trace did not voice his houghts, but a worrisome image gnawed at his in- ides as he looked down at only three imprints of edrolls. He brushed the snow from the charred ends f the burnt-out branches and felt the ashes beneath, lthough he knew Plum had been gone from this amp for over a week. The ashes were frozen in the round.

"We might as well camp here for the night," Trace aid. "It'll be dark in an hour."

# Chapter 11

Two more days found Ox with a major portion of his health back and growing stronger every day. The puncture wound was now no more than a round circle of bruised skin, and the gash in his stomach had knitted back, leaving a lumpy furrow across his belly. As far as his mental state, Ox was the happiest he had ever been.

The snow had tapered off in the past two days, leaving enough places in the shelter of trees and boulders where traces of Plum's trail were evident. After tracking the nine horses for a distance, it became apparent to Trace that if Plum continued in this direction, he would pass somewhere close by the cabin Boss Pritchard and his partners had built above the fork. A chance meeting with Plum and Crown might not bode well for Boss—Trace hoped that the three trappers were keeping a sharp eye.

About an hour before sundown, Trace and Ox reached the rise before the river, where a week before, Plum had waited while Sowers scouted the cabin on the other side. Normally calm in the face of possible danger, Trace felt his pulse quicken when it became apparent that Plum had probably discovered Boss Pritchard's cabin. A quick but cautious climb to the top of the rise confirmed that suspicion. Lying on his belly in the snow with Ox beside him, Trace looked down upon the rough log shack. He counted fifteen horses in the trees behind the cabin. There could be no doubt that the renegades he was tracking were inside. The question that remained was whether Boss, Shorty, and Jake were alive.

"Yeah," Ox suddenly whispered, "that's Plum's old gray he likes so much. And that yeller-lookin' one is Sowers's." After a few moments he asked, "Are we gonna just ride in there and shoot 'em?"

Trace had learned to be patient with his childlike friend. "No, Ox. I don't think that would be too smart. There's too much open ground between here and the cabin. Even a poor shot with a rifle could pick both of us off before we got halfway down the rise. I know the men that built that cabin. I expect we'd best wait till dark and then find out what's going on inside and what happened to the folks that live there." Ox nodded his understanding and approval. "We'll just wait here and keep an eye on 'em till it gets dark," Trace said.

Just as the shadows began to close in, shutting off the last stubborn rays of light, Ox suddenly got up on one knee, and whispered, "There's Crown and Sowers!"

"I see 'em," Trace answered softly. He had watched the two men walk out of the cabin, and go behind it to tend to the horses. He recognized Crown, but he had never seen Sowers before. Now, he wondered, did that leave just Plum and Jamie inside—or were Boss, Jake, and Shorty also in there? And, if they were, were they being held hostage? Or were they even onto Plum's game yet?

"Damn horses ain't findin' much to eat under this snow," Crown complained as he and Sowers searched for willow leaves, brush, and anything else that the horses might eat.

"Hell," Sowers responded, "they's Injun ponies, most of 'em. They can git by on snowballs if that's all there is." He pulled his heavy buffalo coat up around his ears. "Damn, it's cold out here." He crooked a corner of his mouth up in a mischievous grin. "I'da heap rather be with Plum inside with that sassy-tailed little bitch."

Sowers's comment caused Crown to scowl even more deeply than normal, etching heavy lines on his face. He paused to let his mind work on the image of Plum inside where it was warm, probably pawing over the woman. Crown had a powerful need to satisfy his own lust, and it had been a long time since he had been given the opportunity. His rebuff by Bright Cloud back in Little Bull's camp was still fresh in his mind, as well as the castigation that had followed. It was not a question of shame. When it came to his animalistic regard for anything female, humiliation did not exist for Crown. He was hard on women, and that was the only way his sadistic appetites could be sated. And now his mind was on Jamie.

"Don't it bother you some that we're out here freezin' our tails off, while that bastard is settin' in there cozy as can be?" Crown suddenly asked. "Who the hell made him king of the whole damn territory? He oughta pull his share of the load, just like me and you."

Sowers could see right away that Crown was building up to one of his frequent temper fits, and he tried to calm him down a bit. He was not opposed to Crown and Plum killing each other off, but he was not sure he wanted it to happen before spring. It would be easier for him to handle the horses by himself then. "I don't know," he said, in answer to the question Crown had put to him, "I reckon Plum was the one that had the inside track with Little Bull's Blackfeet—I mean, being married to a squaw and all. I never give it much thought. He's just always been the boss."

"Yeah? Well, he ain't got no inside track no more," Crown shot back, his bile rising by the minute. "The Blackfeet kicked us out. We got nobody to count on now but the three of us, and I say he ain't no better than me and you. We're all equal to share in everything—the work, the horses, the plunder, and the damn bitch, too."

Even someone as obtuse as Sowers could see that Crown had finally voiced the one thing that was the burr under his saddle. Sowers knew from the start that the woman would be the cause of trouble between his two partners. The problem for Sowers now was that he was caught between the two of them. From his perspective, both men were to be feared, and he didn't want to be counted as an enemy to either one; at the same time he knew that both men would demand that he take a side. Sowers's only salvation, as he saw it, was to continue to sympathize with whichever of them he was alone with at the time, and back the one that remained standing after the smoke cleared. "Well, it don't seem right," he offered weakly.

"Hell, no, it don't," Crown exclaimed, "and somethin's gonna be done about it. Me and you gotta stick together on this thing. When the time comes for a showdown, I expect you to back me."

"You can count on me" Sowers promised.

"There's gonna be a full moon tonight," Trace said, looking up into the clear, dark sky. "I'd best be getting down there to see what the situation is in that cabin before the moon comes up. It'll be as light as day with the moon shining on the snow."

"I'm gonna go with you," Ox said, checking the load on Trace's extra rifle.

Trace laid a gentle hand on his friend's forearm. "You better stay here and take care of the horses. I

ain't sure you're well enough to move as fast as I
might have to." When Ox started to protest, Trace
cut him off. "I'll need you when the time comes.
Right now I'm just gonna look the situation over,
try to get an idea where everybody is before I make
a move." Ox reluctantly agreed to stay behind while
Trace slipped over the rise and disappeared into the
night.

He made his way quickly down to the river's
edge, then worked back along the bank until he was
behind the cabin. Moving quietly through snow a
foot deep, he came up through the trees where the
horses were collected. A couple of the ponies whinnied softly as he made his way slowly through the
herd, gently stroking a neck or a forelock here and
there to keep them calm. He paused briefly to make
sure no one inside the cabin had become alerted by
the horses before moving on.

Crouching low, he cautiously made his way toward the back of the log shack, moving a few yards
at a time, then stopping to listen. Although there
were no windows in the cabin, he could hear the
voices from inside. Pushing through some low
brush, he moved up to what appeared to be a low
stack of logs close to the back of the building. Behind him, he could see the moon, full and bright,
already inching up behind the trees on the far riverbank.

He remained there for a few minutes, listening
to the voices from the cabin, trying to determine if

one was that of a woman. If she was in there, she was not speaking. The voices he heard were loud and argumentative, and all male. He prepared to move to the cabin wall just as the moon topped the trees across the river, shining brightly over his shoulder. Glancing down, he was stopped abruptly by what he saw before him. The "logs" he had knelt behind were in fact the frozen bodies of three men. It wasn't necessary to identify them, but he brushed the light covering of snow away to reveal the cold, staring countenance of Boss Pritchard, a dark black hole beneath his left eye and a look of rage forever frozen on his face. Trace felt his fist tighten around his rifle in response to the feeling of anger that surged through his body.

*Well*, he thought, *I don't have to guess how many are inside anymore.* Still, he wanted confirmation that Jamie was with them. Leaving the bodies, he moved to the back wall of the cabin and pressed his ear against the logs close to a gunport and listened. He remained there for at least a quarter of an hour before he heard what he was waiting for—Jamie's voice. Although he was anticipating it, actually hearing her speak for the first time in more than a year startled him.

After more than two months of searching, he had found her. Now that he was certain she was there, he had to think about the best possible way to rescue her without endangering her life. As far as the three vermin who had held her captive—if it had turned out that she was no longer with them, his plan would have been simple enough, for Trace was a man of expedient nature. He would simply have blocked the one door and set the cabin on fire. Now he would have to think about it—if cornered, Plum might kill Jamie just out of spite.

As these thoughts ran through his mind, he suddenly heard the door open. He pressed himself tightly against the back wall and propped his rifle against the wall, then took his bow from his back and notched an arrow. Standing in the shadow of the roof overhang, he watched as Crown took no more than a dozen steps from the front of the cabin and proceeded to empty his bladder. It would have been so easy to let an arrow fly, deadly and silent. But Trace wasn't ready to show his hand quite yet, and give Plum any warning of his presence. So he reluctantly relaxed the pull on the bowstring.

He considered waiting until everyone was asleep inside, then surprising them before they had a chance to react, but he abandoned this plan when Crown, finished with his business, went back inside and dropped the heavy wooden bar into place, barricading the door. Boss Pritchard had seen to it that the door to his cabin was stout and secure. Trace would wait until morning. They had to come out sometime, and he would strike then, when he had all three out where he could see them.

\* \* \*

Sowers saw an opportunity to butter his bread on both sides when Crown went outside to answer nature's call. He sidled up to Plum, who was seated upon a stool by the fireplace, cleaning one of his pistols. "I swear, Plum," Sowers said in a confidential tone, "I ain't one to tattle on a man, but I think you oughta know that Crown is doin' a lot of talkin' behind your back."

"That so?" Plum asked, not overly concerned. "What kinda talkin'?"

"Oh, you know . . . talk about sharin' the work, talk about the woman . . . you know, general complaining."

Plum was still not concerned. "Hell, that's just Crown. He's always bitchin' about somethin'. He knows that if he steps outta line, I'll nail his hide to the barn door."

"I know you would, Plum, I know you would," Sowers hastened to reply. "I just wanted to warn you . . . like any friend would."

Plum cocked a suspicious eye in Sowers's direction. He didn't trust Sowers any more than he trusted Crown, especially when Sowers started talking about being his friend. But he kept his thoughts to himself. To Sowers he said, "Yeah, well, I appreciate the warning." Plum had a feeling that there was going to be a showdown between him and Crown any day now. Crown had been getting more and more sullen during the past few days, and he had that dull look in his eyes when he stared at Jamie. Plum had seen that look before, just before Crown carried that Cree woman off into the bushes and killed her. *Dammit*, Plum thought, *he just goes plumb loco when he gets his hands on a woman*. The signs were there. It was annoying to Plum because Crown's gun would be handy in the event of an encounter with the Crows or the Shoshones. But the longer Crown's anger was allowed to build, the greater the odds Plum would get a bullet in the back. *Maybe I'll let him have the woman*, he thought. He had to admit he was not getting much satisfaction from brutalizing her anymore, and he might as well let Crown have her. Maybe it would save him from having to kill him right now.

When Crown had gone back inside, Trace moved away from the back wall of the cabin and retraced his steps to the riverbank, then made his way back up the rise to where Ox was patiently waiting with the horses.

"Is the woman with 'em?" Ox asked as soon as Trace dropped down beside him.

"She's there, all right," Trace answered as he cleared away some of the snow from a little trench between two boulders and prepared to build a fire. It was going to be a long night, and they would need a fire to keep from freezing. Seeing what Trace had in mind, Ox started looking for limbs to put on the fire. "Not too big," Trace reminded Ox. "We don't want to start a fire they can see down there."

When they had a small fire going, Trace got some

jerky from his saddle pack and passed some to Ox.
He found it difficult to hold his emotions in check
as he calmly told Ox what they were going to do.
In his heart he did not want to leave Jamie in Plum's
hands for even one more night, and he had to keep
telling himself that it was best for her chances for
survival. Trace felt certain that Plum would kill her
if he was cornered. He explained to Ox again why
it was necessary to get them all out in the open.
"We've got to wait for daylight," he said, "but I
want to keep a watch on that cabin all night, just
in case they might decide to leave before sunup."
He paused for a moment, then, "How good a shot
are you?"

"I can shoot good," Ox was quick to reply. "I can
shoot better'n Sowers. Plum used to let me do some
of the huntin'."

"Well, you're gonna have to do some shootin' in
the morning, and we can't afford to miss." Trace
had no intention of taking prisoners. As far as he
was concerned, Plum and his partners had already
been tried, and the verdict was death. He cocked
his head and looked Ox straight in the eye. "Are
you sure you're gonna be able to cut down on your
old friends?"

"Plum and Crown weren't never no friends of
mine. I told you, Trace, I didn't know they was bad
men when Sowers asked me to join up. He lied to
me, so he ain't my friend either. Besides, they're
treatin' that woman bad."

Trace stared at the simple giant for a few seconds, wondering if he should just let him stay with the horses. Trace knew he could take Plum and the other two out one at a time if he could be sure Jamie would be safe. But he could not be sure one of them wouldn't kill her as soon as they were aware they were under attack. *No*, he told himself, *the safest way is for all three targets to be out where I can see them.* If Ox could account for one of them, Trace could take care of the other two before they knew what hit them.

Ox, eager to do his part, volunteered to take the first watch, so Trace rolled up in his buffalo robe and went to sleep. Tomorrow promised to be a busy day, and he wanted to be rested when the time came for action.

Inside the cabin there was a great deal of grousing and grumbling. Both Plum and Crown seemed to be in a foul mood, and Jamie did her best to stay out of the way. She especially tried to avoid Crown. He always leered at her, but tonight he seemed to be in a blacker mood than usual, and she felt the intense lust behind his sneering stare. Plum would usually take Crown to task for getting too rutty around her, but tonight he said nothing, although he seemed to be watching Crown closely. There was going to be trouble this night, she could feel it in her bones. Sowers, as usual, skulked in a corner of the little cabin, trying to remain as inconspicuous as she. Her intuition proved to be correct, for Plum and Crown were soon quarreling.

"I'm sayin' we're supposed to be equal partners," Crown fumed.

Plum fixed the sullen brute with a cold stare. "And I'm sayin' we ain't. If it wasn't for me, you'd be sweepin' the floor at Fort Cass, or starvin' to death somewhere, if the Injuns hadn't already lifted your hair."

"Maybe that's the way it was," Crown shot back, "but it ain't that way no more. You ain't got your precious Blackfeet brothers no more. Now it's just the three of us. Ain't that right, Sowers?"

Sowers blanched and mumbled something unintelligible, slinking farther back in his corner. He, like Jamie, could smell brimstone in the confined air of the tiny cabin.

Crown wasn't through. "From now on, we're all gonna share everythin'. By God, I've had enough of you playin' the boss." His eyes were burning black coals of hatred.

Plum did not take Crown's outburst lightly, but he remained calm as he considered the extent of the man's rage. Seeing that it might be in his best interest to make some concession, he decided to offer Crown a trade, knowing full well the real cause of Crown's agony. "Let me git one thing straight with you, Crown. If you don't know nothin' else in that loco head of your'n, know this—nobody salts Jack Plum's tail—and I'd just as soon cut your gizzard out as look atcha. But I'm a reasonable man, so I'll tell you what I'll do. Ain't no part of this here woman your'n, and that's the fact of it—she ain't part of the plunder. There's fifteen head of horses out there, and if we're gonna share all the plunder equal, like you said, then that means each one of us owns five of them horses. Ain't that right?"

"You're damn right," Crown grunted.

"All right, then," Plum continued, "since you're so all-fired rutty over this here woman, I'll make you a trade." Crown's eyes lit up at that, and Plum knew he could name his price. "I'll give you the woman for your five horses."

Crown jerked his head back, anger replacing the fleeting moment of ecstasy he had just glimpsed. "What?" he blurted out. "All my horses? What am I supposed to do, walk outta these mountains? I'll give you one horse fer her."

"I don't think so," Plum replied, smug in his advantage. "She's a mighty fine little woman, and I ain't gonna let her go for one damn horse . . . and that's a fact." He let Crown fume over that for a few moments before adding, " 'Course I don't expect you to walk. I'll loan you a horse to ride as long as you're riding with me."

Crown was almost livid with rage and exasperation at Plum's suggested trade. He wasn't sure that Plum was even serious about trading the woman. He might just be entertaining himself by taunting him. After all, Plum had been mighty stingy about sharing her up to now. Still, Crown's lust for Jamie had risen to near fever pitch, ruling out most practical thought on his part. One basic desire was foremost in his twisted brain—he wanted the woman. He made one counteroffer, having made up his mind that if Plum didn't accept it, he would damn sure kill him and take the woman. "I ain't gonna give up my horse. I'll give you four horses, and that's all." To his surprise Plum accepted.

In her corner of the shack, Jamie heard the consummation of the deal and was devastated by the thought of it. Plum had as much as handed her a death sentence. She had somewhat toughened herself to the brutal treatment at the hands of Jack Plum, had even gotten to the point where she could detach her thoughts from the sickening physical abuse while it was happening. But Crown was a different beast altogether. His sadistic urges could be gratified only by administering pain. She had heard Plum and Sowers talk too many times about the women Crown had killed while satisfying his perverted sexual drives. In her desperation she chanced the usual slap for speaking out and begged Plum, "Please don't trade me to him."

For once, Plum did not strike her for speaking without being told to. Instead, her plea brought a smile to his face. "It's a done deal—you're his'n. I reckon now you wish you'da been a helluva lot nicer to me." The look of distress on her face seemed to bring him a great deal of pleasure.

The lecherous grin on Crown's face terrified Jamie, and she felt her entire nervous system suddenly paralyzed by cold fear. Plum, on the other hand, felt he could relax a bit, knowing that Crown had been pacified for the time being. Sowers, still cowering in his corner, experienced a profound feeling of regret, for now he could be certain he had no chance of eventually taking possession of the woman himself.

"Come 'ere, darlin'," Crown cooed, gloating as he reached for his newly gained property.

Jamie screamed and pulled away from him, trying to dodge under his outstretched arms, but he caught her wrist and pulled her to him, locking her helpless in his powerful arms.

"If you're fixin' to git on her now, put a damn gag in her mouth," Plum said. "I don't wanna have to listen to that screamin'."

While Jamie struggled helplessly, Crown bound her hands together and tied a dirty bandanna over her mouth. When he had subdued her to the point where he could control her with one hand, he proceeded to grope her, pawing her body with sadistic glee, like a great bear. Even Plum was disgusted, while Sowers drooled with lascivious fascination, like a camp dog begging for scraps.

After a few minutes, during which Jamie tried to endure her torment, Crown noticed the stares of the other two men. Like a wolf guarding his kill, he became wary of Plum and Sowers. Resentful of having witnesses to his fulfillment of his innermost pleasures, and suddenly suspicious of Plum's willingness to share the girl, he became worried about a double cross. Plum was trying to catch him off guard, when he was satisfying his sexual desires—that had to be the reason Plum let him trade for the girl. Once the seed took hold in his mind, Crown was certain that Plum was intent upon taking advantage of him—probably with Sowers in cahoots. *Well, we'll see who's the smartest son of a bitch in this game.* Abruptly he stopped the pawing of his helpless victim and announced, "We're leavin'."

"Leavin'?" Plum replied. "Where the hell are you goin'?"

Still holding on to Jamie with one hand, Crown glared at Plum defiantly. "I said we're leavin', and I'll kill the first one tries to stop me." He paused long enough to fix Sowers with a menacing look before shifting his gaze back to Plum.

"Hell," Plum said nonchalantly, "ain't nobody gonna try to stop you. If you wanna freeze your ass off out there, go ahead . . . but I'd at least wait till morning."

Crown's devious mind was suspicious. Plum was being entirely too cooperative. "We're goin' now . . . me and the woman," he stated, waiting for any objection. When Plum's only response was a shrug, Crown shoved Jamie down on the floor. "Git your stuff. We're goin'."

Jamie's mind was in turmoil. She could see the

initial steps of her certain execution being put in motion. The thing she feared most had happened when Plum agreed to the trade with Crown, and now the lust-crazed maniac was going to drag her out in the snow to do his evil. Like a condemned prisoner, she resigned herself to her death. With her hands still tied, she gathered up the few articles of clothing she had. Crown hurriedly packed his parfleche and snatched up his bedroll, keeping a wary eye on Plum as he did so. He made a couple of trips out to the horses with his saddle and belongings before coming in for the last time to fetch Jamie. Plum watched Crown's departure with a show of disinterest, not even offering a comment as Crown picked Jamie up with one arm and went through the door.

When the door had closed behind them, Sowers found his tongue. "That's the craziest thing I ever saw," he exclaimed. "Ain't you gonna stop him?"

"Hell, no," Plum replied. That was his only comment for a long time. Then he added, "He'll be back." Plum knew Crown well enough to believe that he would turn up again when he had finished with the woman—he always did. Crown was crazy when he was consumed by desire, and there was nothing to do but let him have his fill and get over it. He'd be back, all right. Plum felt certain that the only way he would see the last of Crown would be to shoot him—and that day might not be far off.

High up on the far side of the rise, Ox sat, half

frozen and given in to the overpowering urge to sleep. A half hour earlier, he'd thought he heard something, maybe a muffled scream, but after listening for a while, he decided it was nothing more than the wind swirling the snowflakes around his buffalo robe. He pulled the warm fur of the buffalo hide closer around his ears and blinked his eyes deliberately in an effort to keep from closing them altogether. But soon the desire to sleep became too much to resist.

Crown wasted little time in clearing out. Jamie made one attempt to run while he was saddling his horse, and she paid dearly for it when Crown easily ran her down in the snow and struck her sharply across her half-frozen face. The blow was sufficient to leave her stunned and whimpering at his feet while he finished strapping the saddle on.

There were really only two main thoughts in Crown's head as he tied his bedroll and parfleche onto his horse. Foremost was the sadistic anticipation of a pleasure he had fantasized about ever since Jamie had been captured, and the need for some privacy to enjoy it. The second thought that was now developing in his head, as he kept glancing back at the cabin, was to say to hell with the trade he had agreed to. He had the girl now. Plum and Sowers were too damn lazy to even come outside to watch him. There was no one to stop him from taking his other four horses as well. Taking a rope from his saddle, he tied the best four horses in the bunch on a line behind his horse. Anxious to put some distance between himself and the cabin, in case Plum might be planning to double-cross him, Crown lifted Jamie up into his saddle. Climbing on behind her, he started down the river, leading the extra horses behind him. A smug smile creased his face as he pictured Plum when he came out in the morning and discovered that Crown had the girl and the horses too.

It was well past midnight when Trace climbed back up to the top of the rise. There he found Ox sleeping peacefully. He had to shake the huge man several times before he reluctantly opened his eyes. When he found himself staring into Trace's face, he jumped, at once alarmed.

"How long have you been asleep?" Trace asked, making an effort to hide his annoyance.

"I don't . . . not but a minute," Ox stammered, mortified by his failure to stay awake. "I think I just closed my eyes for a second or two." He could read the concern in Trace's face as the rugged mountain man stood over him. "I swear, Trace, I didn't mean to close my eyes."

The look of total despair on his face was too much for Trace. He found it difficult to chastise him. "Never mind," he said after a long pause. "Go on back by the fire. I'll call you when it's time."

Apologetic and contrite, Ox shuffled back down

to the camp and promptly went back to sleep by the small fire. Trace settled himself where he could watch the door of the cabin in the edge of the trees below. Everything appeared to be the same as when he had left Ox to watch it. There was no sign of anyone outside the cabin, and he could just make out the dark forms of the horses in the shadow of the trees behind.

When it appeared that Ox's nap had not done any harm, Trace's irritation with him gave way to thoughts of concern. What could he do with the man? Ox was no more than a child mentally, but Trace wondered if it wasn't more a lack of upbringing and experience than of inborn stupidity. He believed Ox when he said he didn't know Plum and Crown were evil men when he joined up with them. *But what the hell am I gonna do with him?* he wondered, for he had a feeling Ox had latched on to him whether he liked it or not. Trace shook his head firmly to clear his mind. *I'll deal with that when the time comes. I ain't got time to worry about it now.*

The first rays of morning light crept down along the river bottom, and Trace moved behind a runty pine to conceal himself as he continued to watch the cabin. It was only a few minutes later that the dark forms of the horses in the trees behind the cabin began to take on definition. Trace studied the horses for a moment. Something didn't look right. He had counted fifteen horses there the day before.

*Maybe some of them moved farther back toward the water,* he told himself.

The cabin door opened, dragging on the crusted snow, and Trace saw the silhouette of a man standing just inside, obviously taking a cautious look around before stepping out. After a brief pause of no more than half a minute he stepped outside. Trace recognized him as the man Ox called Sowers. Sowers stepped a few paces away from the door by a stack of firewood and emptied his bladder. Then he picked up a couple of pieces of wood from the pile and went back inside. *It would have been an easy shot,* Trace thought as he reminded himself to wait for the right opportunity.

After a short wait, the sun popped over the lower end of the valley, and Trace decided it was time to wake Ox. He made his way down the slope and found Ox sleeping as soundly as a baby. Trace just stood over him for a few moments shaking his head, wondering again if his simpleminded partner could be counted on to do his part when the shooting started. He knelt down and shook the huge man gently. After a moment, Ox sat up and rubbed the sleep from his eyes. When his gaze fell on Trace, he smiled broadly. *Just like a damn duck,* Trace thought. *Wakes up in a new world every day.* To Ox he said, "Time to get up on the ridge. They ought to be coming out soon."

They waited and watched. There was very little activity in the cabin below them. Trace had seen

Sowers come outside before he woke Ox. Later, Plum showed his face for the first time, but there was no sign of Jamie or Crown. And Trace was certain Crown was there because he had seen him the evening before when he had worked his way down behind the cabin. While he continued to watch, Sowers came out again and started toward the trees where the horses were tied. Something was wrong— Sowers stopped when he was only halfway to the trees. He hesitated there for a few minutes, then promptly turned on his heel and returned to the cabin to summon Plum. Moments later, the two men appeared again, conferred briefly, and went back inside. It was obvious to Trace that some of their horses were missing. There was still no sign of Jamie, although he had to assume she was inside the cabin. He decided he had waited long enough—it was time to act.

Trace led Ox down the slope to a clump of bushes half buried in the snow. "Dig in here behind these bushes. Your man is Sowers, all right?" Ox nodded. Trace looked him dead in the eye then. "You understand, now. You aim at Sowers—I'm not going to worry about him because I know you'll take care of him. Right?" Trace wanted to make sure Ox understood the importance of taking the right man. Ox assured him that he would concentrate on Sowers, and Sowers only. "All right," Trace continued. "I'm gonna work my way down behind 'em, and see if I can smoke 'em outta that cabin. When they come out, be careful you don't hit Jamie . . . or me. I'm gonna leave my rifle with you. I can shoot faster with my bow." Ox nodded excitedly and took the rifle from Trace's hand. "Sowers," Trace reminded him one final time before disappearing below the brow of the ridge.

The icy wind, blowing clouds of snow that swirled around him like a ghostly white dust, went unnoticed by Trace, for his total concentration was on the cabin before him. The early-morning sun glistened on the hard snow and reflected in his eyes, causing him to pull his beaver-fur cap low on his forehead. Coming up behind the cabin as he had the night before, he could see that some of the horses were definitely missing. He paused to scan the trees along the riverbank to see if they had simply wandered, but there was no sign of them—and the remaining horses were all hobbled. It gave him pause to consider what that meant, for he now realized that they had been gone since the night before. The obvious conclusion would be that someone had left, probably while Ox was asleep. It was a troubling thought, especially since there had been no sign of Jamie or Crown that morning. He stopped to consider the problem. After a few moments, weighing the possible consequences, he decided to go ahead as he had planned and assume there were four people still inside the cabin.

Moving silently up to the rear wall of the cabin, Trace brushed enough snow away to get a grip on the roof overhang and pulled himself up. Placing each foot slowly and carefully, he climbed up the roof to the short stone chimney. From his high vantage point on top of the cabin, he looked up the rise to the clump of bushes where Ox was waiting. Upon seeing Trace on the roof of the cabin, Ox stood up and raised his rifle, ready to fire. Trace cursed silently. The big simpleton presented a huge target for anyone just happening to glance his way. Trace tried to signal Ox to get down, but Ox simply waved back and continued to stand.

Trace's plan was to heap snow down the chimney, forcing Plum and his partners outside, but before he had scooped up the first armload of snow, he heard the cabin door open below him. He paused to listen.

Plum pushed the door open and peered outside. He glanced back at Sowers, asleep by the fireplace. If Plum had not felt the need to answer nature's call, he would have kicked Sowers awake and ordered him to get a couple of logs for the fire. Since he was going out anyway, he decided to get the wood himself. Now something caused him to pause in the doorway, stunned. Was it a ghost? Plum wasn't sure, but it damn sure looked like Ox standing halfway up the slope in front of the cabin. Plum hesitated, not certain what to do. He had his pistols in his belt as always, but his rifle was inside, next to the fireplace. He blinked rapidly and looked again. Ox was still there. Then, behind him,

he heard the soft thump of a blanket of snow landing on the fire, followed by two more thumps in
quick succession. A movement caught his eye, and
he glanced out in front of the cabin and saw the
shadow of a man standing on the roof, clearly sil-
houetted on the snow. He knew at once what was
happening and realized he had no time to think
about it. His instinct told him he had no chance if
he was trapped inside the cabin. There was no
thought of alerting Sowers to the impending danger. To the contrary, Plum's chances of saving his
own skin might be improved if the raiders remained unaware of having been discovered. So
without pause he slid out the door, hugging the
wall of the cabin, up under the eaves. He moved
quickly to the corner of the shack, hoping he had
not yet been seen. Though hidden from the man
on the roof, he was in plain view of Ox. He managed to round the corner only seconds before Ox's
rifle ball splintered the logs behind him.

Up on the roof, Trace uttered an oath under his
breath and dropped to one knee, an arrow notched,
three others in his left hand. There was no chance
of catching all three men out in the open, since Ox's
premature shot had alerted anyone still inside. Then
below him, inside the cabin, he could hear Sowers
crashing into things as he awoke in a panic. Trace
got ready. In a moment, Sowers came charging out
the door, rifle in hand. He stumbled when the first
arrow hit him solidly between the shoulder blades,

then the second one buried its head deep in his lower back, and he tumbled headfirst in the snow.

Hidden from above, and pressed close to the corner of the cabin, Plum witnessed Sowers's execution. Seeing the arrows protruding from Sowers's back, Plum quickly concluded that they were being attacked by a band of Indians. He didn't waste time wondering how Ox happened to be with them. His immediate thought was to save himself. Frantically searching the trees behind him where the horses were hobbled, he could see no sign of Indians. Maybe he was in luck.

From the front of the cabin, Plum could hear Sowers moaning, and then calling, "Plum, I'm shot . . . help me . . . Plum!"

With no thought at all of helping his old partner, Plum moved along the side of the cabin to the back corner, then he ran as quickly as he could into the trees. *You'll play hell trying to catch Jack Plum,* he thought, grinning in spite of the danger behind him.

Trace waited for only a moment to see if anyone else was coming out before sliding down the roof to the ground, rolling as he landed in the snow, another arrow notched on his bowstring. One glance at Sowers told him there was no danger from that quarter, so he moved quickly to the open door of the cabin. Pulling the pistol from his belt, he bolted inside and found an empty cabin. *Where was Plum?* As soon as he thought it, he heard the sound of a horse bounding through the snow. He charged out the door and rounded the corner of the cabin just in time to see Plum disappear in the trees, whipping his horse mercilessly. In frustration, Trace fired his pistol at the fleeing man, knowing the shot would not reach him.

He would have caught one of the other horses and given chase, but he had a greater concern at that moment—where was Jamie? He ran back around to the front of the cabin just as Ox came stomping down the snow-covered slope, a rifle in each hand.

"Plum's got away!" Ox shouted, pointing toward the river.

"I know," Trace answered. "I'll worry about him later. We've got to find Jamie." He knelt beside Sowers and rolled him over on his side.

Sowers groaned, his lifeblood seeping out around the arrow shafts in his back. He would not last long. Dazed and confused, he looked up into the face of Ox standing above him. "Ox," he rasped, "is that you?" Ox said nothing, but nodded, his simple smile fixed in place. "Am I dead?" Sowers asked.

Before Ox could speak, Trace answered. "Yes, you're dead. Now you must tell the truth. Where is the girl?"

Sowers, fading rapidly, paused to think as if he were trying to remember. Finally he replied, his voice no more than a whisper now, "Crown took her."

"Where?" Trace blurted, but Sowers was gone.

They stood there looking down at the dead man for a few moments. Then Ox stated bluntly, "Crown'll kill her."

There was no time to waste. Trace did not doubt that what Ox said was true, and the man had at least half a day's start—more than that by the time Trace was able to determine which way Crown had gone. Trace sent Ox to fetch their horses and ran to the trees where the renegades' mounts had been hobbled. Most of them had scattered when Plum cut their hobbles, seeking to create a diversion to mask his own escape. The many tracks made a difficult task even harder, for the freed horses had run in all directions, creating a confusion of trails.

On foot, Trace circled the stand of trees, looking for a trail leading away from the cabin. By the time Ox returned with the horses, Trace had found what he was looking for. Ignoring the fresh, sharply defined hoofprints of the scattered horses, he focused on a trail left by at least four horses, maybe more. Their tracks were not so sharply defined, telling Trace that they had been made the night before, and the morning's bright sunshine had melted the edges enough to soften them. He followed the tracks on foot for thirty or forty yards, studying them closely until he was able to confirm that one of the horses was carrying a load while the others were not.

"This is the trail," he told Ox, and he stood up and followed it with his eyes until it disappeared over a hill some three hundred yards downriver.

"What about Plum?" Ox asked. "He's gonna git away."

"Maybe so, but I have to go after Jamie. I may already be too late."

Ox was beside himself with remorse. "I'm sorry I shot at Plum, Trace," he lamented. "You told me to just shoot Sowers, but I thought Plum was Sowers when he come out the door, so I fired. If I hadn't missed, Plum wouldn't of got away."

"Things don't always work out," Trace said as he hurriedly prepared to go after Crown. There was no time to spend on remorse. "Don't fret about it—at least we got one of 'em."

"Yeah," Ox said, and looked back at the dark lump lying still in front of the cabin. "Poor ol' Sowers," he muttered in a fit of compassion for the man he had at one time thought a friend. "It's Plum's fault." Ox looked at Trace, a stern look of indignation on his face. "Plum's a bad man, Trace. He ought not git away."

"Dammit, Ox, it's too bad, but I've got no choice. I've got to find Jamie."

Ox drew himself up to his full height and beat his fist against his chest in a show of bravado. "I can catch Plum for you, Trace. I'll make him sorry he ever treated Jamie that way."

"The hell you can," Trace shot back. Seeing the injured expression on the huge man's face, he tried to soften his words, knowing inside that he didn't have time to reason with Ox. "Plum's sly as a fox.

We need to go after him together—the two of us. Let's find Jamie first." Thinking that would be the end of it, he climbed up on his pony and wheeled him around, ready to ride.

Ox may have been childlike about most things, but he was smart enough to know that Plum had been able to escape because he had stood up in plain view, allowing Plum to see him. If he had remained hidden behind the bushes, both Plum and Sowers would probably have come out of the cabin to see what had happened to put their fire out. Ox felt that he had failed Trace, and he was desperate to do something to make up for it. Plum was an evil man and should not be allowed to escape, so Ox decided this was a way to make up for his mistake. "I let him git away . . . I'll go bring him back," he said with firm resolution.

"What?" Trace asked sharply. There was no time to mince words. "Dammit, Ox, that man'll kill you. He's mean clear through. We'll get him later. Now come on, we're wasting time."

Ox was adamant. "No. You go on—I'm goin' after Plum."

Trace stared at Ox in disbelief. Sidestepping and pawing at the snow, the paint was anxious to get moving, and Trace had to use a great deal of force on the reins to hold him back. Trace could delay no longer. "If your mind's made up, I reckon I can't stop you. You're a grown man, and I reckon you can make your own decisions." He reached over and placed his hand on the big man's forearm. "But, Ox, be damn careful and watch your back. If everything goes well, we'll meet back at the cabin." He released the tension on the reins, and the paint lunged forward a few yards before settling into a gait. Trace looked back one last time and yelled, "If you can't catch him, come on back to the cabin. He'll probably come back to get his horses." Trace couldn't imagine a man like Plum giving up and hightailing it that easily.

# CHAPTER 12

Jack Plum was not one to be run off by anyone, leaving horses and all his possessions behind. And he was not at all content to play the role of the victim. Back at the cabin, he had realized immediately that he was in a trap, and he had no choice but to escape as quickly as possible. Thinking his attackers were Indians, he had run for the horses, cutting their hobbles as he pushed and shoved his way through them, hoping his pursuers would stop to chase the animals and leave him be. To make his getaway, he jumped on Sowers's horse—the only one with a halter still on—and dashed out along the snowy riverbank. Flogging the animal mercilessly, he scanned the bluffs above him for signs of pursuing Indians trying to cut him off. Even as he ran for his life, he was already planning his retaliation against the raiders.

As his horse pounded along the frozen riverbank, it suddenly registered that no one was chasing him. Not only that, but he also realized that he had heard no war whoops or scalp cries. He slowed the toiling pony to a walk, then finally to a halt, while he listened, straining to catch any sound on the wind. All was silent. A tiny suspicion wormed its way into his mind. He couldn't say for sure that there were any more than two men who had jumped Sowers and him. He had seen Ox on the slope, and the shadow of one man on the roof. *That weren't no damn war party*, he told himself, as he jerked his horse around and stood facing the trail he had just made in the snow.

*Only two men*, he thought. *Ox, that simple fool, but who was the other? Crown?* "Nah," he muttered, "Crown's long gone. He won't come back till he's finished with the woman." He decided it didn't matter who the other man was, he was as good as dead as far as Plum was concerned. And Ox—that fool might have come back from the dead once, but Plum was determined he wouldn't make it twice.

Trace pushed his pony hard, pausing only for short rests to keep from riding the paint into the ground. While he had some worrisome thoughts about Ox going after Plum, his mind was almost totally consumed with his concern for Jamie. Too much time had passed since Crown had taken the girl from the cabin. Anything could have happened by now, and he chastised himself for not making his play the night before. He tried not to picture the terror she might be facing, but it was difficult to erase the thoughts from his mind. For most of the long weeks he had searched for Jamie, he had strived to keep the girl's fate out of his thoughts, knowing that getting caught up in his anger and despair could cause him to become careless. But now, as he doggedly followed the trail in the snow, he found it more and more difficult to control his anger. *What if Jamie is dead?* he kept asking himself. Would it be possible to extract enough pain from Crown to subdue the fire of his anguish?

When darkness fell, he paused to rest his horse and build a small fire to warm himself. A few hours later, when the moon rose over the valley, he was in the saddle again, following the trail brightly lit in the moonlight. Crown had evidently sought to put plenty of distance between himself and his partners back at the cabin before stopping. Trace had come upon no campsite so far, so he knew he was going to have to push even harder if he wanted to overtake Crown before he made camp. At least he had not found any signs that would indicate Crown had stopped. And he figured that as long as Crown stayed on the move, Jamie could not be suffering too much.

How much more could she endure? Jamie rode now on one of the spare horses Crown had taken, her hands bound together, the horse's halter tied to the back of Crown's saddle. Slumped forward, her chin almost resting on her chest, she rocked with the horse's steady rhythm, her swollen and bruised face throbbing with each step the animal took.

She had finally been pushed to the point where she vowed to take no more abuse without fighting back, but her defiance was short-lived. When Crown had thrown her on his horse in the middle of the night and left Plum and Sowers, she had violently struggled against his childish groping of her body. When he struck her for her resistance, she struck back at him. Her defiance tended to please him, and he retaliated by pulling her off the horse and whipping her viciously with a willow switch. Even then she spat at him, determined that though she might be destined to die shortly, she would not go passively.

Crown pushed on through the night, not stopping even when the sun found them the next morning. Not until well after the noon hour did he decide to stop and make camp. This was the time she most dreaded, because up to that point he had restricted himself to his immature pawing and fondling. She knew with fatal certainty that he was saving her torment until he made camp. *How can I defend myself?* her weary mind asked. Crown was a powerful man, and she had no weapon other than her hands and feet. But she was determined to do what she could to fend him off.

As soon as he selected his campsite, Crown built a fire. When it was burning satisfactorily, he grabbed Jamie and dragged her over to a tree, where he bound her securely, grinning broadly at her feeble efforts to fight against him. Instead of assaulting her immediately, he got back on his horse and rode back the way they had come. He retraced their trail for almost a mile until he came to a high ridge where he could look over his backtrail for a considerable distance. He didn't trust Plum, and he had to make sure he wasn't being tailed. For as far as he could see, there was no sign of any living thing. The moaning of the wind as it whistled through the valley seemed to confirm the emptiness. Crown smiled. Everything was just as he wanted, and he joyfully anticipated the evening of pleasure awaiting him.

Jamie strained against her bonds until she was exhausted. It was no use, Crown had made sure of his knots. He would soon be back, and the heinous moment she had lived in fear of would be upon her. Knowing in her heart that he would certainly kill her when he was finished with his sadistic pleasure, she tried to will herself to be strong and to resist to the end. Even as she fought to strengthen her resolve, she felt the tears streaming down her face, and she whispered into the cold white emptiness, "Mama, I'm scared," a phrase she had not uttered since she was a little girl.

She heard him coming, his horse breathing hard with the exertion of plowing through the snow, and she felt her body grow numb with dread. In a few moments, he pulled up and dismounted, leaving the saddle on the exhausted animal. The evil grin spread across his grimy face was enough to tell her what lay ahead for her, and she cringed as he stood over her.

"Now, Miss Prissy, there ain't nobody to bother us," he gloated, "and you gonna git rode like you ain't never been rode before."

Summoning all the courage she could muster, she spat through swollen lips, "Don't you come near me, you filthy pig, or you'll wish you hadn't."

Crown laughed, delighted. "That's right, honey, spit and claw like a damn wildcat. The rougher it is, the better I like it." He stood over her for a long moment, leering like a glutton about to partake of a feast. She steeled herself for his assault, but he only laughed again and said, "First I'm gonna git me somethin' to eat. I'd give you somethin' too, but it'd be a waste of good buffalo jerky, 'cause you ain't never gonna eat agin after we're done tonight."

Jamie strained against her bonds, the rawhide thongs cutting deeply into her wrists. Amused by her efforts to free herself, Crown watched while he ate, chewing the tough jerky until tiny rivulets of saliva formed at the corners of his mouth. "Now tomorrow I might have me somethin' besides buffalo— maybe some of this haunch." He reached over and grabbed for her bottom. She jerked away from his reach, moving as far away as the rope that bound her to the tree would permit. He laughed and said, "You know, I et a Cree woman once, but I ain't never et no white woman."

He got to his feet and stood over her again. In a sudden lunge, he bent down and grabbed her breast. She screamed and kicked him hard between his legs, causing him to double up with a loud grunt and back away to recover. She had hurt him, but not badly, and he glared at her, fury raging in his eyes while he waited for the pain to subside. She stared back at him, her eyes glazed with terror, knowing his retaliation would be brutal.

His recovery took no more than a few minutes, and his rage increased with every second. Moving near her again, he snarled, "You're gonna rue the day you ever done that," and struck her hard with his fist against the side of her face. Her chin snapped around with the force of the blow, sending her brain reeling. Before she could recover, he methodically rained a series of blows on her face and head until everything went dark and she slipped into the black void of unconsciousness.

When she awoke, it was to a world of pain. Darkness had fallen, and Crown had built the fire up until it was a roaring inferno. She tried to move, but found she could not. Her head was still in a fog, and she was not aware at first that he had dragged her over to two small trees. Her hands, no longer tied together, were strapped one to each tree, stretching her arms apart so that she was spread out on the snow. When her mind began to clear, she became aware of the blood caked on her face and the dull pounding in her brain. Nauseated from the blood she had swallowed, she knew then that she was beaten. There was no longer any will to resist, or even to survive. Evidently there were many degrees of dying, and she was sure that she must be already in the final stages.

Crown sat staring at her, waiting for signs that she was coming to. He was afraid for a while that he had killed her in his rage and thus deprived himself of the torture that brought him his greatest pleasure. He smiled when he saw her stirring—he would give her a few minutes more, so she would be fully aware of the hell he planned for her. When she had been unconscious, he had ripped away part of her clothing, amusing himself with crudely groping her helpless body while he waited for her to revive. He might have done more, but he was still sensitive from the kick she had given him earlier, so it was necessary to delay his pleasure for a while. But now he was ready.

Though she was conscious, Jamie's mind was spinning wildly, back and forth between reality and a misty shroud of half-light in which Crown appeared to be a ghostly image. She was no longer sure he was even real until he grasped one of her ankles in each hand. Then the pain returned as her head started to clear, and she became fully aware of what was happening. Holding her legs apart, he dropped to his knees and forced his body closer to her. Staring horrified through swollen eyes, she was haunted by the repulsive image of Crown's sinister face, gloating over his conquest. Then suddenly his face was no longer there.

The butt of the rifle smashed against the side of Crown's face with such force that it sent the surprised renegade sprawling. Holding his rifle by the barrel, Trace had swung it with all the strength he had. The impact with Crown's head was sufficient to splinter the rifle stock, sending pieces of the wood flying and making a sound louder than the crack of a rifle shot.

Crown rolled over, dazed for only a moment before he struggled to his feet and prepared to fight. Ignoring the stabbing pain of his broken jaw, he drew a long skinning knife from his belt and slowly advanced toward Trace. In a sudden spark of memory, he recognized Trace as the meddling stranger who had spoiled his opportunity to take the Murdock family's wagon back on the Wind River. In spite of the pain it caused him, he managed a crooked grin as he moved cautiously to Trace's right, holding the Green River knife in front of him and moving it back and forth, taunting.

Crown was a powerful man, thick through the shoulders, with legs like tree trunks. He had killed more than one man in hand-to-hand fights, and he was confident of the outcome of this contest.

However this time he faced the lightning-like fury of the Mountain Hawk.

Trace watched with cold and unblinking eyes as the menacing hulk advanced slowly but confidently in a half-crouch, tensed for a sudden attack. *Come on*, he thought, *bring it to me*. Trace could have ended it earlier, quickly and without endangering himself. A rifle ball in the back would have done the job. But to satisfy a rage that had been smoldering for many weeks, he had to rip this vermin's life from him with his own hands.

Suddenly Crown attacked. Lunging at Trace, he thrust viciously with the long knife. Much too quick for Crown, Trace easily avoided the wild charge, stepping aside and catching the renegade with another solid smash of his rifle, which landed squarely on Crown's nose. The blow stopped Crown in his tracks, and he dropped to his knees, dazed. The remaining piece of the wooden rifle stock now dangled from a single splinter. Trace unhurriedly broke it off and tossed it aside. Although he appeared to be calm and methodical as he slowly circled the injured man, Trace was actually a volcano of vengeful fury. Swinging the broken rifle like an axe, he brought it down on Crown's skull. Crown was driven down into the snow, face first. Trace stepped back and waited. After a few seconds Crown, battered and bleeding, struggled to get up. Holding the rifle by the trigger guard now, Trace calmly walked around to stand before Crown, who was now on his knees again. His nose was splintered and flattened against his face, and blood flowed into his dingy beard. Crown stared, confused and disoriented, realizing that this was his moment to meet death's dark angel. Trace put the

barrel of the rifle up to Crown's face and held it
there for a moment. Then he pulled the trigger.

It had been too long. Jamie was afraid to believe
her nightmare was over. Her body was racked with
the pain of so many brutal beatings. Her face was
swollen and bruised, and she felt sick inside, having been nourished that day with nothing more than
her own blood, flowing from the cuts in her mouth.
She stared at the man hurriedly cutting her bonds,
uncertain of what was happening. And then the reality of it slowly penetrated her confused mind.
"Trace?" she whispered, barely making a sound.

Still locked within the grip of his overpowering
fury for the loathsome monster who had tormented
Jamie, Trace was unable to move for a moment. The
sound of his name on her battered lips snapped him
out of his trance and caused him to pause and gaze
into her eyes. He stifled a gasp when he read the
hurt in those gray, pleading eyes. "I've come to take
you home, Jamie," he said softly, and he gently
wrapped her torn clothing around her, covering her
exposed skin. Then he picked her up in his arms
and carried her over by the fire to warm her.

"Trace?" she whispered again, her voice that of a
small frightened child.

"Yes, it's Trace," he answered. "You're safe now,
Jamie, I'll take care of you." He made no attempt to
express the hurt that he felt for her—it went beyond
the limits of the spoken word. He felt her arms

tighten around his neck and her body press close to his chest, and she began to cry—tears of relief but also tears of despair. Still afraid to believe her ordeal was over, she held on to Trace with all the strength she had left while the agony of the past months flowed out with her tears. Trace held her until he felt her body relax.

He placed her gently on a bed of pine boughs and covered her with his thick buffalo robe, then sat by her side until she drifted off to sleep. His heart went out to the slight figure who had suffered such brutal treatment at the hands of Plum and Crown. As he watched her sleeping, he noticed a gradual quickening of her breathing, followed by a restless fit of movement back and forth, and he guessed that she must be dreaming. As the restlessness increased, she began moaning softly. Suddenly she cried out in her sleep and Trace pulled her close to him to comfort her. "No! No!" she cried pitifully and struggled against his arms. Finally she screamed, "No!" defiantly and began to hammer her fists against Trace's chest.

"Easy, Jamie," he murmured rocking her gently in his arms. "You're all right now. You're with Trace. It's just a bad dream." After a few moments, her eyes flickered, then opened, and she stopped struggling. She stared into his face for a long moment before starting to sob. Trace felt her body go limp as she let him cuddle her. It was enough to break his heart, to think of the torment she must have suffered. In a little while she stopped crying and was quiet. He rocked her gently until she began breathing heavily again and he knew she was asleep.

Looking at her face, he realized that he would have been unable to recognize her, even without the horrible mutilation of her face, for she was barely more than skin and bones. *We've got to fatten you up,* he thought.

"Trace!" she rasped as soon as he moved.

"I'm not gonna leave you alone. I'm just trying to find something to eat." He knelt down and put his hand on her hair, stroking it until she lay back again. "I don't have much to give you but dried buffalo. I reckon that'll have to do until I can hunt us up something." Fresh meat was what she needed, but he knew he could not leave her alone.

"Trace," she called again.

"Yes," he replied.

With her eyes still closed, she asked, "Why in hell didn't you come after me?"

He was surprised by the question, but encouraged to hear her tone. Maybe there was still a spark of the old Jamie in her yet. "I came as quick as I could," he answered simply. "You weren't that easy to find."

The next morning Jamie was much improved, having benefited from the first night of uninterrupted sleep she had enjoyed in weeks. It would be some time yet before she even approached her full strength, though. Trace stressed the necessity for fresh meat, and she reluctantly permitted him to leave her and go hunting, but only after he loaded Crown's rifle for her. He would hunt with his bow because it was silent, but also because his Hawken was out of commission until he could fashion a new stock for it. When he rode out of their camp, she was sitting with her back against a tree, the rifle across her lap and Trace's pistol in her hand.

They spent two more days in the camp that Crown had established. Jamie began to get much of her strength back, nourished by the heart and liver of the mule deer Trace had killed. There was no mention of the frozen body lying at the bottom of a deep gully some twenty-five yards away. Trace decided that if Jamie felt the need to talk about her ordeal with Crown, she would broach the subject herself.

"Pretty bad, huh?" she blurted out and pushed her chin up, thrusting her face forward. "It's getting better. Some of the swelling must have gone down around my eyes, 'cause it doesn't seem like I'm squinting through a crack every time I try to look at something."

"You're coming along just fine," he assured her, thinking to himself that he doubted she would ever fully recover. The beatings had been too brutal. There were wide cuts on her cheeks where the skin had apparently split under the impact of Crown's fist— and there were old scars too, no doubt left from Plum's brutal attentions.

She watched his face carefully when he answered her, then asked, "How bad is it?"

"It's not bad at all, considering the beatings you musta took." He couldn't bring himself to tell her the truth. He was thankful that she had no mirror to see the destruction for herself. "You just need some healing time, and you'll be as sassy as ever."

She started to smile, but winced with the resulting pain from the split in her lip. "You always were a poor liar, Trace McCall," she muttered and lay back to rest.

As soon as he thought Jamie was able to travel, he saddled the horses and packed up their camp. Reluctant to climb into Crown's saddle, Jamie tried to explain to Trace the fearful feelings she had in the presence of anything that had belonged to the evil devil who had tormented her so. Trace understood what she tried to convey, and he had a great deal of compassion for her. But there was a matter of practicality to be considered—it would be a hell of a lot easier for her to ride with a saddle than bareback. He tried to convince her that the man's things couldn't hurt her—they were just *things*. Besides, as far as his saddle was concerned, Crown's evil was in his mind, not in his ass, so the saddle couldn't hurt her. In the end Trace switched saddles, putting his on Jamie's horse and using Crown's himself.

Jamie was further alarmed when he told her that he was not taking her back to Promise Valley right away. He explained that there were a couple of loose ends that he was obligated to tie up. Foremost was the matter of Jack Plum. That was a matter he had promised himself that he would take care of. He might not be required to take any action, depending upon whether or not Ox had been able to run Plum to ground. But he seriously doubted that Ox could have succeeded. Plum was far too clever for the simple giant. Trace hoped, for Ox's sake, that the big fellow had not caught up with Plum. Regardless, he had to return to Boss Pritchard's cabin because he had given his word to Ox that he would meet him there.

Jamie was astonished to learn that Ox was still alive. His wounds had appeared to be mortal when Plum had left him beside the trail to die. While she wanted desperately to go home, still she felt indebted to the big man who had tried to help her escape, so she did not plead with Trace to abandon Ox.

There were other reasons why Trace wanted to return to the cabin. He had been studying the sky that morning, and he didn't like the look of the clouds moving in from the north. There were a few high mountain passes between here and Promise Valley, and he didn't relish the idea of getting cut off by a snowstorm. It would be better to have a warm cabin in which to wait out the storm, stocked with provisions to last until spring if necessary. *It wouldn't hurt if Jamie had a little more time to heal up some before I take her back to her daddy, anyway,* Trace thought, but he did not say that to Jamie.

# CHAPTER 13

Almost certain now that there had been no more than two men who had attacked them at the cabin, Plum worked it over in his mind. The more he thought about it, the more his anger erupted inside him. *Two men!* he thought. *And one of them a half-wit.* If he had known there were only two, he would have gone back inside and retrieved his rifle. He and Sowers could have held them off from the cabin. He cursed himself for not taking a shot at the bastard on the roof, but he had thought he barely had time to escape an Indian war party. *We'll see who scalps who now, by God!* He turned his horse toward the bluffs above him and started working his way back. Below him, on the riverbank, Ox followed his trail. The two men passed within a hundred yards of each other, neither aware of the other.

Ox followed the obvious tracks in the snow, moving cautiously, stopping often to search the way ahead with his eyes before proceeding. Plum was as sly as a fox, as Ox was only too well aware. Trace had warned him to be careful and not take any chances, but it had been an unnecessary warning. Ox knew that Plum was the meanest man he'd ever seen—maybe with the exception of Crown. But that was the main reason Ox had insisted upon leaving Trace and going after Plum. His conscience was bothering him pretty badly—not just because he had fired prematurely back at the cabin, allowing Plum to escape, but for more serious reasons. He had stood by and done nothing to help Jamie when Plum was treating her so cruelly. If he had known that Jamie wasn't really Plum's wife, he might have stood up to the man. But he would make up for it now. He would follow Plum all the way to Canada if he had to.

Ox had tracked Plum through the snow for no more than three miles when his trail suddenly turned away from the river and climbed up into the bluffs. Following doggedly after him, Ox was surprised to find that once he had gained the top of the bluffs, Plum had turned around and was now headed back the way he had come. *Going back for the horses!* Ox thought. *Trace said he would.* He whipped his horse for more speed. He should have known that Plum would never leave all his horses and plunder. He wished then that he had waited back at the cabin for him to show up.

Ox couldn't tell if he was gaining any ground on Plum or not, but he knew he was within half a mile of the cabin, and there was still no sign of him. He would have to be very careful now. It wouldn't do for him to run up on Plum by surprise. Coming to the rise where he and Trace had kept watch on the little log shack below, Ox got off his horse and continued on down the slope on foot. Careful and alert, he took his time descending toward the cabin, his rifle charged and cocked. Before passing the clump of snow-covered bushes where he had hidden before, waiting for Sowers to come out, he paused and took a good look around. He saw smoke coming from the chimney and behind the cabin, in the trees, he saw that three of the horses had wandered back— Ox couldn't tell if they had been hobbled or not. It looked like Plum figured everybody was gone and he was left with all the plunder.

This called for some thought on Ox's part. It was apparent that Plum was in the cabin. And if Plum was watching the slope, he would be sure to see Ox long before he reached the bottom. Ox needed the element of surprise. Plum was fast and he was slick, too dangerous to be given any advance warning. Ox looked around him, trying to find a better way to advance on the shack. The best, he decided, would be to circle around to the back, the same way Trace had gone when he sneaked up to the cabin. If he stayed low, he could use the bushes for a screen for most of the way until he reached the pines that started halfway up the slope. Once he reached them, he could make his way down to the river and come up through the cottonwoods behind the cabin.

Because of the snow and the circuitous route Ox had to take, more than half an hour elapsed before he reached the trees where the horses were. Plum had hobbled them, he noted, and there, up close to the cabin, he saw Sowers's horse. *Ol' Sowers ain't gonna like that*, he thought, forgetting for the moment that Sowers was dead. Making his way slowly toward the cabin, Ox held his rifle before him, ready to fire at the first sign of movement from inside. At the back corner of the log structure, he stopped to listen. There was no sound but the wind and the heavy thump of his own heart as it beat against his chest. Inch by inch, he worked his way along the side of the cabin, placing each foot carefully to avoid making noise on the hard-crusted snow until he reached one of the small rifle ports that Boss Pritchard had cut on each side of his cabin to shoot through in case of attack. Slowly and silently, Ox stuck the barrel of his rifle through the port, just far enough to push aside the hide covering. As the wind swirled around the cabin, sweeping smoke from the chimney down around him, he peeked inside. Plum was rolled up in a thick robe, sleeping before the fireplace. Ox would have shot him then, but the port was not wide enough to bring his rifle to bear on the sleeping form—and he could not risk a miss. As slowly and quietly as he could manage, he withdrew the rifle barrel from the port and continued along the side of the cabin until he reached the front.

At the door now, he paused again and readied

himself for the attack. The element of surprise was extremely important. Checking his weapon once more, he stood with one hand on his rifle and the other on the door handle. One deep breath and he suddenly yanked the door open and stepped inside, firing into the form lying before the fire. The crack of the rifle echoed inside the tiny cabin, the sound reverberating off the log walls. Not waiting to assess the damage of his first shot, Ox dropped the rifle and pulled the pistol from his belt, sending another lead ball after the first. Two shots dead center, and the form did not move. Ox knew at once that he had been tricked. In a panic now to reload his weapons, he turned to find Plum pointing a rifle directly at his head.

"Well, now, if it ain't my old friend Ox." Plum's tone was heavy with sarcasm. "I wouldn't," he cautioned when Ox started to raise his empty pistol, "I'd put a ball between your eyes before you could swing it." When Ox dropped his hand to his side, Plum continued talking. "How many times have I gotta kill you? I thought you woulda learnt the first time that it don't pay to double-cross Jack Plum. And now you've done shot a good buffalo hide full of holes. Why, I halfway think you was planning to do me some hurt."

"I was gonna kill you. You shouldn'ta been so mean to that woman, Plum," Ox scolded. "You're an evil man." He stood there waiting, like a calf before the slaughter.

Plum grinned. "Well, I can't argue with that. I was just hopin' that it was that other son of a bitch trackin' me insteada you." He motioned with the rifle for Ox to step outside. "Who the hell was he, anyway?"

Ox hesitated. Would Trace want him to tell Plum who he was? Ox didn't know, and he was intent on doing the right thing for once. Finally he made up his mind that he didn't have to tell Plum anything. "He's my friend, and I ain't gonna tell you his name. He don't make fun of me like you and Crown do."

Plum smirked. "So he's your friend, is he? Well, you overgrown simpleton, let me tell you what's gonna happen to your friend—I'm gonna track him down and kill him. Whadaya think of that? I'm gonna cut his heart out and eat it."

Totally distressed by Plum's cruel taunting, the childlike giant could not see that he was simply being goaded into a suicidal attack for no other reason than to provide entertainment. "You've hurt enough people," Ox said, the excitement rising in his voice. "You leave Trace alone."

"Trace, is it?" Plum jeered. "I figured it might be that bastard the Injuns think is a damn hawk or somethin'. Well, your friend is gonna soon be a dead bird. I'm gonna string his guts up over a tree for the buzzards to eat . . . right after I'm done cuttin' you up for coyote bait."

Ox could stand no more of it. Blind with rage, he suddenly let out a frustrated bellow, lowered his head, and charged like an angry bull with one thought in his mind—to protect Trace McCall. Plum never wiped the smile from his face as he pulled the trigger and deftly sidestepped the charging bull. Although the rifle ball split dead-center, right between Ox's eyes, his momentum carried him rushing past Plum, and he crashed heavily to the ground. Unhurriedly, Plum drew his skinning knife from his belt and, grabbing Ox by the hair, pulled his head back. He slit the big man's throat from ear to ear.

"Now, you stupid son of a bitch, let's see you come back from this one."

Ox's corpse was too heavy to carry, so Plum tied a rope under his armpits and used his horse to drag it around behind the cabin, where he laid it beside those of Boss Pritchard and his two partners. He kicked a little snow over Ox to speed up the freezing process and make sure he wouldn't begin to smell before the spring thaw. Plum still planned to occupy the cabin until then.

His thoughts turned now to the man Ox had been so determined to protect. The name Trace meant nothing to Plum, but his common sense told him the odds were good that he had already met the man. Thinking back, he recalled the tall sandy-haired mountain man who had spoiled his plans to murder Paul Murdock's family and steal his wagon. He had thought at the time that the man might be the same one that the Blackfeet called Mountain Hawk. Now he was even more convinced. Who else could it be? There had been no other evidence of a lone white trapper in these parts.

Plum felt an urgency to deal with this mountain man who had now shown up twice to complicate his life. He had the sense to realize that Trace would not be as easy to dispose of as the moronic giant now lying underneath the snow behind the cabin. A little more cunning would be required perhaps, but Plum welcomed the challenge. The quicker the Mountain Hawk was dealt with, the sooner Plum could settle in the cabin and wait out the winter undisturbed.

Plum studied the hundreds of tracks the horses had stamped in the snow. He was as good a tracker as most of the Blackfeet he had ridden with, and he knew what he was looking for. Trace had obviously split off and followed Crown and the girl, so it was no chore to find the fresher tracks of one horse and rider, following Crown's older trail. As he gazed toward a point near the river's bend where the tracks disappeared in the distance, Plum considered the man he would stalk. Trace was tracking Crown. What would likely happen if he caught up with his old partner? It was even money, in Plum's mind, that Crown would get the best of that fight. On the other hand, if this Mountain Hawk happened to get the best of Crown, he might just take the girl and keep going. This possibility caused Plum to think about Jamie again. Maybe he had been a mite hasty to give Crown free rein with her. It was bound to be a long winter, and it would have been handy to have a woman to keep him warm. Then his sensible mind told him that if Crown was still alive, it most likely meant that both the mountain man and the girl were dead. *I reckon we'll just have to see what's what. But I want that damn woman back.*

Jamie lay still, wrapped in a warm buffalo hide, the hair side turned in to make a soft and snug bedroll. She had been awake now for several minutes, reluctant to open her eyes to acknowledge the morning. Her sleep had been deep and healing, free from the nightmares that had filled her dreams over these many weeks. Without opening her eyes, she knew that Trace was close by. She could hear him as he put wood on the fire and set a pot of snow in the ashes to make water for the coffee he had found in Crown's pack. It was a good feeling—to know Trace was near. The wounds on her face and body were tender and painful still, but she didn't care anymore because she knew she was safe. Finally she relented, giving in to the bright ray of sunshine that had focused on her face, and opened her eyes.

"I was beginning to wonder if you were gonna sleep all day," Trace said cheerfully when he glanced back and saw Jamie stirring.

She started to smile, but winced when the effort reminded her of her battered lips. "I think I could sleep right through the day if I didn't have to pee," she frankly admitted.

Leaving the coffeepot to heat in the coals, he moved to help her up. "Don't get too feisty now," he warned when she got to her feet too quickly and staggered a little. "You've took a helluva lot of punishment. You're gonna have to build your strength back up." He supported her with a hand on her arm. "Think you can make it?"

She assured him that she could, and after taking a moment to steady herself, she took a dozen tentative steps away from the fire and squatted in the snow. Realizing at once what she had done and feeling suddenly embarrassed, she asked him to turn his back. Then she glanced back at him and discovered he had already done so. She was overcome by a sense of shame. For months she had been treated with no more respect than that given a camp dog, forced to relieve herself with someone watching her, usually making lewd remarks. Though degrading and humiliating, she had had no choice, and in time she became numb to the gawking of her captors. Now things were suddenly different, and she felt ashamed to have sought no privacy in Trace's presence.

Finishing as quickly as possible, she moved back to the fire, her steps still unsteady, humiliation flushing her face and tears gathering in her eyes. She started to apologize, but before she could speak, Trace interrupted.

"It's all right, Jamie. I understand. I know what you had to go through."

She nodded silently, her tears spilling over and streaking down her bruised cheeks. He took her arm and gently lowered her back onto her bedroll. "I reckon you've been as close to hell as a body can get without dying, " he said, looking deep into her eyes. "Well, that's all over now. We'll have you back to your old self in no time." He endowed her with a great big smile. "Especially with my cooking." Forgetting her split lip again, she did her best to mirror his grin.

In spite of Trace's constant reassurances that she would be good as new in no time at all, Jamie knew that there was a wound deep inside her that she would never recover from. She felt a pox inside that had soiled her very soul—a feeling of rotting shame that no amount of cleansing could expunge. How then, could she even hope to recover her life? Of what value were her dreams of Trace McCall now? Through no fault of her own, she had been ruined, abused and ridden like a brood mare until there was no trace of decency left to her.

Sensing the cause of her sudden reluctance to talk and her growing despondency, Trace tried his best to take her mind off the treatment she had endured at the hands of her captors. He talked of her father and Buck Ransom, of the Bowens and Reverend Longstreet, and the other families waiting to welcome her back to Promise Valley. Nothing seemed to lift her spirits, and he feared that she was slipping into a permanent state of melancholia. The rode that day in virtual silence. Trace, not inclined to talk much himself as a rule, found it difficult to press a reluctant Jamie into any positive conversation. He soon gave up trying, and they rode on through the quiet of the snow-covered mountainsides.

While Jamie's thoughts were weighed heavily with guilt—for reasons she could not explain—still she was determined to piece her life back together. Her sadness came from the feeling that she must say farewell to the part of her that had embraced hopes of a life with marriage and children. In her mind, those prospects were lost forever. But there were other things to live for. She could go back to the valley and help build a home for her father. They could develop the little piece of land they had settled, plant crops, maybe even raise some cattle. Her life was not ended. One thing she promised herself, however; she would never be taken alive by Indians again. When she glanced ahead at the tall, straight figure of the mountain man, rocking easily with the motion of his horse, she no longer felt the old familiar tug on her heartstrings, but she was sure she would always have special feelings for Trace McCall.

Even though he was eager to return to the cabin to meet Ox, Trace made camp early that afternoon. Jamie was holding her own, but he knew it was best to stop and let her rest. He was further hampered by leading four extra horses, not counting the one

Jamie rode. Even making slow time, though, the
would reach the cabin before noon the following day

Seeking a sheltered spot up under the bank of th
river, Trace discovered a shallow cave that had bee
carved out by the waters during times when the rive
was high from spring flooding. He got a fire starte
and made a place for Jamie to rest at the back of th
small alcove. Once he had her settled comfortabl
and had prepared something for her to eat, his nex
chore was to gather enough cottonwood limbs t
strip for the extra horses he had to feed. From th
looks of them, it appeared that Crown had neglecte
feeding them for several days.

After the horses were fed and left to paw aroun
under the trees that lined the riverbank, Trace se
tled himself by the fire and began roasting his sup
per. Saying nothing for a long time, Jamie watche
the sandy-haired young man as he turned the stri
of meat over the flame. Finally she broke her silenc

"Trace, I want you to teach me how to shoot
gun," she said.

Somewhat surprised by her statement, he smile
and replied, "I thought you already knew how t
shoot—just aim the gun and pull the trigger."

"I don't mean that," she responded quickly. "
know how to do that. I mean, I want you to shov
me how to load it and clean it, and how to hit wha
I'm aiming at." She had made up her mind that sh
was not going to remain a helpless female in th
event of another crisis.

Trace thought back over the years to a time when amie was more tomboy than girl. She had gone unting with him once, and she had fired a rifle that lay. As he recalled, she had not proved especially andy with the weapon then. He couldn't help but mile when he pictured her reaction when her shot ad miraculously hit the target. "I suppose you hould learn a little about guns," he said. In his opinon, every woman west of the Missouri should know how to handle a rifle. "I'll show you how to load it and keep it from fouling, but I 'spect we better wait ill I get you back home before we do any target hooting."

He spent the better part of an hour teaching her o load and aim Crown's rifle. He showed her how o clean it and how to handle misfires and jams. She practiced aiming at various trees and rocks, and hefting the weight of the weapon. "When we get back o Promise, we'll do some target practice. That's the only way to get to know the rifle's habits—like a endency to shoot high or low, left or right."

By the time the shadows lengthened, connecting with those on the far side of the river, she felt very comfortable with her rifle. She was not bothered by he fact that it used to be Crown's rifle, as she had been with his saddle. Somehow a rifle seemed less personal than a saddle. Trace, relieved to see her thinking about something other than the pain she had suffered during the last few months, recognized he first signs that she was going to be all right again.

He excused himself to check on the horses, feeling that Jamie's wounds—even those deep inside—were on the way to healing.

She watched him as he disappeared over the top of the bank and into the trees, tall and straight, striding effortlessly and as natural as any animal born in the mountains. *It's going to be damn hard to put you out of my mind, Trace McCall.* Sighing inwardly, she brought her thoughts back to the river and concentrated on the icy ripples tugging at the rocks at the water's edge. A movement at the edge of her vision caused her to start, and she felt her heart skip a beat. Alert now, she peered at a clump of brush on the far side of the river. She could have sworn she saw something move there. At first afraid, she started to call Trace, but hesitated lest it was only the wind blowing the leaves. But there it was again. This time she saw a definite moving of the bushes, and she began to back slowly farther up under the bank, never taking her eyes from the spot on the other bank.

While she watched, her heart racing, a small gray head poked through the brush and drank from the river. "Damn!" she whispered. "A deer—you scared the hell outta me." Relieved, she almost laughed out loud. Then she realized it was the perfect opportunity to test her proficiency with the rifle. Moving very deliberately so as not to startle the unsuspecting animal, she measured the powder and poured it down the barrel, selected a lead ball and a patch,

amming them down, and picked a percussion cap
ut of the skin pouch. Ready now, she very slowly
ocked the hammer back and brought the rifle to her
houlder. Remembering what Trace had told her, she
ook a breath, held it, and slowly squeezed the trig-
er.

She felt the butt slam against her shoulder as the
harp crack of the rifle split the evening calm, scat-
ering a brace of birds nesting in a nearby bush, their
vings beating a staccato retreat into the trees. The
udden explosion brought an involuntary squeal
rom Jamie herself. She almost squealed a second
me when she saw the deer drop instantly, its head
till in the water. Filled with newfound confidence,
he rose to her feet and was about to wade out into
he chilly water when Trace appeared on the bank
bove her, panting from running through the snow,
is rifle ready, searching for the point of attack.

"Jamie! What the hell . . ." He stopped himself
rom saying what he was thinking. It was a dumb
hing she had done—that rifle shot could be heard
or miles, announcing their presence to every Indian
n the territory. Seeing the look of alarm in her eyes,
e knew that it was pointless to scold her. The se-
iousness of her thoughtless action had just occurred
o her.

"Trace, I'm sorry. I wasn't thinking. Damn, I'm
orry." She glanced quickly to all sides, expecting to
ee hostiles converging upon them.

He said nothing for a few moments while he con-

sidered the probability of an Indian hunting part
being in this section of the mountains. *What's dor
is done,* he decided. Finally, he spoke. "Pretty goo
shooting, but I reckon you'd best let me go fetc
your kill for you." He turned to head for his hors
"There's a better place to ford the river downstrear
a ways," he explained. Pausing at the top of th
bank, he added, "I expect it would be best to g
after game with my bow after this."

Jamie was furious, mostly with herself for bein
so stupid—but she was also a little mad at Trace fc
taking her blunder so calmly. He should have raise
holy hell with her, for shooting at a deer. Instead h
quietly let it pass like a benevolent and patient fathe
It was difficult to explain her feelings. It was jus
that she had finally resolved never ever to depen
on anyone to take care of her again. It was the rea
son she asked Trace to teach her to shoot in the firs
place. Frustrated, she picked up a stone and threv
it into the fire, sending sparks flying to land sizzlin
in the snow. Within fifteen minutes, Trace appeare
on the other side of the river, riding bareback on hi
Indian pony to retrieve the deer.

Trace watched Jamie while she reloaded her rifle
"This time, don't shoot it unless there's an Injun or
the other end of it," he said, grinning broadly. "Nov
I'm gonna take a little ride around this river bottom
to make sure we ain't got company coming to ea

some of that deer you shot." Her expression told him that she didn't appreciate his humor.

Guiding the paint up a snowy draw to the bluffs above the river, Trace made his way downriver beyond the point where he had forded to retrieve Jamie's deer. There were no tracks in the clean white expanse of snow but his own. He stopped there on the bluff and listened, turning slowly to look in every direction before moving on. There was no sign of another living thing for as far as he could see in the growing gloom of evening. Soon it would be dark, so he crossed the river and scouted the other side to a point well above his camp. By that time, it was no longer possible to see farther than a few dozen yards, so he returned to the shallow ford and crossed back to the other side.

When he returned, he found Jamie seated by the fire, her back to the steep riverbank, the rifle resting across her knees, keeping a sharp lookout. "It's me, Jamie," he called out when he rode into the trees where the horses were hobbled. "Don't shoot that damn rifle." After taking care of the horses, he began skinning the deer Jamie had killed. "I almost waited too late," he said. "He's damn near froze already."

# CHAPTER 14

Plum jerked back hard on the reins and listened
He smiled to himself when he was sure that he
had heard the unmistakable sound of a Hawken rifle
Crown had a Hawken. Plum had heard the distinct
crack of that rifle on more than a few occasions
Turning his head to minimize the whistling of the
wind around his fur cap, he strained to catch any
further sounds. One shot, that was all. He couldn't
be sure, but it seemed to have come from upwind—
hard to say how far, maybe three or more miles. Feeling confident that he had found his prey, he dug his
heels in his horse's sides and loped off down the
ridge toward the river. There would only be another
hour of daylight, if that much, so he hurried to close
the distance before darkness forced him to make
camp for the night.

Trace sat before the fire. While Jamie sat peacefully watching him, he worked away at a piece of
pine, whittling it into the rough shape of a rifle stock
It would not be a pretty thing, but it would have to

do for now. When they returned to Promise Valley, he could have Buck make him a new stock. Buck was handier than most when it came to working with his hands. "Well, that ain't too bad," he said, holding the half-finished carving up for Jamie to see. Having no drill to make holes for the screws, he took some rawhide thongs and tied the new stock on as best he could. The original stock had been attached to the frame with a couple of wedges and two screws to secure it. Trace's repaired version was a sight different from Mr. Hawken's original. He stared at his handiwork for a long time before raising the rifle to his shoulder to get the feel of it. Frowning, he said, "It'll have to do."

Putting the rifle aside, he turned to look at Jamie. The way her bruised and battered face looked, it was hard to believe that she had actually improved in the past couple of days. The thought of the abuse she had suffered caused the rage to rise in him, and he was almost sorry he had not drawn Crown's death out over a longer period of time. He could feel the anger burning inside him when he remembered that Plum was still out there somewhere. When he had left Ox to chase Plum, Trace's one thought was to get to Jamie as quickly as possible. Nothing else had mattered at that point. Now that Jamie was safe, he realized that he would have no peace of mind until he had settled with Plum. He should not have permitted Ox to go after Plum. The man was too dangerous. But Trace hadn't had the time to argue. Ox was determined to go. *I hope to hell he gave up right away and went back to the cabin to wait for me.* He felt responsible for the big simpleton. His thoughts were interrupted when he realized Jamie was staring at him, apparently having read the anger in his eyes.

"What is it?" she asked, concern in her voice.

"Nothing," he said quickly, his stern expression relaxing into a smile. "You'd best get some sleep. We'll be riding out early in the morning."

She moved back to the rear wall of the shallow cave, and Trace covered her with a heavy fur robe. Then he put some more wood on the fire to make sure her little alcove was snug and warm. Once he was satisfied that she was settled in for the night, he scaled the bank to take a good look around. He still had some concern over the thoughtless shot that Jamie had taken earlier. But even if it had been heard, they were probably better off where they were than they would have been if he had decided to stay on the move. At least this way they wouldn't be caught out in the open if a war party came searching for the source of the rifle shot. The camp he had picked was well protected, situated as it was up under the riverbank. From their position he could make it extremely costly for anyone who attacked them. His only concern was for the horses, as there was not enough room for them under the overhanging ledge and he had had to hobble them in the trees close to the water. He told himself that he was probably unnecessarily concerned about the possibility that a

hunting party was anywhere nearby—there had
been no sign of any other human being for days.
But he was well aware that it never paid to assume
you were alone in the mountains, especially in Indian country.

Satisfied that there was no sign of Indians near
their camp, Trace walked along the steep bank of
the river toward the stand of cottonwoods where he
had left the horses. Darkness was already descending upon the narrow valley, and he was careful to
watch his step. One misplaced foot and he might
find himself sliding down the steep bank to land in
the river, some twelve feet below him. The shallow
water close to the bank was covered over with a thin
layer of ice, so it would be a chilly bath indeed. The
thought made him shiver.

After checking on the horses, and spending a little extra time stroking the paint, Trace made his way
back along the bank to his camp. He took a moment
to tend the fire, then checked to see that Jamie was
sleeping peacefully. Kneeling before the frail and battered girl, her knees drawn up in a protective position, Trace shook his head in silent compassion. He
studied her face, now relaxed in slumber, no longer
frowning and twitching with haunting dreams of her
captivity. Though she now seemed free of such out-
ward signs of her ordeal, still Trace feared she would
always carry the scars inside from what she had endured. Shaking his head again, he swallowed hard,

wishing he could tell her that they would all go away.

He wrapped his blanket around himself and lay down before the sleeping girl, positioning himself between her and any attack that might come. With his rifle and pistol within easy reach, he tried to catch a few hours' sleep.

Trace awoke to an overcast sky. Heavy clouds formed a dark ceiling over the narrow river valley, and in the air there was the definite feel of snow on the way. It seemed that his earlier hunch about the weather might be accurate, making it all the more urgent to reach the cabin as soon as possible. Glancing over at Jamie, he saw that the girl was still fast asleep, still in the same curled-up, protective position she had assumed the evening before. *I'll let her rest while I go get the horses*, he thought, knowing that she needed all the rest she could get. As quietly as he could, he left the recess under the bank and climbed up on top.

Jack Plum pulled the heavy robe back from his face so as not to restrict his eyesight. It would be daylight soon, and he needed to be alert. Crown should be coming out of that hole under the riverbank before long—that is, if it was Crown under there. Plum was intrigued to find out just who would climb up the bank to go for the horses. This Trace fellow had definitely caught up with Crown, there was no doubt about that, because both Crown's horse and a strange paint pony were hobbled with the others in the cottonwoods.

Plum had spent most of the previous afternoon searching for their camp, and it was after nightfall when he stumbled upon the horses tied in the trees. Even then, he didn't locate the camp right away. Crown, or Trace, had picked a good spot to camp in, Plum had to admit. It changed his plans considerably, for he had intended to murder whichever one he found while he slept. With the camp up under that bank, it would be far too risky to try to surprise him. If Plum had his choice, he would prefer that it be Crown who had survived the clash with the Mountain Hawk. He had promised himself the pleasure of killing his longtime partner for many months now, and he was really hoping to settle the man's hash once and for all. He had been content to let Crown finally get his hands on Jamie. But the sullen bastard couldn't be satisfied with the trade they agreed to. He had to run off with the horses, too—picked the best four out of the bunch. And one thing Jack Plum would not stand for was for anyone to steal his property.

The question he was now anxious to find the answer for was the welfare of the girl. The more he thought about Jamie, the more he wanted her back. When he conjured an image of her white and frail body, cringing in mortal fear of his advances, he found himself literally salivating. *If that bastard has*

*done kilt her, I'm gonna make a gelding outta him before
I kill him.*

"Come on, dammit," Plum mumbled as he rubbed
his hands together vigorously in an effort to keep
them warm. He had removed the wolfskin mittens—
plunder from the Kutenai raid—only minutes before,
and already his fingers were stiff and frozen. He was
tired of waiting. Sitting in a hole burrowed out of
the snow behind a log, he waited, his rifle ready and
a heavy buffalo robe over his head with snow raked
up over it, making him almost invisible from a distance of fifty feet. He had positioned himself carefully so that he had an open shot at anyone on the
riverbank below him. The waiting game was hard
on Plum, for patience was not one of his virtues and
he was getting angrier by the minute.

At last his patience was rewarded. Soon after first
light pierced the leaden sky above him, he spotted
a head above the edge of the bank. Moments later,
a man cautiously climbed up and knelt on the bank.
He remained there for a full minute, looking up-
stream and down before rising to his feet. It wasn't
Crown! A wry smile formed on Plum's face. *Well,
now, lookee here. Ol' Crown warn't the he-bear he thought
he was.* Plum grudgingly admitted a newfound respect for the man the Blackfeet called Mountain
Hawk. Any man who got the best of Crown—even
if he bushwhacked him—was a man to take seriously, and a man best eliminated, as far as Plum was
concerned. It might not bring the satisfaction that

killing Crown would have, but there would be a certain amount of pleasure in getting the man who had put Crown under.

Plum readied his rifle and waited patiently for Trace to start along the riverbank toward the horses. He was in no hurry. There was a clearing of at least twenty yards between Trace and the trees where the horses were hobbled. There was no need to rush the shot. He rested the three-foot barrel of the rifle on the log before him to steady his aim. He would take no chances of missing the shot, for it might be a dangerous mistake to miss this mountain man.

At last Trace started toward the horses. Plum set his sights for the middle of the open space before the trees and waited, the smile still present upon his face as Trace left the cover of the bushes that obscured Plum's vision. His target in the open now, Plum laid the front sight on Trace's chest, then led him about a half a step. *Sometimes it takes a little while, but Jack Plum always squares a debt,* he thought, for he had never forgotten Trace's interference with his plans to murder Paul Murdock and steal his wagon. He slowly squeezed the trigger, and the Hawken barked sharply, sending a .50-caliber ball on its deadly mission. A fraction of a second later, Plum grinned widely as he saw the solid impact of his shot spin Trace around and drop him in his tracks. As Plum got to his feet, he saw the body disappear over the side of the bank. No fool to rush in immediately, Plum first took the precaution to reload his rifle before making his way cautiously down the bluffs to the riverbank. Ready for any surprises, he inched his way up to the steep bank, taking note of the rifle lying in the snow, and peered carefully over the edge. There was no body, but there was a clearly trampled trail in the snow leading down the bank to a sizable hole in the thin ice of the shallow water. Plum held his rifle ready to fire as he stood watching the hole in the ice intently. He waited for several minutes to be sure Trace didn't pop back up. *Unless he's a by-God fish, he ain't coming up,* Plum thought, satisfied that his kill had been confirmed.

Now his thoughts turned immediately to the girl he suspected was hiding under the bank, waiting for Trace to return. "Ain't she gonna be tickled to see me, " he said maliciously, almost laughing out loud at the thought. He promptly picked up Trace's rifle, turned on his heel, and followed Trace's tracks back to his camp.

In the hollowed-out alcove under the riverbank Jamie was awakened by a sound—of what, she was uncertain. A rifle shot? She couldn't say for sure. Her mind struggled to rid itself of the heavy fog of sleep. She saw then that she was alone, and felt somewhat reassured. Trace was out there somewhere, so if indeed it was a shot she had heard, it may have been him, firing at a deer or some other game. *I'd better pee while I've got the chance,* she thought, and quickly went to the far edge of the hollowed-out cave to do so.

Back down the river, desperately clinging to a handful of roots and grass directly under the rim of the steep bank, Trace lay in the hollow left by the log that had been there moments before. He had been spun around and knocked over the bank by the heavy blow of a large-caliber rifle ball in his shoulder. He had stumbled a little just before the ball hit him, and that had probably saved his life. As it was, however, he was in a desperate way. The shoulder was already numb, and he knew that before long the real pain would set in, rendering his arm useless.

He knew he had been lucky, and only his quick thinking had prevented his assailant from searching up under the edge of the bank where Trace would have been easily spotted. When he rolled over the rim of the bank, Trace had landed almost on top of a large driftwood log. Seeing his only chance to escape, he dislodged the log, sending it rolling down the bank and through the ice. Luckily the water was just deep enough under the ice for the log to roll away from the edge of the hole, causing Plum to assume it was Trace who had gone through the ice.

Jamie was just completing her business when she heard footsteps crunching the frozen snow near the mouth of the shallow cave. "Wait a minute, Trace!" she quickly called out. "I didn't expect you back so soon."

"That's all right, darlin', I reckon I've seen it before."

Jamie froze, still squatting on her heels. There was no mistaking that voice. Her brain was suddenly sent reeling, and for a few moments she found it impossible to move, as if her body had become paralyzed. Afraid to turn to face the voice, she prayed that it was a dream, and closed her eyes, squeezing her eyelids together tightly. Plum spoke again.

"Ain't you happy to see your ol' sweet husband again?" Plum asked, chiding the terrified girl. Thoroughly enjoying her torment, he continued to taunt her. "I'm even gonna forgive you for runnin' off with your boyfriend out there. You don't have to worry 'bout him no more, though—he's laying under the ice in the river. 'Course, I'm gonna have to whup you just the same, so's you'll know not to do nothin' like that agin." The evil grin left his face and, deadly serious now, he commanded, "Now, git up from there, and git over here."

Jamie felt as if the roof of the cave was crashing down on her. It was no nightmare—Plum had found her! Too weak to move at first, she somehow staggered to her feet, holding on to the wall of the cave for support, and finally turned toward the sneering Plum. As she stood there on unsteady legs, her feelings of defeat and despair gradually turned to anger, and suddenly all the months of torment and shame at the hands of the evil Plum rose up inside her like a white-hot flame. She made a choice as she stood facing the leering countenance that she hated with all her heart. She would no longer be afraid of this scum, and she would no longer submit to his torture, even if it meant death. She knew from experience that hell could be no worse than living as Jack Plum's slave.

"Git your ass over here," Plum repeated, his eyes narrowing as he showed his anger at Jamie's lack of response to his commands.

"You can go straight to hell," Jamie replied calmly. She took a step sideways toward her bedroll and the pistol Trace had given her.

Following her eyes, Plum saw the barrel of the pistol protruding slightly from under the heavy buffalo robe. It brought a gleam to his eye, and he grinned slyly. "Well, well, I do believe you've got some notion about that pistol, ain'tcha, honey?" He raised his rifle and held it on her. "You go ahead and try fer it. I'd just as soon shoot you down as not."

Feeling the strength returning to her legs, her will resolved, she met his cruel gaze unblinking. Very deliberately, she took another step toward the pistol, her eyes locked on his.

The grin faded from Plum's face. Puzzled by the girl's show of defiance, he warned her, "I don't know what you think you're doin', but if you take another step toward that pistol, I'm gonna cut you in two." To illustrate his intent, he cocked the hammer.

Jamie's gaze was icy as she continued to stare at

the suddenly confused Plum. She took another step, and he raised the rifle, threatening. He didn't want to kill her, but he had no choice if Jamie went for the pistol. The woman had gone crazy. He considered the possibility of rushing her, but it was plain that she could reach the pistol before he could reach her. *Dammit*, he concluded, *I'm gonna have to shoot her.* She was only two steps away from the buffalo robe now, and was poised there, still gazing coldly into his eyes. He was unable to understand that Jamie had determined to die rather than be with him again, and that she was equally determined to kill him as well. She took one more step, and his hand tightened slowly on the trigger.

"Plum!" The voice came from behind him, and Plum whirled around to find Trace McCall standing at the edge of the cave, his left arm hanging limp at his side, blood dripping from his fingertips, a pistol in his other hand. Though shocked to see Trace still alive, Plum reacted instantly, bringing his rifle up and firing. He was fast, but the Mountain Hawk was faster. Both weapons discharged almost simultaneously, the ball from Trace's pistol slamming into Plum's chest, causing his shot to smack into the wall of the cave a foot wide of its target.

Plum staggered a few steps backward before regaining his balance. He realized that he might be mortally wounded, and his face was a mask of rage. Seeing that Trace had no other weapon but a knife, Plum dropped his empty rifle and pulled his pistol from his belt. "Damn you!" he spat and leveled the weapon at Trace, who was poised to attack. But before Plum could pull the trigger, he was struck in the back by a slug from Jamie's pistol.

The impact of Jamie's shot caused Plum to jerk the trigger and miss Trace as the Mountain Hawk quickly sidestepped, closing the distance between the two in the blink of an eye. Using his good shoulder, Trace plowed into the wounded renegade, sending him sprawling on top of the campfire. With screams of rage and pain, Plum rolled out of the fire and tried to scramble to his feet. Filled with her own rage, and fueled by a lust for long-awaited vengeance, Jamie grabbed a flaming stick of wood from the fire. Moving very deliberately, with both hands on the burning limb, she delivered a smashing blow against the side of Plum's face that sent the struggling man back down.

Trace started to move, then seeing the drama before his eyes, he paused, allowing the tormented girl to extract her own vengeance. Though Plum was dying from his bullet wounds, he was lucid enough to know his fate, and he attempted to drag himself out of the cave. Unhurriedly, Jamie followed him. When he had gotten to the mouth of the cave, she methodically delivered blow after blow with the still-burning limb upon Plum's skull until there was no longer so much as a quiver from his battered body.

Finally it was over. She put her foot against the dead man's back and rolled him over the brink of the riverbank, watching as his body bounced and tumbled down the bank into the icy water. When she turned to face Trace, her face was still twisted with rage, and she stared at him with eyes wild and unfocused. For a moment, he feared she had gone over the brink with Plum's body, into a world of madness. A few moments passed as the two of them stood transfixed, staring at each other without her really seeing. Jamie's face slowly relaxed, the anger seeming to recede, and she became aware of him again.

"You've been shot," she finally uttered, and quickly moved to minister to his wound.

At the time, Trace was not fully aware of what had taken place in those terrible moments. He only knew that it struck him that Jamie demonstrated an unusually calm and steady demeanor as she instructed him to sit while she tended the wound in his shoulder. He would have expected her to be weak and perhaps weepy after such a terrifying incident. It would be sometime later, that Trace would look back upon the events of this cold gray morning, and realize he had witnessed a transformation in Jamie. Gone from that moment on was the frail, fearful girl, replaced by a hardened, confident woman with the steel to make her own way in this wild country.

# CHAPTER 15

It had already begun to snow when Trace and Jamie started out that afternoon, headed for Boss Pritchard's cabin above Three Forks. For most of the journey, the pair rode in silence, deep in their individual thoughts. Trace, at the head of the column of horses, had his left arm in a sling that Jamie had fashioned for him to take the strain off of his shoulder. He had been lucky. Plum's rifle ball had ripped through the muscle, but had broken no bones. Jamie had cleaned it as best she could and wrapped it carefully. And while it was sore and painful, it appeared that it would heal.

Of more concern to him was the question of Jamie's welfare. Occasionally, when he looked back at the somber young woman, now riding with a pistol strapped to her side as well as Crown's Hawken rifle within easy reach, Trace was amazed at her stony countenance.

As for Jamie, she felt a peace within her soul that surprised even herself. There were scars deep in her mind that would never fade away, but she was now confident that she could face the rest of her life on her own terms. No longer feeling the shame that had recently drowned her in despair, she had adopted an attitude of self-reliance that needed no other individual to survive. She was somewhat chagrined to find she could now gaze ahead at the broad shoulders of the young mountain man on the paint pony without feeling a wistful longing. *Maybe you've finally grown up, girl.* She smiled as she thought it. Up ahead of her, Trace happened to look back at that moment. Seeing her smile, he grinned in return, and she gave him a little wave of her hand.

By the time they reached the cabin, the snow was at least two feet deep in the valleys, and deeper on the higher elevations. As Trace had feared, the cabin was empty. They both had hoped that they would find Ox waiting for them, but they soon discovered his frozen body lying next to those of Boss Pritchard, Shorty Whitehead, and Jake Watson. After Trace took care of the horses and started a fire in the fireplace, he took a shovel from the corner of the cabin and covered the stack of frozen bodies with a mound of snow. "That'll have to do until the ground thaws enough to dig," he told Jamie.

There was nothing left to do but settle in and wait out the weather. They had a snug cabin, with firewood already cut, even a supply of frozen meat buried outside the cabin door. They both agreed things could be a whole lot worse.

During the next few days the snow never let up,

piling up almost to the eaves of the little cabin. It was necessary to open the door frequently to ensure that it didn't get blocked by a buildup of snow. Trace was kept plenty busy raking the snow off the roof, keeping the woodpile accessible, and providing feed for the horses they had accumulated. It was a full-time job for a one-armed man, but Jamie did her share to help him. He had harbored some concerns that returning to the scene of some of Jamie's torment might be too much for the girl to endure, but she showed no signs of stress, which was a great relief to him. In weather like this, he was mighty thankful for the cabin. Boss Pritchard and his two partners had done a masterful job of constructing a cozy dwelling.

For the first week there was a minimum of conversation between the two. A lot of healing was required before Jamie could release all of the bitterness stored up after the long weeks of brutal abuse at the hands of her captors. The peace she had experienced after Plum's death was enough to carry her through the cold, snowy days. After a week, the storm moved on, and a glimpse of morning sun seemed to bring her out of her shell. Soon she was close to the Jamie that Trace had known before she was abducted.

This improvement in Jamie's frame of mind was a welcome sign to Trace, although it also served to create a new concern for him. As Jamie became more and more her old self, Trace began to feel a little uncomfortable because she gradually took on more of a woman's role in their daily existence, and Trace was reminded of the declaration she had once made that she would make him a good wife. Though it had been long ago, he had never forgotten it. She did not now mention it. Still, he couldn't help but wonder if it was on her mind and she might be waiting for him to broach the subject.

As Trace made his way through the snow, walking down the riverbank to find food for the horses, his thoughts were far from the bundle of cottonwood branches he was carrying. His arm was out of the sling now, but it still hung almost useless, making it a struggle to keep the frozen limbs together. Jamie was in the cabin, cooking their supper. He was torn between the image of a dark-eyed Snake girl that he had carried in his mind for years and an obligation he felt building up inside him for Jamie.

He tried to counsel himself as to what he should do. *Dammit,* he argued, *Jamie's as fine a woman as a man could want for a wife.* She had been through hell, and after being with Plum she had to feel used and possibly that no man would want her. That part was not what bothered Trace. His reluctance was born of a love for something and someone else. His heart went out to Jamie, however, and in the end, he decided to do what a decent man should do.

"What's the matter with you?" Jamie asked, as she watched Trace push the boiled meat around on his plate. "You got some complaints about the cooking? 'Cause if you have . . ."

"No. No complaints," he interrupted before she could tell him to cook his own supper. "I've just been thinking, that's all." He put his knife down on the edge of the tin plate. "You know, Jamie, you and me have been friends for a long time." Sensing a seriousness in his tone, she stopped chewing and gave him her full attention. He mustered up his courage and finally blurted out, "You reckon you and me oughta get married?"

At first she seemed to have no reaction to his blunt proposal. She said nothing, simply gazing into his eyes, as she formed her reply in her mind. When she spoke, it was without excitement. "Trace, you know I love you, and there was a time when I wanted nothing more in this world than to be your wife. I'm sorry, but things are different now. I guess you're about the most decent man I know, but I don't want a man in my life anymore. I hope you're not too hurt by this, but I don't think it would be a good idea for you or me." She paused to watch his reaction. "I hope this won't damage our friendship, because I truly do think of you as my closest friend."

"No," he assured her, "nothing will damage our friendship." He hesitated, still finding it hard to believe he had misjudged her feelings so completely. "I hope you know it didn't make any difference to me . . . you know, about Plum and all."

She smiled. "I know." She paused. "And Trace,

thank you for asking me. I'll always treasure that," she added, knowing in her heart why he had proposed marriage and that she would always love him for it. But she no longer had a desire to be tied to any man, even a man as decent as Trace McCall.

Neither of them commented on it, but both Trace and Jamie felt great relief in the days that followed. The winter months became a partnership between two friends, a needed period of healing for both as the cold weather clamped its icy grip upon the river valley. Finally, one day Trace came back from hunting with word that the snow had cleared the mountain passes. It was time to leave for Promise Valley.

It had been a peaceful time for Jamie and Trace, but both were ready to say good-bye to Boss Pritchard's cabin. The ground was still too frozen to dig, so the day before they left, Trace brought rocks from the river to construct a mound over the bodies behind the cabin. It wasn't much of a monument to three honest mountain men and one innocent soul, but it would have to do. Trace felt bad about Ox. The poor simpleton didn't deserve to die like that, but in these harsh mountains, things didn't always work out the way they should. When the last stone was in place, Trace and Jamie started out, driving their small herd of bony, undernourished horses, before them.

Buck Ransom held the worn length of rope up to inspect it for signs of weakness. He frowned as he examined it, as if the rope had personally offended him by wearing out. "I reckon I'm gonna have to buy me some new rope when I git to Fort Bridger," he mused aloud as he laced the offending line around the pack he was securing on his horse. His intention was to set out for Bridger on his way to Fort Laramie to meet a wagon train he had agreed to lead to California. He was in no hurry. It would be weeks before the folks he had contracted with would arrive at Laramie. But early signs of spring had caused a ripple in his bloodstream, and he had an itch to be in the saddle again.

The winter had been a hard one, with more snow than usual, causing Buck to spend more time inside his cabin than he cared to, and he longed for some company. It wasn't that he had not talked to another soul all winter. At least every few days or so he saw Reverend Longstreet or Travis Bowen, usually when he took some venison or elk by after a hunting trip. Less often, he saw Jordan Thrash. But talking to Jordan always depressed Buck. He had never seen a man go downhill so quickly. Ever since Jamie had been carried off by that band of Kutenais, Jordan just seemed to sink into deeper and deeper despair, and Buck wondered if he was going to just give up and die. It made Buck uncomfortable to be around the man.

So he was packing his horses early because the company he craved was that of other men like himself—trappers and scouts, mountain men and scalawags—men who had tasted the pure essence of life that could be found only in the high country. He felt sure he could find a few of the old free trappers hanging around Fort Bridger, suffering with winter itch, same as he was, looking for someone to swap lies about the old days when beaver was still plentiful. A week or two of that, seasoned with a few quarts of Louis Vasquez's throat-skinning panther piss, was what he needed. Maybe Bridger himself would be there. Buck was looking forward to it. After that, maybe he would be ready to meet up with his train of settlers.

He was absorbed in thoughts of the old days when a movement off in the north end of the valley caught his eye, and he paused to consider what manner of traveler might be approaching from that direction. Squinting while he tried to decide if he should be fetching his rifle or not, he determined that there were two riders, driving about fourteen or fifteen horses. He dropped the end of the rope he had been holding and walked over to the corner of his small corral. Stepping up on the bottom rail to get a better view, he watched the riders, just now passing the ashes of the old Tyler place.

"Well, I'll be go to hell . . ." he blurted out when the riders got close enough for him to recognize the familiar form riding easy on the paint pony. "Trace!" Buck yelled, and then he realized who the second rider was. "And Jamie," he said softly. "Praise the Lord!"

Buck jumped down from the fence and ran to his horse. Without taking the time to saddle it, he threw on a halter and leaped on its back. With a sharp kick of his heels, he was off at a gallop to meet his friends, yelling his best rendition of a Crow war whoop.

Trace and Jamie pulled up to watch the wild charge of the old mountain man, wide grins on their faces as Buck came on at a dead run, his horse splashing up mud from the soggy valley floor. He soon slid up to them, leaning against the reins, his buckskins spattered with mud.

"I swear, Buck," Trace said, "you've scattered our horses all over hell."

Off his horse before it came to a complete stop, Buck roared in mock indignation, "Scattered your horses? To hell with your horses!" He reached up and grabbed Trace by the shirt.

Laughing, Trace let himself be pulled off his pony, landing on top of Buck and knocking both of them to the ground. Scrambling to their feet, they hugged and slapped each other on the back vigorously. Buck finally calmed down enough to turn his attention to the girl who sat quietly smiling at them.

"Jamie," Buck said softly, his eyes searching hers, trying to see what condition she was in, dreading what he might find. "Welcome home, honey. Are you all right?"

"I'm all right," she assured him, her smile warm and genuine.

Buck was anxious to hear every detail of the story,

but he contented himself with waiting until the girl had a chance to see her father. "Come on," he said, hopping up on his horse again. "I'll help you round up your horses, and then I'll go over to Jordan's with you. Lemme run by and put my packhorse in the corral, and we'll take this little lady home." He pulled back on the reins, pausing. "Unless you wanna put the horses in my corral—it's kinda small, but it'll do till you have time to fool with 'em."

Trace answered. "No. We'll drive 'em on over to Jordan's. Half of 'ems Jamie's anyway."

"Suit yourself," Buck replied loudly. Gracing Jamie with a wide, toothy grin, he declared, "What a glorious day!"

A tearful reunion followed between father and daughter. The shock of seeing his daughter again after all but giving her up for dead was almost too much for Jordan Thrash. After the initial embrace, he had to sit down to keep from collapsing. He looked into Jamie's face, feeling the hurt in each of her faint scars, blaming himself for each one. Knowing what was tearing her father apart inside, Jamie quickly assured him that she was all right now and that she had never blamed him for her suffering. It would have been useless for him to try to help her when the Indian war party took her.

While father and daughter reunited, Trace and Buck put the horses away. When they were all in

Jordan's corral, Buck sidled up to Trace. "They's a mighty poor-lookin' lot," he allowed.

"I reckon," Trace replied. "They've had a hard winter."

Buck couldn't contain his curiosity any longer. "She had a pretty rough time of it, I reckon."

"She did," Trace answered.

"She'll be all right, though? I mean, the girl's got spunk . . . she'll be all right, won't she?"

Trace smiled. "She'll be fine."

Buck was losing his patience. "Well, dammit," he finally blurted out, "are you two . . . is there anything goin' on between you two?" When Trace did not answer right away, Buck pressed. "Accordin' to what you told me, you spent the whole dang winter together in that cabin. You mean to tell me that nothin' went on?"

"Well, I'll tell you, partner, it ain't none of your business, but I know you'll bust if you don't find out. I asked her to marry me, but she turned me down."

"Well, forevermore . . ." Buck was flabbergasted. He had always assumed that Trace and Jamie would wind up together. Now he didn't know what to think. "She turned you down?" he asked, not sure he had heard correctly. Trace nodded. "Turned you down," he repeated, slowly shaking his head. Then, "Well, she's got more sense than I give 'er credit for."

They both laughed at this and started back toward the house, where Jamie was now busy making a pot of coffee. There was no more conversation before reaching the cabin that Jordan had rebuilt, but Buck was working something over in his mind. He had decided it was best not to say anything about a conversation he had with a little Snake girl back in the fall at Fort Bridger. A lot of trappers sired offspring with Indian girls and rode away thinking nothing of it. Trace McCall was not that kind of man, and Buck knew it. Now that things were not as Buck had assumed between Trace and Jamie, he wondered if he should let Trace know about his Indian son. It was a worrisome thing for Buck. He was going to have to make a decision about it. *I'll decide on it tomorrow. Now ain't the time.*

"What are you aimin' to do now?" Buck asked, as he approached the open cabin door. When Trace did not answer, Buck turned to see if his young friend had heard him. "Never mind," he murmured. His question had already been answered. Trace Mc-Call had stopped several paces behind him, distracted by the long, lonesome call of a mountain hawk.